Bryan Collier lives with his wife and two cats in the UK. He has a BSc in Electronic Engineering from Coventry University and an MBA from Bristol Business School.

He was an Electronic Engineer for twenty years, before taking his MBA and becoming a self-employed Business Consultant. Among his interests he lists: ancient history, quantum physics, crossword puzzles, sudoku, playing guitar, and cooking. This is his first book.

He is currently researching his next novel.

2012
A CONSPIRACY TALE

Bryan Collier

Matador
9 De Montfort Mews
Leicester LE1 7FW, UK
Tel: (+44) 116 255 9311 / 9312
Email: books@troubador.co.uk
Web: www.troubador.co.uk/matador

ISBN 978 1906510 541

Typeset in 11pt Stempel Garamond by Troubador Publishing Ltd, Leicester, UK
Printed by Cromwell Press Ltd, Trowbridge, Wiltshire, UK

Matador is an imprint of Troubador Publishing Ltd

This book is dedicated to Oscar and Dylan

ACKNOWLEDGEMENTS

The author would like to thank the following people: Zecharia Sitchin, Laurence Gardner and David Hatcher Childress, whose books inspired the vision for this work, my mother, Marguerite for her contribution and patience, and my wife, Julie for her unending support and excellent ideas.

I would also like to thank my friends for their feedback on the story concept and, in particular, Mark Hows for the cover design and artwork.

PREFACE

The year is 2008 – a period of great unrest. Governments are out of touch with the people, fear of terror is at an all time high, and the planet's resources are at an all time low.

This is a story of ordinary people with some extraordinary talents and a desire to seek out the truth.

"The truth that makes men free is for the most part the truth which men prefer not to hear."
Herbert Agar.

PART ONE

"In the business world, the rear-view mirror is always clearer than the windshield."

Warren Buffett

CHAPTER ONE

Head Office of IDSys, Cambridge Science Park, England

Mitchell Webb, CEO and founder of IDSys, sat behind his desk in his office on the second floor of the purpose built research and development facility in Cambridge and tried to control his excitement. In the next few minutes he would know if his company's bid to design, manufacture and supply Radio Frequency Identification Devices (RFIDs) to the British Government had been successful. This was the big one. This was what he'd been waiting for, ever since he started the company some six years earlier on the back of his patented technology for vehicle tracking systems. Mitchell's father had died when he was twelve years old and his mother had struggled to send him to university. Unlike the other students, Mitchell had put in excessive hours of study, avoided the Union bars, and worked on assignments with a dedication rarely seen by students of his age. He was determined to succeed for both his and his mother's sake. Unfortunately, Mitchell's mother had died in his final year at university and never got to celebrate his achievements. His patent for vehicle tracking systems had been instrumental in raising the capital he needed to start his own company, and its success had enabled him to move the business into their current premises at the Cambridge Science Park, two years ago.

At forty-two, he was fairly young to be heading up such a large organisation, with manufacturing sites and service offices around the UK. Although slightly greying at the temples, he still looked a lot younger than his years and this, he felt, was often a disadvantage in business. Nonetheless, at six feet two, he was an imposing figure, and he kept himself in good shape in his home gym. He had never married. '*Married to his work*', some said, but he had never been comfortable in serious relationships and, if truth be known, he hadn't met a partner that ever showed any interest in his work – apart from the obvious financial benefits. He was what previous generations would have termed *a self-made man*, but he never forgot his background; on the contrary, it was his driving force and the root of his tremendous will to succeed.

Mitch's office was large but austere. Apart from his desk, it contained a simple meeting table for up to six people and a couple of two-seater leather sofas. On one wall hung a 32" LCD TV, which could receive satellite television programmes, as well as containing a computer port for presentations and meetings. The office was only accessible through a smaller outer office, where his secretary and personal assistant sat.

He switched off the History TV programme on the Mayan Calendar he had been watching sporadically, and thought to himself, *If the world's gonna end in 2012, what has it all been for?* He wondered if some future civilisation would examine this one and jump to the conclusion that *we* had predicted the end of the world in 9999, because our electronic calendars only had four digits for the year. *People get so carried away with this prophecy of doom crap,* he concluded. He often tuned in to the satellite history channels when he had spare time, though he was bored to death with documentaries about Nazis and Sharks. *Although,* he mused, *the two seem to have a lot in common.*

He pressed a button on his desk phone, "Sarah, hold all calls except the one I'm expecting from Mister Shackelford."

His mouth felt dry and he fumbled in his pocket for a Tic-Tac. Eighteen months of presentations, demonstrations, tenders and meetings in dusty government offices, and it all came down to this phone call. He knew his company was in the best position to win the contract, but he still worried about their lack of Government contacts and whether the old boy's network would scupper him. Preston Shackelford had been his main contact at the Home Office and seemed a straight-up guy, but you always heard of contracts going to companies with serious political connections.

The phone buzzed and he felt his palms grow moist. The voice of his secretary cut through the silence. "I've got Mister Shackelford for you, Mitch."

"Thanks, Sarah. Put him through."

The phone went dead for a second then hissed back into life. Momentarily, he wondered if he should have had his project team available in case there were any last minute technical queries, but he decided this was not going to be that kind of call. *They should be in the lab anyway*, he reassured himself.

"Mitchell Webb," he announced, trying to keep his voice flat.

"Hi Mitch, Preston Shackelford, Home Office. Hope you're well."

"I'm fine, thanks Preston, how about you?"

"I've been worse, but damned if I can remember when."

"Oh ..." Mitch began and his heart sank as he feared bad news on the horizon.

"But to business. As you know, the decision regarding the placement for the RFID chips contract was debated today, and we have Government approval to place an order for the first phase."

Jeez, he's a cold fish, thought Mitch, fighting his emotions. His stomach did a back flip. Then his logical mind jumped in: *first phase? Are they going to start playing silly buggers at the last minute? All I want to know is who's getting the contract?* He could imagine Shackelford sitting behind his large, old fashioned ministerial desk, enjoying Mitch's discomfort. He looked like a typical civil servant; obligatory pin-striped suit, trousers worn a fraction too short so that when he sat down, you could see the tops of his socks and his bony white legs. He had an annoying habit of talking with half-closed eyes when he was about to deliver disappointing news. He tried to bring an image of Shackelford into his mind to see if his eyes were half-closed or not.

"I'm pleased to inform you, Mitch, that your proposal has met with approval. I'll be faxing the 'terms and conditions' through later this evening," Preston continued.

"Excellent!" Mitch exclaimed, "I mean, that's great news. We won't let you down".

"I know you won't Mitch. Your solution was technically superior to the competition and it gives us the greatest flexibility going forward."

"Er... you mentioned something about the *first phase...*"

"A minor formality Mitch. We can't release all the funds in one go for a programme of this complexity. It'll all become clear when you receive the contract. I must add that it has been a pleasure working with you and I look forward to continuing our relationship."

"Me too, Preston. Will you be overseeing this programme personally?"

"At a high level, yes. But I'd like you meet some of the other interested parties. I'll get my people to contact your secretary to arrange a meeting in the next few weeks."

"No worries."

"Well, congratulations again, Mitch. I'll be in touch."

"Okay... and thanks for everything, Preston."

Abruptly, the phone went silent and Mitch was left to try and pull his thoughts and emotions together.

"Yes! Yes! Yes! We did it!"

He had to tell the team immediately. Thumping the intercom button on his desk, he tried to calm his voice again. "Sarah, I'm expecting an important fax to arrive in the next hour or so; please let me know as soon as it comes in. Are the guys in the lab?"

"The red light's on over the door, so someone's in there at least. I assume this fax will be from the Home Office?"

"Damn right, we got the contract – all leave is officially cancelled until further notice!" Before she could respond, Mitch was through the door to her office. With a grin a Cheshire cat would be proud of, he winked at her, punched the air, and headed down the stairs to the development lab on the first floor.

Sarah had been with the company since its launch. A youngish forty-six year old, she was an attractive woman. At five-foot-six she was not particularly tall, but she had an elegant posture and that, with the heels she wore, made her appear taller. She was always smartly dressed, usually in a stylish skirt in black or grey with a neat shirt. She kept a smart black jacket on a hanger behind her office door, in case she had to attend a meeting, or greet an important visitor. Sarah was very good at this type of work; with an easy, cheerful personality to which people warmed quickly. Apart from his old university mate, Simon, he trusted her more than anyone else in the world.

On his way down the stairs, Mitch saw one of his test technicians, Duncan Wood, coming out of one of the offices on the floor below. "Duncan, meet me in the main lab, I've got some news. Grab anyone else who's not in there already," he called after him, barely able to hide his excitement. He stopped at Simon's office to see if he was around. *Empty! Damn!*

Robin Kirk was running through a design simulation in the lab. He'd been an RF design engineer at IDSys since leaving University with a BSc in Electronic Engineering three years ago. He had initially worked on the second generation of vehicle tracking systems, but had progressed onto the RFID programme eleven months ago. He knew his future would be secure if they won the Home Office contract, but couldn't help feeling that they were getting into something that was going to test his ethics significantly. From what he knew about the programme, the RFID chips would be implanted into people's hands, just below the skin, and would carry identification information that could be remotely accessed via radio waves in a bid to counteract terrorism. His girlfriend and best mate had ribbed him incessantly about 'Big Brother' and 'The Nanny State' over the vehicle tracking systems. *At least I'm not making weapons,* he had countered. Still, he wasn't sure how they'd react to this latest development.

The door buzzed and the red indicator light momentarily flicked on and off, bringing him back to earth with a bump. Mitchell Webb burst into the room like a man caught short at a real ale festival, closely followed by Duncan Wood and Sandra Faye. "Gather round, boys and girls," he commanded, catching his breath.

"Have we got it?" the voice from the far corner of the lab was Simon Rockwall, IDSys Project Manager and Mitch's right-hand man.

Mitch paused until he was sure he had everyone's ear. "You bet your sorry asses we got it! As soon as the fax confirmation arrives, I'm taking you all down the pub to celebrate. Simon, come with me, I want to go over some of the detail before tomorrow's press announcement."

As the two men left the room Rob sat back down at his bench and thought to himself, *this is it then - we just got into the public control business.*

CHAPTER TWO

Shelby Taylor stared at the image of a double helix on her VDU. She was comparing different mouse strains to determine which were susceptible to a particular disease and which were not. Single Nucleotide Polymorphisms, or SNPs (known as "snips"), are single genetic changes, or variations, that can occur within a DNA sequence. More than 8.3 million of them have been discovered in the fifteen different mouse strains alone. Shelby had been at DNATech for the past five years and she absolutely adored her job. She was not at all what you would expect from a Lab Assistant; small, dark-haired, with a trendy 'bob', and a blinding white smile. If you saw her in the street, or at a night club, you would never guess that she was a lab rat.

Shelby had been what some would describe as a '*gifted child*'. She sailed through her early school years and was very popular with the teachers and her class mates alike. She had an aptitude for both the sciences and the arts, and was equally proficient on the sports field. In her first year of secondary school, things started to go slightly wrong for her. She found it hard to concentrate on lessons; her mind jumping from one subject to another. It was around that time that Shelby started having strange dreams. They rarely made sense and she would often wake up in the night feeling confused and sometimes terrified. She would try to encapsulate her strange visions in her paintings, which were highly advanced and beyond the abilities of most children of her age. At her parents' direction, she had attended therapy and was incorrectly diagnosed with Attention Deficit Disorder (ADD). Possessing a great desire to make a difference in the world, Shelby struggled her way through university, finally attaining a second class degree in Biology. The position at DNATech was only her second real job since leaving University and, despite her difficulties with concentrating, she was determined to do well.

The lab was a class 1 clean room and occupants had to enter through a small air-lock, where they donned protective overalls and shoes. The inside of the lab looked like a top-of-the-range modern kitchen, complete with stainless steel worktops, and an astounding number of cupboards. The main difference between this lab and a kitchen was that there wasn't an oven, but a wide range of scientific analysis and measuring equipment instead.

The door opened and her Lab Supervisor, Kim Denton, entered the room. "How's it going, Shelby?"

"Okay. Just another 5 million snips to compare," she smiled.

"Thank God for computers. Listen, Shelby, you know we talked about carrying out some experiments with bio-chipped mice for the Home Office?"

"Uh huh."

"Well, we finally got the go ahead. An engineer from a company in Cambridge will be coming down this Friday to give us the low down on a new bio-chip they've developed, and we're to work with them to conduct some tests on a batch of mice. It's all fairly routine stuff, are you able to pick this up?"

"Sure. Let me have the details and I'll get onto it as soon as this finishes." Shelby was well aware that Kim didn't think very highly of her, but she was determined to prove herself.

Kim passed a blue folder to Shelby, containing the meeting schedule and proposed test scenarios.

"I take it we'll all be having one of these chips in the not so distant future?" Shelby enquired, as she swivelled on her chair.

"If the tests bear out. It's for our own security. You know how difficult it's been lately. If it's not terrorists, it's animal rights activists."

It's a crazy world, thought Shelby, *where the animals have more rights than the humans.* Shelby was quite comfortable using lab-bred mice for her experiments, but she disagreed strongly against using chimpanzees and other 'higher order' animals in tests. That's why she was so pleased to be working at DNATech – they never conducted experiments on anything else. When she looked up, Kim had already left the lab and was in the airlock taking off her clean room attire.

Kim Denton walked down the hall and straight into the Director's office. It was an ornately decorated room with a thick carpet and a large wooden desk, inlaid with green leather. To the left of the desk there were three visitor's chairs and to the right, a large laser printer. Mark Runnels was a large man with a ruddy complexion. He favoured small rectangular glasses; looking over the top of them made his face appear even larger than it was. As he sat going through reports at his desk, Kim pulled up a chair and planted herself in front of him. Kim did look like a typical lab technician. With a mass of greying curly hair, kept under control by the copious use of hair pins and clips, she had a narrow, pale face, made to look even narrower by the over large spectacles she wore most of the time. She had never got on with contacts – they irritated her eyes. Kim was allergic to most things found outside of the Lab – so being cooped up in a 'clean-room' for ten hours a day suited her down to the ground.

"Shelby will be handling the tests for the bio-chips, Mark," she said.

"How much does she know?" said Runnels without looking up from the reports.

"Only what we decide to tell her," replied Kim defensively.

"Will she be a problem when we start the transmission tests?"

"She'll stick to monitoring the results. She's not so good at making speculative conclusions. She'll just record what she sees."

"And the engineer from IDSys?" Runnels looked over the top of his glasses.

"He won't be needed by then."

"Fine. I'll report progress to powers that be. Oh, and thanks Kim. You will be rewarded for your loyalty to the firm." He paused for a second or two, then added, "I've got to go to a meeting tomorrow. Would you be able to take some files over to Gellar for me in the morning?"

"Of course. Is there anything else you'd like me to take care of?"

"No, no. That will be all. Just tell them that I sent you." He passed Kim a sealed box file marked, *'Runnels – c/o Gellar'*.

Kim smiled as she rose from her seat and left the Director to his business. *I'd better be well rewarded*, she thought to herself.

CHAPTER THREE

Head Office of IDSys, Cambridge Science Park, England

Mitchell Webb and Simon Rockwall sat in Mitch's office reading the Home Office contract for the RFID programme.

"We've done it, Simon. This is the big one." Mitch was staring at the order number and authorised spend on the front page of the fax. He was already doing the mental arithmetic.

"This *phase one* shite bothers me, Mitch. We need to make a press statement in the morning to try and boost our share price as much as possible, if we're to have even an outside chance of raising the capital to launch a new production site for this baby," said Simon.

"I know. I've got Alan working on it. I'm sure we can move some of the smaller orders around in the meantime. I mean, who cares if we piss off a few of the small guys doing this? This is the big one. This is me and you retiring at fifty, Si. This is: *fuck you, venture capitalists, me and Simon have made it big time.*"

Simon wasn't really listening. He was speed reading the contract, looking for show stoppers. "Oh, crap!" he spat, as he turned to page four and quickly absorbed the information.

"What...?" Mitch was still soaring.

"No press conference tomorrow and strictly '*need to know'* status."

"What?" Mitch repeated. "How the fuck are we supposed to raise the capital to start production?"

"Oh, that's already been sorted. They have a company in China that we need to engage with right away," Simon answered.

"China? But we always manufacture over here."

"If we sign this Mitch, we have to follow their plans."

The two friends looked at each other for several minutes hoping for a sign. They had been close since university. Mitch had studied for his

11

degree in Electronics at Nottingham University at the same time Simon was reading Business Studies. In contrast to Mitch, Simon was shorter and stockier with spiky black hair that he kept cropped close to his scalp. He was excellent at business negotiating and had stopped Mitch from screwing up on more than one occasion. He had been a Godsend dealing with the bureaucracy of the Home Office, and could do an impression of the Prime Minister that even Shackelford seemed to find amusing. Mitch valued his friend's advice and rarely made a move without discussing it with him first.

Finally, Mitch scratched his head and said, "So we can't go public with this, but they'll supply a manufacturing facility?"

"Looks like it."

"So we don't need to fund the manufacturing operation, but we still see the same profit from the devices?"

"Apparently, but I'm no lawyer Mitch."

"Crap! Today was supposed to be the best day of my life," *or the worst,* he remembered. "It seems to have fallen somewhat short of the mark."

"Look, Mitch, I think we should go with it. We still hold the patents. The USA and Europe, - hell, even Japan and Australia will be jumping on the band wagon and we could sell billions of the little buggers," reasoned Simon.

"Well, the USA have their own programme, but yeah, we could still mop up the rest of the world," Mitch conceded.

"So what do you say?"

"I don't know Simon. What about the moral implications? I mean, can you live with being known as one of the guys who instigated the removal of people's civil liberties?"

"Mitch? Wake up buddy. It's too late for that. Jeez, we should never have tendered in the first place if you were gonna go all fluffy about it later." Simon shook his head in disbelief. "It's not like they're compulsory for everyone. Only people travelling outside of the European Union and immigrants will be required to have them. And like you said, America are going to introduce them themselves anyway."

Mitch thought for a minute. "Fuck it! Let's do it! Tell Sarah to book a room at the Swallows and order some snacks. I'll tell the team it's *need to know* and get them to sign a new 'Non-disclosure Agreement'. I'm not over the moon, and that Shackelford character gives me the creeps, but this is what I set the company up to do, and I'll just have to live with it. So will they!"

"Guess I'd better brush up on my Chinese," joked Simon, as he rose from his chair.

When Simon had closed the door behind him, Mitch walked over to the window and looked down on the car park outside. *Every one of the cars down there represents an IDSys employee, and their futures are in my hands*, he contemplated. *I hope to God I've made the right decision.*

CHAPTER FOUR

Underground cavern, somewhere on Earth

Lord Enki kicked off the side of the pool and began his ninety-ninth length. He diligently completed one hundred lengths each morning before breakfast. As he heaved his large frame out of the pool, he noticed his reflection in the glass doors overlooking the courtyard. Despite his huge number of years, he was still in good shape. His skin was a little grey, but nothing that a few supplements couldn't put right. He slipped on his robe and looked out of the glass doors. His daughter was in the covered courtyard playing with the maid. In common with all of the families in the colony, they had only the one child. It was their way.

"Atrahasis, where are you?" he called, as he eased his bulk into one of the recliners around the pool.

"A thousand apologies Lord," effused Atrahasis, charging into the room in a panic. He placed a tray on the table next to his leader.

Enki dismissed his excuses with a wave of his hand. "What progress has been made?"

"Much has been achieved since you last enquired, Lord."

"Such as?"

"The control chip is now in progress and phase two will soon be initiated."

"How will it be deployed?" Enki enquired, as he swallowed the preparation Atrahasis had made for him.

"Don't worry, the terrorist atrocities of late have made millions fear for their security. In the New World, they are already experimenting with them and we have plans to increase the terrorist activity in Europe which, when complete, will have people queuing up for implants."

"Very good. We need to keep spreading disinformation to the wider population. We cannot fail this time. We have become diluted and weak." He studied the webbed skin between his long fingers as if it was the first time he'd noticed it.

"Everything is following your timescale, Lord. Our influence over the media has been highly successful in de-sensitising the populous to all manner of extra-terrestrial existence, and the strategic placing of the Sumerian, Babylonian and Mayan relics has created a huge amount of interest in the earliest civilisations amongst the creationist and evolutionist sceptics alike. Most of the world's population now has some expectation of the return of Jesus, Buddha, or Krishna, or of impending destruction by an asteroid …or the return of Planet X. Anxieties are running high."

"Excellent. Now I must rest. Wake me again when you have substantial progress to report."

Enki leapt up the staircase to his bedroom two steps at a time and dimmed the lights once more. As he drifted off to sleep, he felt satisfied that the situation was under control.

CHAPTER FIVE

The Golden Hind, Public House, Cambridge, England

Rob weaved his way through the drinkers in the garden and made his way to the bar, hoping he was the first to arrive so he could down a pint before the others got there. He was a pretty average guy; average height, average weight, with average tastes. Some even said *average intelligence*, but he was thrilled when Mitch had given him his break at IDSys – he had been given complete autonomy over his designs, and had proved himself to be a more than competent RF engineer on several occasions.

The old gang, friends from work or university and Rob's old mate from school usually met up on a Friday evening for a few drinks before they moved on to their ever diverging personal activities.

Rob spotted a table near the entrance to the garden; away from the 'families with kids' waiting for a table in the restaurant-come-conservatory. *Jeez, how things have changed from the smoke filled bars of my youth,* he lamented. *In those days pubs were the solace of beer swilling men, girls looking for a good time; getting slashed on Bacardi, gin or vodka, and yes, the occasional underage students; spending their grants on a few bizarrely named cocktails. Nowadays, they all seem to be gastro-pubs or theme bars.*

Charlotte Moore, Rob's girlfriend for the last seven years, was the first to arrive. He had first met Charlotte at six-form college when they were taking their A levels, but it had taken the best part of six months before they became involved with each other. As their relationship blossomed, they both applied to do their further education in Birmingham, so they could be together. Rob was to study Electronic Engineering, whilst Charlotte had chosen Social Science. Their relationship had grown stronger and stronger during their time in

Birmingham, but now things were becoming a little stressed. Charlotte didn't like the student attitude that Rob and his pals still embraced for the most part, and she was becoming more and more reluctant to take part in their *silly plans*. She wanted to settle down, get a nice house; without lodgers, plan for the future, and save as much of their hard earned money as possible. Okay, Rob agreed that life would be less complicated without Gideon living in their spare room, but who would he solve the mysteries of the universe with if he went?

"Over here Charlie," Rob called, spotting her entering the bar.

She looked gorgeous, as usual. Wearing a summer top and skirt that greatly enhanced her figure, and a pair of spectacular high heeled sandals, Charlotte never failed to make an impression. With her short blonde hair and fresh-faced smile, she could still turn heads whenever she entered a room.

"Hi," she called, as she made her way through the families and non-smokers, who had filled the rest of the seats since Rob had arrived. "Am I the first to arrive?"

"Just you, me and Gideon tonight I'm afraid, unless Sue's coming. Vodka and tonic okay?" Sue was a friend of Charlotte's from work.

"Vodka and Red Bull, please hon. No, Sue can't make it either. She's baby-sitting her sick cat."

Making his way to the bar, Rob wondered how he could tell Charlotte that IDSys had won a Government contract, without going into any details about the RFID chip. It certainly meant that they'd be staying in Cambridge for at least the next three to four years. Worse than that, how could he tell Gideon? He'd go off on one of his, *'they want to turn all of us into Borg'* speeches.

Gideon Mycroft arrived on his bike and chained it to the pub garden fence, before looking up and spotting Rob and Charlotte sitting by an open window overlooking the beer garden. *Getting their passive smoking allowance through the window now are they?* he mused.

Charlotte was the first to spot Gideon's arrival. "Here's your favourite conspiracy theorist, darling," she chided.

"Wha...? Oh, Gideon's made it then?" Rob said, catching on slowly.

Gideon Mycroft was Rob's best mate from secondary school and they'd stayed in touch even after they'd moved to Cambridge; to the point that Gideon was currently lodging with them, while he looked for a suitable job. Gideon was one of life's late developers; he still had that laid back *Hippy* look with slightly longer hair than most, a large range of black tee-shirts, and a tendency to use words like 'cool', 'sweet' and 'dude'. At twenty-five, he still wasn't sure what he wanted to do, but he was passionate about what he believed were government cover-ups. He would spend hours on the PC in Rob and Charlotte's study researching secret societies: the Illuminati, the Skull and Bones, and the Freemasons, to name but a few. And there was no shortage of information out there to whet his appetite. With two highly successful parents, who seemed perfectly happy to 'fund' their only child until he discovered what he wanted to do with his life, Gideon was in no hurry to change.

"Hi Mister and Missus Hart, it's your faithful servant Max," announced Gideon as he arrived at their table.

"What have you done with Freeway?" enquired Charlotte, playing along.

"Oh, he's guarding the Rolls – I came down on my bike, Missus H."

"Well, thank you Max," interjected Rob. *Gideon spends far too much time watching repeats of old American TV shows*, he thought, getting slightly irritated. "Here's a twenty. Get me a lager and Charlie another vodka and Red Bull. Oh, and whatever you're having."

"Cheers boss. Because it can be 'moyder' working for you two," joked Gideon.

Rob looked out across the beer garden and wondered how he could tell them about his *good news* without incurring their wrath. Gideon was a complete conspiracy theorist and Charlotte was a total human rights fanaticist. *Why should I be made to feel guilty for doing a job that I really like? I mean, it's not like I'm designing stuff to harm people. If anything, it'll make people's lives better. Safer at least. Anyway, if I wasn't doing it, someone else would be.*

Gideon returned with the drinks on a tray. "So big fella, any news on that big secret contract your company has been working on?" he enquired, as he dumped the tray of drinks on the table.

"Well, it looks like we may have got a contract to proceed with the first phase of something," Rob replied, abstractedly.

"Wow. I'm glad I don't work in something so vague as to be completely meaningless, dude," Gideon said, provokingly.

"Oh, come on guys. It's Friday," interjected Charlotte, fearing the beginning of an argument; very likely these days when the three of them were alone together.

"I'm just a lowly design engineer who does what he's told. What's new in the world of conspiracy, Gideon?" Rob enquired, hoping to change the subject.

"Well, the latest news is that they're putting fluoride in the water to control our minds," said Gideon with a mischievous look in his eye.

"Right, and how long have they been doing that?" asked Rob, suspecting that this was a Gideon wind up.

"Oh, I'm not sure. Since the early seventies in some areas, I think. Apparently they can throw a switch and make us do things that that we don't even know we're doing, by secret signals from mobile phones."

"But at least we have nice teeth," offered Charlotte, in an attempt to lighten the mood a little.

"No, but seriously, dudes, the Government here, and in the US, are up to no good. I mean, why are we subjected to chemicals in the water, chemicals in our bread, forced vaccination at birth, tracking of our mobile phones, not to mention the shit you're into – tracking of our vehicles, chip and PIN ... need I go on?"

"Gideon, you don't have a vehicle – unless you call that two-wheeled shopping trolley a vehicle. You don't have a chip and PIN card, and you haven't been vaccinated against anything," snapped Rob.

"I have to eat bread and drink water, though!"

"Yeah, but it's not life threatening, is it?"

"How do you know? I read that fluoride is actually more poisonous than lead," asserted Gideon, before taking a huge gulp of beer.

"Gideon, you can't believe everything you read on the Internet," argued Rob. "Most of the stuff is written by cranks."

"Says the man who believes everything he sees on that flat-screen TV in the corner of the room. You do realise that 90% of what is broadcasted is propaganda, don't you?" countered Gideon.

"No, but I do know that 78% of statistics are made up on the spot," replied Rob sarcastically, before taking a long satisfying swig of his lager.

"That's right, make a joke out of it. We live in an age of information overload. Most people can't take it all in. That's what they rely on when they spread their lies. They expect us..."

"Gideon! Do you know what you'd find if you looked up *paranoid* in the Oxford English Dictionary?" interrupted Rob.

"No. My name, I suppose," said Gideon, sullenly.

"Ha ha. No, you Muppet! You'd find a definition of the word *paranoid*. But, maybe your name should be there too."

"Guys, guys, please! Not tonight! Let's go back home and have dinner... and relax!" pleaded Charlotte.

"The problem with Gideon is that he's a *'glass half empty'* person, said Rob defensively.

"And I suppose you'd say the glass was half full," snorted Gideon.

"No, I'm an engineer. I'd say the glass was too big."

After dinner, Charlotte and Rob sat in their lounge flicking through the Sky channel selector, trying to find something to watch. Gideon had already gone to bed, claiming he had paperwork to attend to. "Why were you so hard on Gideon tonight?" Charlotte enquired.

"It's just his conspiracy shit gets on my nerves sometimes."

"He's been like that since we've known him. Why do you let it wind you up? Most of the time he's only saying it for effect."

"I dunno. I guess it's because there's stuff going on at work that makes some of what he's saying have a ring of truth about it."

"What, like your Government contract?"

"Nooo," Rob lied. "Gideon spends too long watching videos on YouTube and finding conspiracies in everything. You know, he actually told me that he believes that giant reptiles are running the planet, and that the President of the USA is the Anti-Christ."

"So, do you think it's time to move on? Get another place?"

"Jesus, Charlotte!" snapped Rob. "I'm in the middle of a huge project. I've probably got to go to back and forth to China for the next few months. I don't need to be thinking about moving house, moving towns, or whatever!"

"Okay. Calm down. I was just wondering. China sounds interesting. Will you be allowed guests?" she asked hopefully.

"Ha ha, I expect Mitch's budget will stretch to the odd visit," he smiled, feeling a little calmer after his outburst.

Why am I feeling so touchy? he thought. *It must just be nerves about getting this design right. Thank God I've got Charlotte to keep me grounded.* He slipped his arm around her shoulders and kissed her on the head in silent thanks.

After Rob had gone up to bed, Charlotte got her herself another cup of coffee and sat down at the kitchen table. She felt exhausted; she hadn't been sleeping too well recently. Only last night she had found herself lying in bed for hours, listening to Rob snoring and watching the bedroom curtains billowing slightly in the breeze.

She tidied away the remains of their dinner and decided to do the washing up, rather than leave it until the morning. *I wonder what's got Rob so edgy about work*, she thought. She knew Mitch was a demanding boss, but he wasn't an ogre. She decided that what they needed was a holiday on their own, and resolved to pick up some brochures when they went shopping tomorrow.

CHAPTER SIX

The University of Cambridge, England

Alexander Wells fine-tuned his telescope to the constellation of Orion. "This is crap. I need to be in the South Pole to see anything decent," he moaned. Setting the built-in camera to five minute intervals, he moved across to his PC. *If I can prove my hypothesis that the Asteroid Belt was originally another planet, my Ph.D's in the bag*, he reminded himself.

He'd become interested in the theory that the Asteroid Belt may have been a planet originally and that it had been in a collision with another astral body which had shattered it into fragments after reading about 'Planet X' on the Internet. Some people refer to this interloper as Nibiru, after the Sumerian texts that describe such an encounter with a planet they called Tiamat.

According to Sumerian legend, this catastrophic collision created not only the Asteroid Belt, but Earth itself with Tiamat's moon becoming our own Moon in its present orbit. It is also speculated that Nibiru, if it existed, may have been responsible for the peculiar spin of Uranus, which appears to be lying on its back, compared to the other planets. Nibiru, it is said, returns to our solar system every 3,600 years, with catastrophic repercussions.

What really caught Alex's imagination regarding the Sumerian texts he had been studying, was that this early civilization from 3,000 BC appeared to have a much better understanding of our Solar System than we do today. They knew, for example, of the existence of Uranus; not re-discovered until 1781, Neptune; not re-discovered until 1846, and Pluto; not re-discovered until 1930. Not only that, they knew that all of the planets in our solar system circled the Sun – a notion that Galileo was condemned for by the Catholic Church as late as 1616.

Interestingly, NASA had recently launched a probe, named Dawn, to study the Asteroid Belt and to look for clues about the formation of the solar system. Dawn's first target was Vesta, the fourth-largest asteroid in the region and the only object in the asteroid belt visible from Earth with the naked eye. It has an iron core and signs of lava flows on its surface. Vesta also has a gaping crater, so deep it exposes the asteroid's mantle. After six months of observations, Dawn would leave orbit and begin a three-year trek to the dwarf planet Ceres, the king of the Asteroid Belt. Though relatively close to Vesta, icy Ceres, it was believed, formed under vastly different circumstances. It may contain water-bearing minerals and possibly a weak atmosphere. *Lucky for me, my thesis will be marked before Dawn can either prove or disprove it.*

Now that's strange, he thought, as he compared the pictures of the Asteroid Belt he had from yesterday with today's. He ran his program to calculate the mass of the fragments in this region again, and looked at the two sets of figures. They appeared to show that a section of the Asteroid Belt was increasing in mass. *Could some of the fragments be joining together?* he contemplated. *What would cause that? This could be worth monitoring,* he decided, and set about adjusting the telescope to concentrate on the area in question. No sooner had he set up his new experiment than his mobile sprang to life with the theme from the X-Files. The screen displayed 'Gideon calling'.

Alex had met Gideon last year at an Astronomer's convention in the city centre. Gideon, obviously, was there by mistake; believing it to be something to do with Astrology. They'd met at the bar during the first interval and found, surprisingly, that they had a lot in common. They ended up skipping the rest of the lectures and spent the rest of the day chatting about all the wrongs in the world. They discovered that they were both huge fans of the X-Files; a popular TV series in the 90's, starring David Duchovny and Gillian Anderson. In fact, they had both adopted the theme tune for their ring tones.

"Hi Gideon. What gives?" he responded, setting his mobile to 'speaker mode'.

Gideon's voice echoed from the tiny built-in speaker, "Hi Alex. Just wondered if you were still on for the UFO Symposium tomorrow night?"

"You bet. They got that guy from America giving a lecture on ancient aliens and the Sumerians and shit."

"Ha ha, have you found Nibiru with that telescope of yours yet?"

Alex tutted. "Firstly, if it was out there it would be too far away to see, even with this baby, and secondly, I don't think it still exists." *At least not in one piece,* he thought.

"Okay dude, you're the expert," conceded Gideon. "I've got some things to check out on the Internet first, so I'll meet you in the bar at seven, bye."

Alex turned his phone off and went back to his calculations. He liked Gideon, but was a little wary of getting drawn into his conspiracy theories. *All that paranoia; it just can't be healthy,* he warned himself. Although he and Gideon hung out together fairly regularly, he'd never actually met Gideon's other friends, nor the couple that he lodged with. *I wonder what he's got to hide,* he thought. *Shit, it really is catching.*

The following evening

The UFO Symposium was all they had anticipated and more; the speaker from America had an impressive set of slides and animations about the ancient Sumerian civilization. Whilst Alex had found their knowledge of Astronomy and advanced mathematics fascinating, Gideon had enjoyed the theory that an alien race, called the Annunaki, had visited earth with the intent to mine gold for their own planet. Needing slaves for the mines, the Annunaki had carried out genetic experiments and had created modern humans by mixing their own DNA with the indigenous Hominids. In exchange, these beings had taught the first humans how to create and sustain a civilisation, helping them to cultivate plants and farm animals. Man had changed from a hunter-gatherer to a farmer in an incredibly short amount of time, and the American speaker claimed the Sumerian texts explained why.

Eventually the aliens had bred with the humans, creating hybrids, who became 'demi-gods' and ruled over the human race. Their advanced civilisation and technology had apparently been destroyed in a nuclear war between factions of the demi-gods around the time of the Great Deluge. In fact, the speaker had claimed that the nuclear war may have been the cause of the flood.

Finally, two excited and slightly inebriated young men, each carrying a four pack of lager, bundled into Alex's flat in the student letting area of Cambridge. It was small by most standards, comprising of only three rooms: a single bedroom, a bathroom, and a main room; containing a small kitchen, a dining table and a sitting area.

24

"Shhh," admonished Alex. "Don't make so much noise. The guy upstairs is a right miserable git."

"Sorry Alex," replied Gideon as he picked up the heavy ashtray he'd inadvertently knocked off the small coffee table in Alex's kitchen-diner-lounge.

"What a night!" exclaimed Alex, opting to sit in the single armchair furnishing the room.

"That guy sure seemed to know his stuff, but aliens? What do you think about that?" marvelled Gideon, sinking back into the under-sprung sofa with his can already at his lips.

"Maybe, but you'd think that if these Anu-watsits really existed, there'd be more evidence of them around today."

"Annunaki," corrected Gideon, "and the evidence *is* around today. That's what he was showing us. Those Sumerian cylinder seals are still around today, aren't they?"

"Yeah, but I mean, what happened to all their technology and stuff?" pondered Alex.

"Buried somewhere in Iraq, I guess. What they didn't take with them. Maybe they're Saddam's real Weapons of Mass Destruction. I've always thought it strange that by the time the Americans got there, the Imperial Baghdad Museum had been completely ransacked. Something like 100,000 items went missing. I guess there's no point in the aliens coming back for their stuff now," said Gideon.

"Ah, but did they leave?"

"They must have...or they'd still be running the planet," reasoned Gideon.

"It sure as hell explains how the Sumerians knew of the existence of the outer planets of our Solar System. I was nearly blown away when that guy explained that they even knew the colours of Uranus and Neptune. I mean, that's only recently been confirmed by Voyager 2," said Alex, wiping some spilt beer off the arm of the chair with his sleeve. "And how the hell could they have known about Pluto? You can't even see it with the most powerful telescopes we have today!"

"What about all that stuff about them creating humans from caveman DNA?"

"Well, I've never believed in Darwin's theory – it would have taken too long," replied Alex, opening his second can. "Fancy a spliff?"

"Yeah, go on then. Don't make it too strong. I'm gonna look up that bloke he mentioned on the Internet when I get back. Sitchen wasn't it? Do you reckon his translations of the Sumerian tablets are accurate?"

"Well, that's the key question isn't it? But there's no need to rush off, dude. We can look him up here," replied Alex, sweeping his arm around the room in the vague direction of his laptop, which was sitting on the corner of a self-assembled dining table. "But, getting back to my point about Darwinism - it would have taken billions of years for evolution of the kind he describes. And I'm just not convinced that the Earth is that old."

"How come? I thought the Earth was like 4 billion years old," said Gideon, suddenly becoming interested again.

"That's what they teach us in school. But have you ever done the maths?" asked Alex. Gideon shook his head, as he ripped up the cover of a Rizla packet to make a roach. "Exactly – no-one ever does. But here's the thing: Earth's spin is slowing down at a rate of about one second per year. That means that 120 years ago there were 2 minutes more every year. 1.2 million years ago there were an extra fourteen days each year. Where's this leading? Well, 4.8 million years ago, there were an extra 56 days each year. That's an increase of 16% on the current year. If you go back 30 million years, the Earth would have been spinning at twice its current rate. That means only six hours of daylight, followed by six hours of darkness each day, and winds of well over 300 miles per hour on a regular basis. You've seen the destruction that 150 mile an hour winds can cause these days. How could Dinosaurs have survived in those conditions? Nothing could survive back then, let alone 60 million years ago."

"So why do they tell us Dinosaurs roamed the Earth over 60 million years ago?" asked Gideon.

"You tell me. Probably because they can't explain how the Dinosaur fossils got here if the Earth isn't at least as old as that. But, you know what? Actually, there's evidence that suggests the Earth is only two million years old in reality," Alex concluded.

"Really, what is it?" said Gideon, passing the 'joint' to Alex.

"There's something called the *Helium Problem*. Which suggests that all decaying material on the planet emits helium. Now, this helium can't escape the Earth's atmosphere very easily. If you calculate how much helium there is in the atmosphere today, the Earth can't be much older than two million years. No-one can fathom it," Alex explained. "I'm not saying that the *Universe* isn't 4 billion years old, just that the Earth and Moon, in their present configuration, can't be more than two to thirty million years old at the most."

"Shit, dude. That's amazing," said Gideon. Alex wasn't sure if he was referring to his theory or the cannabis, which was now taking effect.

Having finished the 'joint', they meandered their way across the room to the laptop. "Have you got broadband on this...?" started Gideon.

"Of course, dude." Alex wiggled his mouse and the laptop's display sprung to life.

"Hey, what's that you're working on?" asked Gideon, appearing at his shoulder.

"Oh, just some stuff for my Ph.D on the Asteroid Belt."

"Sweet. You don't think it was created by the collision of Nibiru and... what was it?"

Alex looked a little embarrassed. "Well, it's one possible theory – even before the Sumerian texts came to light. Ask any astronomer and they'll tell you that everything that happens in Heaven and Earth is cyclic: pole changes, ice ages, maybe even the Big Bang itself. What goes around, comes around. No reason to discount planetary collisions."

"You *do* think it could be possible then?" grinned Gideon. "What about the return of Nibiru or Planet X in 2012?"

But Alex wasn't listening. He was looking at the results of his latest mass calculations. "Shit. This can't be right."

"What is it?"

"Er... well, it's kinda hard to explain."

"You can tell me, I'm a doctor," joked Gideon.

Alex laughed. "Well according to these calculations, the area of the Asteroid Belt that I'm studying appears to be putting on weight."

"Aren't we all, dude?"

"But this can't happen. I mean, this is the reverse of what has been happening for millions of years."

"What does it mean, Alex?"

"I don't really know. I'm going to have to have my figures checked by my professor." He clicked on his telescope viewing window and groaned. "And I'm going to have to be quick about it; the whole region will be obscured by Mars in a few days."

Gideon had already lost interest. "Google Sitchin. S-I-T-C-H-I-N."

CHAPTER SEVEN

Underground cavern, somewhere on Earth

Enki switched off the CNN broadcast and parted his thin grey lips in a sickening smile. The cavern appeared spartan, but behind the walls was a complex array of monitors, communications equipment and computers. He waved his hand in front of a panel and the doors to the communications room slid open.

"Atrahasis, when does the Bilderberg Group meet again?"

"They are sending out invitations for…let me see…" Atrahasis flicked through the timetable he was holding in his gnarled hand. "…Yes, here it is; 22nd August, …in London," he added.

"Good. Make sure they get updated on the current situation, and Atrahasis…"

"Yes, Lord?"

"I want that European incident to happen as soon as possible."

"Yes, Lord."

"We were so close in 1940," he lamented. "We underestimated the will of the New World and relied too much on that fool Hitler. It's frustrating that it has taken this long to get ourselves back into a position of strength. At least this time we have global communications to assist us. Now, what is being done to distribute the elixir to the citizens?"

"I think you will be very pleased, Lord," Atrahasis replied, fearfully. "We are providing the special ingredients to a global soft drinks manufacturer for inclusion in their latest health drink, and to a toothpaste company as an additive to their 'enamel strengthening' products."

"Will we get enough penetration with only two delivery systems?"

"We will in Europe and the New World. In the Old World we will be introducing similar Halaal products and, to be efficient, we will add some to the main supplier of ground cayenne pepper and salt in the region. Our mathematicians calculate that we will reach over 80% of the target population within the desired timeframe."

"What of the others?"

"Co-incidentally, they are concentrated either in areas of natural disaster or in densely populated regions. Our forecasters inform us that we need a 30% reduction in the overall population for your plan to be successful. I believe that a combination of earthquakes, tsunamis and floods will deliver the required results. Of course, your brother will need to be successful with his graviton experiment to ensure our total success."

"Things may not be as bad as I first thought," decided Enki. "Again, we must manage the disinformation to avoid widescale suspicion. When will my brother be in contact again?" he added.

"That is a little more difficult to predict, Lord. The conditions should be correct for the end of the year."

"And the NASA satellite has been launched and is making its way to Mars?

"Yes, it will orbit Mars and head on to Vesta."

"Let's hope my brother has prepared well. You may leave me in peace, now. I have much to contemplate. I want you to take charge of this personally, Atrahasis. Take my cloak and meet with the Council of Three Hundred."

"Very well, Lord."

CHAPTER EIGHT

Frankfurt Airport, Frankfurt, Germany

Rob disembarked from the plane and headed for the nearest information board. His connecting flight to Hangzhou Airport wasn't for two and a half hours, so he decided to relax with a beer in the first class lounge. Frankfurt Airport, like most hubs, was extremely busy at this time of day, but the first class lounge was relatively peaceful. He noted that the lounge was a good eight or nine gates away from his flight, but he was in no particular hurry. He found a quiet corner, where he could keep an eye on the information screen, and settled down to read the novel he'd bought at Heathrow. It was his first visit to China – his first time flying first class too. Simon was meeting him at Hangzhou Airport with his driver. They both had rooms booked at the Ramada Plaza, close to the West Lake. He would be assessing a manufacturing site close by, before taking an internal flight to Tianjin, to look at another facility on one of the TEDA (Tianjin Economic Development Area) sites. It looked like he was in for a tiring few days, and he had to be back in a week's time to meet with the DNATech people.

Rob checked his watch: a little over an hour until his flight. *Might as well have another beer*, he thought to himself. *At least I don't have to drive at the other end.* As he got to the bar, he heard his name over the public address system.

"Last call for Mister Kirk on flight UE119 to Hangzhou..."

What? It's not for another hour, he thought to himself. Then it suddenly dawned on him. *Holy crap. I forgot about the time difference between London and Frankfurt.* Grabbing his things he dashed out of the lounge, back onto the main concourse. *Oh shit, this is all I need. The first time they let me out on my own and I miss my damn flight*, he cursed as he ran towards gate 22. The gate attendants were about to close the barrier to the plane. "Hold up," he shouted. One of the attendants looked at his watch, then at Rob, who was still three gates away. He shook his head, and re-opened the barrier. Rob skidded to a stop and fumbled with his documents.

"We were just about to have your bags taken off the plane, Mister Kirk," said the attendant, as he checked his boarding pass and passport.

"I know, I'm really sorry," pleaded Rob, explaining. "I forgot about the time difference from London, it was such a short flight."

The attendant waved him through dismissively. By the time Rob got to his seat, he was sweating buckets and his lungs felt like he'd been breathing sulphuric acid. As he looked round, he noticed that there were only nine other seats in first class. Several of the other passengers eyed him as if he'd just walked on board completely naked. The steward brought him a glass of champagne and a bowl of nuts.

The captain's voice came over the speaker:

"I'm sorry, ladies and gentlemen, we will be delayed by ten minutes due to the late arrival of some passengers."

Rob wanted the spacious first class seat to swallow him whole. *Oh my God. I've got to spend the next fourteen hours with these people, and now they all know that I'm the reason for the delay*, he thought. He busied himself trying to work out how to operate his personal TV.

The rest of the flight was, thankfully, uneventful. He'd been well looked after. The food was excellent – served on china plates. He watched a couple of good movies *and* managed to sleep for several hours. The first class cabin was quite spacious and he got up and stretched his legs a few times.

Hangzhou Airport, Hangzhou, China

As Rob lined up to pass through immigration, he marvelled at the cleanliness of the airport. There seemed to be cleaners everywhere. *The immigration officials look like they're Red Army in their smart uniforms and insignia*, he thought. Having passed through immigration, he collected his bags and lined up behind the other passengers to clear customs. Coming out the other side, he realised he had a clear view of the reception parties and noticed, much to his amusement, that he was probably a good foot taller than most of the other passengers around him. Simon waved from behind the barrier and he headed in his direction.

"Hiya, Rob. Good flight?" Simon asked, taking one of Rob's bags from him and handing it to the Chinese man standing next to him.

"Yeah, no problem," he lied.

"The car's outside. It's about twenty five miles to the hotel, so we should make dinner. This is DQ," he added, introducing his driver.

"DQ?" whispered Rob, as they followed the driver to the car.

"I know," answered Simon. "Probably the closest pronunciation to his real name."

After another excellent meal in the hotel restaurant, he finally collapsed on the bed back in his room and rang Charlotte.

The Ramada Plaza Hotel, Hangzhou, China
The next day, he met Simon for breakfast.

"Make the most of the hotel food," Simon warned him. "The stuff they serve in the factory canteen is almost inedible."

"It's really weird," said Rob. "I'm not used to being somewhere where most people don't speak a word of English."

"They hotel staff aren't bad, but we've got an interpreter at the factory. I'll introduce you to her. She's probably the most important person you need to meet," he laughed. "I've picked up a few basic words, but not enough to have a conversation."

"What about the driver? Er...PQ."

"DQ? No, he's hopeless," confided Simon. "He knows *hotel, airport* and *factory*...Oh, and *slow down*, which is quite useful, the way they drive over here. I taught him that one myself," laughed Simon. "I was coming back late from the factory one evening, and DQ obviously wanted to get home, so he was speeding down the dual carriageway and a damned beeper kept going off. Anyway, I had a splitting headache, so I asked if he could go any quieter. Next thing, the damned fool has speeded up."

"How come?"

"Well, I found out the next day from Diana – she's our interpreter, by the way – that *quieter* sounds like their word for *faster*," chuckled Simon. "I was shouting QUIETER, and he thought I meant FASTER. But don't worry; I'll be with you most of the time."

On the way to the factory, Rob got to see first hand what Simon had meant. Unlike in England, where the Highway Code is law, in China they seemed to make the rules up as they went along. People were cutting off corners, driving on the wrong side of the road, ignoring traffic signals. It seemed to Rob that the bigger the car, the greater 'right of way' you were granted. When they came off the dual carriageway, they nearly collided with a man on a strange three-wheeled contraption coming the wrong way. DQ expertly swerved round him as if nothing had happened.

"Phawr," said Rob. "What do those things run on?"

Simon laughed. "I know. Smells like rotten cabbages doesn't it? Wind the window up."

As they approached the industrial area, Rob noticed the huge plumes of smog hanging over the buildings, and the sunlight became hazy. Simon noticed Rob's expression.

"Fossil fuels," he said, by way of an explanation. "Must be what it was like in the London smog years ago."

Hangzhou Communications, Hangzhou, China

When they reached the factory, Rob was introduced to Diana and then shown to the office of the factory owner, a Mister Chen. Mister Chen spoke very few words of English and Rob was grateful for Diana's interpretation skills. Rob explained, via Diana, that he was interested in their test facility and would like to see their equipment.

It was several hours later, when Diana said to him, "You take lunch now, yes?"

"Er... okay. Where are we going?"

"Mister Chen wants to take you to restaurant. It oldest restaurant in Hangzhou," she stated, proudly.

Rob was relieved not to be eating in the canteen after what Simon had said earlier.

"Is Simon joining us?" he enquired.

"Mister Rockwall is busy. He say you go alone."

Louwailou Restaurant, Hangzhou, China

The restaurant was magnificent. Huge vaulted ceilings with gold coloured beams, luxurious red curtains and the whitest tablecloths Rob had ever seen. Several of the other diners seemed to be wearing the uniforms he'd seen at the airport.

"This State run restaurant," Diana explained. "Mister Chen know manager. He get us very good seat."

Mister Chen smiled at the mention of his name and led them to an exclusive table away to the side of the other diners.

Diana talked Rob through the menu, trying her best to explain what was in each dish. Mister Chen occasionally chipped in and between them they ordered lunch. Being the guest of honour, it befell to Rob to eat the fish's head when it arrived, much to the amusement of Diana and Mister Chen. Rob suspected that they never tired of this ritual with their English and American visitors. Recognising chicken, Rob started to fill his plate. Diana kept the conversation going, expertly switching from English to Chinese and back again.

Enjoying a plate of freshly cooked eels, Rob picked up what looked like a vegetable from a dish that had just arrived.

"Mmmm, these are good," he said, smiling and nodding at Mister Chen. "What are they?" he asked Diana.

"They come from sea. Vegetable, I think," she replied. She spoke to Mister Chen in Chinese. "I think perhaps they used to have a head," she announced politely.

Finally, the waiter brought out two small glasses of drink for each of them and arranged them on the table. One was dark and one was pale, but slightly cloudy. Diana explained that it was snake blood and snake bile. *You bastard Simon,* thought Rob. *So that's why you didn't want to join us. Oh well, bottoms up.*

After dinner, Diana offered to take Rob sightseeing on the West Lake. Mister Chen had to return to the factory. Rob decided it would be rude to decline, so he thanked Mister Chen for his hospitality and set off with Diana to find a boat. The tour lasted about two hours and Rob was exhausted by the end of it. Diana had been the perfect tour guide and had explained everything to him, including several Chinese legends. As they were crossing one of the small bridges to take the boat back to the mainland, a small child and his mother were coming in the opposite direction. The child pointed at Rob, said something in Chinese and hid behind his mother's legs. Diana giggled as they passed and said something to the woman in Chinese.

"What was that all about," enquired Rob.

"He say '*look mama a giant*'," she replied with a smile.

Back on the mainland, Diana put Rob into a taxi and told the driver to take him back to his hotel. She also told Rob how much to pay him when he got there.

Later, when he met up with Simon in the hotel restaurant for their evening meal, Rob asked, "How the hell can you get any work done when all they want to do is take you out to lunch and show you around all the time?"

Simon replied, "You'll get used to it. It's not so bad in Tianjin. They're a bit more work savvy. And they speak more English up there. What did you think of the factory?"

"We've got our work cut out getting them up to speed," Rob admitted.

"So when do you fly back?" asked Simon, tucking into a huge steak.

"Oh, I've got a meeting with DNATech in a week's time, so next Wednesday should be fine," answered Rob. "I'm glad this hotel serves English food," he added, pouring vinegar over his chips.

"Well make sure you leave yourself time to pick up something for your wife," advised Simon. "The shops in Beijing are pretty good. I'd get my flight home switched to there, if I was you."

"Er... we're not married," said Rob awkwardly. "But, you're right. She'd go mental if I didn't take something back. I saw some rather nice kimonos in the hotel shop."

"They're cheaper in Beijing. I'll get Diana to sort out your flight. You'll love it."

CHAPTER NINE

Head Office of IDSys, Cambridge Science Park, England

Mitchell closed the weekly programme meeting at 11.30am on the dot and sent his team back out to their work stations.

"Sarah, stay behind please. I've got some letters for you to respond to." Mitch whispered, as the others left the boardroom.

"Okay."

Mitch waited until they had all left before he spoke again. Sarah, in the meantime, cleared the table of documents that people had left behind and wiped the whiteboard clean. *What would I do without her?* Mitch thought as he contemplated someone walking into the boardroom and reading the notes / action points from this morning's meeting.

"Thanks, Sarah. I'm forever forgetting the secret nature of this project."

"These are different times for the company, Mitch. Mister Shackelford is hardly off the phone. Do you remember when we had that irritating truck hire guy on the phone every week, asking..."

"Yeah," he smiled. "But this is different. Shackelford virtually owns us at the moment. I can't leave the country without his say so."

"Really?"

"Well yeah, virtually." Mitch paced to the window to look over the Science Park that he once thought announced his arrival in the world of electronic design. Now it felt like a prison. He remembered the real reason he'd asked Sarah to stay behind. "We're not going to cope with our current staffing levels, Sarah, so I'd like you to contact our agencies and see what they've got."

Sarah took out her notepad. "What are you looking for?" she asked.

Mitch scratched his head. "Well, with Simon and Rob spending so much time in China, I really need to backfill them. Do you need any extra help yourself?" he asked.

"Well, the admin has increased quite a bit lately. I could do with someone to help me process the expenses and the timesheets, I suppose," she replied appreciatively. "The question is...where are we going to put them?"

"That's what I've been trying to work out," Mitch admitted. "We can't afford to move to bigger premises – not until the Government releases more funds, anyway. Would you mind looking at the floor plan? – I think we're all going to have to give up some space. Simon can share my office."

He could tell by the look on Sarah's face that she was concerned. "I'll look at the floor plan again," she said. "But it's not going to go down well with the troops."

"I know, but we all have to make sacrifices. It won't be forever. Anyway, let me have the CVs when they come through and we'll see."

Sarah looked at her watch. "You haven't forgotten that you've got a meeting with Mister Shackelford at 12.15, have you?"

"No, Sarah, I haven't. When he arrives, send him to my office, and have the staff restaurant send up a buffet – I can't stand having to entertain him in town. Here're the letters for reply. I've marked up my responses."

Not for the first time, Mitch was wondering what he'd got himself into. Everything had been fine at the start, but now things were going from bad to worse. The programme was on schedule (just), but the interference from the Government was beginning to feel more and more like a takeover bid. He was already using the Government's preferred manufacturer in China, despite the unfavourable reports from Simon Rockwall and Robin Kirk. Simon was permanently based out there – at least for the foreseeable future, and Rob, who had just returned from their Tianjin site, was travelling out there at least one month out of every three. Extensive testing was being carried out at DNATech, at the Government's request, and last minute specification changes were on the point of throwing the project into complete meltdown.

On top of everything, Shackelford and his scientists had produced a modification to the RFID chip that his designers were to incorporate before going into production.

He was just about to enter his secretary's office when he heard Rob from the stairs below.

"Mitch! Can I have a quick word?" Rob called up.

"Oh, Hi Rob. It'll have to be quick – I've got a meeting in fifteen minutes."

They both entered Mitch's office and Sarah said she'd bleep him when Shackelford arrived.

"So what's the problem Rob?" Mitch asked, without inviting Rob to sit down.

"Well, did you know about the changes to my RFID chip design that the Government have requested?"

"Yeah, they've provided schematics, haven't they?" Mitch carried on sorting out his paperwork.

"Well yeah, but I've got only two days to re-layout the substrate to take on board their amendments," complained Rob.

"Can it be done?" Mitch asked.

"If I put in a couple of long days, I guess so."

"Thanks Rob, it's appreciated. You guys are all on bonuses when we get paid."

"It's not that, it's just that the modification they're making is to include a receiver as well as the transmitter circuit I designed."

"So? I expect they need to update the information on the chip from time to time," Mitch reasoned.

"Well, that's usually done using the magnetic interface we designed for the vehicle tracking system. Not by remote RF signal."

"So what are you saying, Rob?"

"This modification means they can update the chip remotely, over large distances, without the user being aware," Rob replied.

"And the problem is?"

"It's just not what was described in the original requirements specification, Mitch."

"So we make the changes and we bill them for it," Mitch said, getting mildly irritated.

"But..."

"Rob, I haven't got time for this. Shackelford is on his way. Design the chip to do whatever he wants. Just make sure we track any changes they make, and charge them accordingly."

The buzzer went and Sarah's voice announced the arrival of Preston Shackelford.

"I'm sorry, Rob. I've got a meeting," Mitch said, signalling that the conversation was over.

Rob left Mitch's office with an uneasy feeling in his stomach. *Am I the only one who's bothered about this?* he thought. *Devices that can only transmit information is one thing. But devices that can receive instructions, without the individual even knowing, is a completely different matter. I've never seen Mitch so blasé about this kind of thing before.*

Mitch had barely sat down when Sarah entered with Shackelford, who was carrying a large briefcase. "Nice to see you, Preston," Mitch said, as he came around his desk with his hand outstretched.

"Likewise."

"I thought you guys had red briefcases," said Mitch, nodding at the worn-out briefcase at Shackelford's side, in an attempt to lighten the mood.

"Dispatch boxes. Only the dispatch boxes," Shackelford grumbled, as he lowered himself into Mitch's visitor's chair.

"Have you come for a personal update on the programme, Preston?" said Mitch, deciding to stick to business after all. *This guy's obviously had a sense of humour bypass,* he told himself.

"On the contrary, Mitch, I've come to update you." Shackelford reached into his briefcase and pulled out a wad of documents and placed them on the desk in front of Mitch. "The rest of the team are pleased with your progress, Mitch, and you've been invited to join them at an... er... at an exclusive meeting in August."

Mitch glanced at the top document containing a list of invitees and exhaled slowly. "Very exclusive. I'd have thought these guys were well out of my league."

"Not any more, Mitch. Not any more."

"What goes on at these...er...meetings?"

"The great and the good discuss current issues and decide what they can do to put them right collectively. There are often break-out sessions for particular problems to be resolved, but on the whole it's an opportunity to meet with like-minded individuals, play some golf, eat well and make influential contacts."

"Does the Queen of the Netherlands *play* golf?" asked Mitch incredulously.

"Haven't a clue. I don't get invited to such grand functions. I'll leave you to browse through the documents at your leisure. Needless to say, these documents are highly sensitive – *eyes only*, yes?" With that, Shackelford rose from the chair. "Oh, by the way Mitch, don't be alarmed. You may hear this group of individuals being referred to as the *Bilderberg Group* in the press and the like, but it's just a load of nonsense dreamt up by disgruntled executives and nobodies who don't get invited."

"The Bilderberg Group? Who are they?"

"As I said, just some media invention designed to cause problems. Don't bother to see me out, my driver's waiting for me in reception."

As the door closed Mitch looked over the list of invitees again and his stomach flipped. These people were serious operators. Several of them, he noted, were chairmen and CEO's of large, global organisations, others were royalty, senior politicians, international bankers, with a few celebrities thrown in for good measure. He sat back down at this desk and googled *'the Bilderberg Group'* on his desktop. Wikipedia had the following to say:

> *"The Bilderberg Group or Bilderberg conference is an unofficial annual invitation-only conference of around 130 guests, most of whom are persons of influence in the fields of business, media, and politics.*
>
> *The elite group meets annually at exclusive, four or five-star resorts throughout the world, normally in Europe, once every four years in the United States or Canada. It has an office in Leiden, South Holland, Netherlands. The Bilderbergers met from May 31 to June 3 at the Ritz-Carlton Hotel in Istanbul, Turkey for the 2007 meeting.*
>
> *The original intention of the Bilderberg Group was to further the understanding between Western Europe and North America through informal meetings between powerful individuals. Each year, a "steering committee" devises a selected invitation list with a maximum of 100 names. Invitations are extended only to residents of Europe and North America. The location of their annual meeting is not secret, but the public and press are strictly kept at distance by police force and private security guards. Although the agenda and list of participants are openly*

available to the public, it is not clear that such details are disclosed by the group itself. Also, the contents of the meetings are kept secret and attendees pledge not to divulge what was discussed. The group's stated justification for secrecy is that it enables people to speak freely without the need to carefully consider how every word might be interpreted by the mass media." [1]

Well that all looks pretty innocuous, he thought. He put the documents in his briefcase to take home and digest in his own time.

Sarah popped her head around the door and said, "The buffet's arrived, but I guess you won't be needing it now?"

"No, take it over to the boys in the lab; they'll manage to make a hole in it, I'm sure!"

Sarah laughed. "I'll whip it down now."

After his discussion with Mitch, Rob had returned to the lab. Duncan and Sandra were laughing about something.

"Hey, what's up, Rob?" enquired Duncan, noticing Rob's downbeat manner.

"Nothing really. Mitch has got that Shackelford geezer in with him again. I've never seen him so wired."

Duncan laughed. "Me and Sandra call him 'Sir Humphrey'. Get it?"

"Yes. Very funny, Duncan. Listen, I don't suppose you can stay behind tonight for a couple of hours to help me check some new designs?"

"They're not making more changes, are they?" Duncan looked at the time. "I suppose I can manage a couple of hours."

The red light over the door blinked on and off and Sarah came in pushing a trolley of food in front of her.

"Hey, what's this? Buffet food not good enough for Sir Humphrey?" Duncan quipped.

The next morning, Mitch was in his office early. A short time later he heard the door to the outer office close and he knew Sarah had arrived for work. He took the documents that Shackelford had given him yesterday from his briefcase and set them out on his desk. Pressing his

[1] http://en.wikipedia.org/wiki/Bilderberg_Group

intercom button he said, "Morning Sarah, can you get me Simon on the phone in China – he shouldn't have left yet." A few moments later, a well recognised voice came through on the speaker phone:

"Hi Mitch, how's it going in sunny Cambridge?"

"Not bad, how're things you're end?"

"Bloody hot. The air-conditioning in the hotel's on the blink again. But you don't want to know about that. We finally got the production line producing our vehicle tracking chips with a decent first time yield. Another few weeks and we'll be ready for production of the new RFID chips."

"That *is* good news. When are you planning to fly back?"

"I should be back early next week...anything the matter?"

Mitch hesitated, then said, "I've had a rather unusual invitation."

"Oh yeah. Who from?"

"A bunch of people calling themselves the Bilderberg Group. Heard of them?"

"No shit! The Bilderberg Group *are* an elite bunch. What do they want from you?"

"I guess it's to do with our RFIDs," ventured Mitch.

"Well, you've starting mixing with people in high places while I've been away."

"I don't suppose I should duck out then?" Mitch ventured.

"Are you crazy? These guys are amongst the most influential people in the world. If not *the* most influential."

That's what I was afraid of, thought Mitch. "Sure could do with your help on this one, buddy. I mean, what do I say?"

"When is it?"

"Not until mid-August."

"Have they given you an agenda?"

"Sort of – I got a pile of documents on stuff I've never heard of mainly." Mitch toyed with the documents on his desk.

"I'll take a look at it with you when I get back. Jesus Mitch, this could make you a billionaire in no time."

Or make me 'persona non gratis' for the rest of my days, thought Mitch.

"Don't talk to anyone else about it until I get back," said Simon suddenly.

"Don't worry. I don't intend to. Do you know they keep the meeting venue a secret up until a few weeks before it's due to be held?"

"They don't want the publicity."

"All I know is it's to be in London this year."

"Don't even mention *that* to anyone. You'd get crucified if they found out that you'd leaked anything like that," warned Simon.

"I know, I know. This stuff's going in the safe tonight."

"In the meantime, you'd better brush up on your secret handshakes."

Mitch paused. "What, you mean like the Freemasons or something?"

"Bound to be plenty of them around. You be sure to let me know if they try and get you to roll up your trouser leg and do strange things with chickens," laughed Simon.

"Oh, very funny, Simon. What's that noise in the background?"

"Ha ha. That, my friend, is the bell telling the workers that the bus has arrived to take them home," Simon chuckled.

"I'd better not keep you then," joked Mitch.

"Yeah, right. You know full well that I've got my own driver. You should see the way they drive out here. I'm surprised they don't make their cars with a steering wheel in the middle, the lack of attention they pay to what side of the road they're supposed to be on."

"I thought the bicycle was the preferred mode of transport."

"Now *that* you have to see. I don't know how they manage to miss each other."

The two friends continued to chat about Simon's adventures in China for another half an hour or so. At the end of the conversation Mitch's mood had greatly improved.

As soon as Simon had hung up, Mitch took the pile of documents, shoved them in a company folder, scribbled Bilderberg on the front, and put it in the safe behind his desk. *I suppose I've got to get used to mixing in these circles.* Mitch had never been keen on the placing of contracts based on who you knew, rather than what you knew and how well you did it.

CHAPTER TEN

Head Office of DNATech, St. Albans, England

Shelby Taylor and Robin Kirk went over the testing schedule for the second time. They had been working together on and off for the last two months and had got on famously from day one.

"What do *you* make of these transmission tests, Shelby?"

"I suppose they're to make sure there are no ill effects from all of your funny radio waves."

"Is it normal to use fifteen different DNA strains?"

"It is if you're looking for behavioural differences."

"Why would they be interested in behavioural differences? Surely we're just talking health issues in our case?"

Shelby rubbed her nose as she thought about Rob's question. "Maybe they just want to be sure they're not being sent raving mad," she offered finally.

"I wish they'd let me monitor the results as well."

"Why?"

"Just for peace of mind, I suppose," Rob replied hesitantly. "RF signals can do strange things to people – just look at microwave ovens."

"But you must be sure of your own design...."

"I am when I'm the one who's designed it, but this..."

"You didn't design this?" asked Shelby, feeling slightly alarmed.

"Most of it, yeah. But not this receiver bit. That was the Home Office boys and they've been pretty tight-lipped about what it actually does."

As soon as he'd said it, Rob felt pretty foolish. It was Gideon's paranoia rubbing off on him, he was sure.

"Am I in any danger running the tests?" Shelby asked, growing concerned.

"No, of course not. You'll be screened the whole time. It's the little miceys who'll get it," said Rob, reassuringly.

They sat in silence for a few minutes with their thoughts. It was Rob who eventually spoke first.

"Hey look. I didn't mean to scare you. I'm sure everything is fine. I've never worked on something like this before. Usually we're only tracking and recording information from vehicles."

"So these things can send information as well as receive it?"

"Of course. That's their main function. At least I thought it was until they hit me with the receiver design."

"I never thought I'd have an issue with privacy laws etcetera, but the more I think about this, the more uncomfortable I get. Can you live with this okay, Rob?"

"Now you're starting to sound like my mate, Gideon."

"I take it that's not a good thing?"

"That really depends on your point of view."

Their meeting finally concluded around noon, which gave Rob plenty of time to get back to Cambridge.

"Listen, Shelby," Rob said, as he packed his notes into his briefcase. "I think it might be a good idea if you visited us at IDSys next Friday to see the equipment, and for me to walk you through a few things in our lab."

"No problem. Can we make it after lunch though, as I've got a meeting with my boss in the morning?"

"Yeah, great. Say, two o'clock? I'll mail you a map. It's pretty easy to find."

"Okay, thanks Rob. It'll make a change to get out of this place."

Later that evening

Shelby had a restless night; she had been experiencing strange dreams over the last few weeks and tonight was no exception:

She was leaving work and appeared to be the last one to go; as per usual. She surveyed the car park, which was empty of cars, and began to walk home. It was dark and still. The street seemed to stretch out before her like a runway. She felt the first spots of rain, and realized she wasn't wearing a coat; in fact she was dressed in only a short cotton nightdress. The rain was starting to get heavy and she felt the cold go right through her. As she looked round for somewhere to shelter, she saw a large white building, with pale green doors, just off to the side of the street. She started to run towards the entrance of the building. The doors were open when she reached them and she stepped inside to take shelter. She found herself inside an elevator. She tried pressing several of the buttons, but nothing happened. Then, just as the panic began to well up inside her, the lift started to descend. The doors opened and she walked towards another set of doors in front of her. She opened the doors and saw a room full of unoccupied workstations; rows and rows of vacant workstations.

She awoke with a start.

CHAPTER ELEVEN

2nd Floor, Palace of Westminster, London, England

The phone on the antique desk began ringing and the occupant of the office waited two rings. The phone went quiet, then, seconds later starting ringing again.

"Hello?"

"Is that extension 333?"

"No, it's extension 322."

"Are you alone?"

"Yes."

"Good. I have some information for you. Last night the President of the United States, the Canadian Prime Minister, and the President of Mexico signed the North American Union agreement. The Extended European Union is expected to be agreed within the next few weeks and the African Union soon after. The Asian Union agreement needs to proceed at a faster pace to keep to the desired timetable."

"How am I to speed things up from here?"

"There will be a terrorist attack at the heart of Europe, which will achieve two things. Firstly, it will strike enough fear into the hearts of the Europeans that they will practically beg their Governments to introduce bio-chip identity devices. Secondly, it will make it easier to consolidate the European Union. The Bilderberg Group is meeting in August and will move things along from their perspective. Four of our top investors will be funding a new film to be directed by Spielberg or Lucas, or someone, putting a positive slant on the New World Order. If the Asian Union can't step up the pace, we'll make sure they don't pose a problem."

"Very well. I assume there will be no terrorist survivors this time?"

"No. We've learnt from our previous mistakes. But there are a couple of small problems. We need to cover our tracks at IDSys once the devices have been tested and are ready for production. I understand the design engineer isn't entirely happy with our little modification."

"Shall I take care of that?"

"No, far better if we use another party. We don't want anything tying Westminster to any IDSys issues. Send me the details of the design engineer by the usual method and we'll take it from here. There is the matter of the Astronomy student however."

"Who's he? What's he done?"

"His name is Alex Wells from the University of Cambridge and it looks like he's discovered our graviton particle project in the Asteroid Belt. Fortunately for us, he reported his findings to his professor and he's not sure what he's stumbled across."

"And the professor informed you, naturally. Okay, I'll arrange to have it cleaned up."

"Thank you."

"What about the girl at DNATech?"

"I've been assured that she doesn't pose a problem. Not very bright, by all accounts."

A few minutes later the conversation was concluded and the phone receiver was replaced. The man rose from his desk and went to the window to look out across the Thames. *Finally, we seem to be making some progress*, he thought. There was a knock at the door.

"Come."

"Ah, there you are, Minister, good."

CHAPTER TWELVE

Head Office of IDSys, Cambridge Science Park, England

The drive up to Cambridge was fairly uneventful. Shelby had programmed her Sat Nav just in case, but preferred to leave it switched off unless she got into difficulties. She was more concerned about her car than finding her way. The salary at DNATech wasn't great and, although she found her six year old 1.6L Vauxhall Astra handy for around town, it wasn't so hot for motorway driving.

The meeting with Kim earlier had left her feeling that there was a lot going on behind the scenes that she was not being told about. She had assumed that the testing she would be performing would consist of two batches of mice from the fifteen different DNA strains – one control group and one group with the implant. However, Kim had informed her that there would be a third batch that would also be implanted. When she asked what the difference was between the two test batches with the implants, she was told not to concern herself, it was simply an additional test scenario for their client, who would interpret her results as they saw fit. She had only seen this done before when they were testing combinations of factors and she couldn't help wondering what the new batch had that made them different from the other implanted mice. She wondered if she should discuss it with Rob, but quickly ruled that out, deciding it would be unprofessional.

Anyway, it was a nice day to be out driving; the sun was out and there was a refreshing breeze coming through her open window. She knew the trip should only take her an hour or so which gave her time to stop off at a service station for a bite to eat.

When Shelby arrived, Rob met her in reception and, having signed her in at security, led her up the stairs to the first floor laboratory.

"We're meeting with Simon Rockwall, our Programme Manager,

first," he said, as they climbed the stairs. "Then I'll take you to the lab to see the equipment."

"Okay," she smiled.

They entered a small meeting room with a rectangular desk in the centre and seating for eight people. The room was equipped with the usual paraphernalia; conference phone, flip-chart, white board, laptop projector and refreshment bar. Simon was already pouring himself a coffee, and offered to pour out two more. Once they were settled, he passed around his project plan and started the meeting.

"I'm pleased to see that you guys have kept on top of things while I was in China. The production facility is now up to speed, the radio frequency tests are complete and we've passed the emissions tests," he summarised. "So, it's all down to you, Shelby. Once we get the go ahead from your lab, we can go into mass production whenever the Home Office is ready."

"We're on schedule to begin testing next week, provided we take delivery of the equipment on time," replied Shelby. They both looked at Rob.

"No problem. We'll run through the set up and operation after this meeting, and I can bring it down to you early next week."

"Actually Rob, let Duncan install it. I've got other work scheduled for you. Now, if you'd like to look at the updated plan in front of you, I'll take you both through it," Simon instructed.

After the meeting, Rob walked Shelby through the operating procedure for the equipment and introduced her to Duncan, who would be helping her with the installation and set up at DNATech. "It's all pretty straight forward, Shelby," Rob said, showing her how to run the test program. "It's fully automated and you'll know when the tests are complete when this message comes up." He pointed to the display.

"We've designed this Faraday cage, so only the mice will be subjected to the RF signals," said Duncan helpfully.

After a tour of the facility, Rob took Shelby up to Sarah's office where they had prepared some operating manuals to assist her in performing the tests. "Remember, if you have any problems, just give me a call on my mobile," said Rob.

"I'm sure I'll be fine, and thanks for the manuals."

"Oh, I nearly forgot. You'll need the key codes for the receiving tests. Do you know where Mitch keeps them, Sarah?"

"They're in his office safe. He's not in today, so just nip in and get them. Here's the combination. I have to remind him to change it every week." Handing Rob a slip of paper, she turned to talk to Shelby and Rob went into Mitch's office.

Being familiar with the layout, Rob went straight to the safe behind the desk. *I hope we don't get too many of these Government contracts,* he thought to himself, *all this secrecy is a pain in the neck.* He opened the safe and flicked through the files looking for the familiar buff folder which the Home Office had provided, containing the codes to unlock the RFID receiver. As he moved the heavy cashbox to one side to check the top shelf, he accidentally knocked a folder onto the floor. The contents spilled out. *Damn,* he cursed under his breath. As he picked up the sheets of paper he noticed the invitation. *Meeting of the Bilderberg Group on 22nd August in London,* he said to himself. Most of the names meant nothing to him, but two or three stood out like he'd been smacked in the head with an iron bar. *There're some serious heavyweights going to this,* he thought, sliding the paper back into the wallet and returning it to the shelf in the safe. Finding the folder he needed he re-locked the safe and left without giving it another thought.

As he saw Shelby out of the building, he noticed that most of the others had already left. Looking at his watch he realised it was 6.45pm already. "Sorry for holding you up so long Shelby. Looks like you'll be quite late getting back to St. Albans," he said, apologetically.

"Oh, that's okay, I've not made any plans this weekend," she replied, as she opened her car door.

"Drive carefully," he offered and turned to go back into the building.

I've had to cancel my plans for this evening as well, he thought as he went back up to the lab to finish off.

By the time he was ready to leave it was dusk. As he shut the main door behind him he noticed he was the last to leave. He could see the night security guard behind his desk in reception through the large glass doors. His car was parked in the far right-hand corner of the car park. *Trust me to park next to the only broken light,* he thought.

As he moved across the empty car park a tall, moving shadow caught his eye to the left, but as he looked across he couldn't see anything there. The hairs on the back of his neck stood on end momentarily, and he admonished himself for being so jumpy. He thought immediately of what Gideon had told him the other night: '*You know those Sat Nav's, Rob, well did you know that they can download instructions to them to make you go where they want you to go?'* 'Yeah, right,' Rob had responded. But Gideon had continued: *'How many times have you used one and ended up in the wrong place? Think about it'. Gideon and his damned conspiracy theories!* That was what was spooking him. He got in his car and started the engine. Much to his relief, there was no explosion.

Rob and Charlotte's flat, Cambridge, England

Rob and Charlotte's two-storey flat was only a few minutes drive from the Science Park. He and Charlotte shared the main bedroom with its en-suite bathroom, and the small study on the first floor, whereas Gideon had the spare room on the ground floor next to the lounge. There was also a small kitchen-diner, with another bathroom off the back. Parking in the street was a problem and Rob circled the block a couple of times before he found a space not too far away from their front door. A large dark blue or black car slowed, then sped up the street. Had that car been following him when he went round the block? He couldn't remember.

By the time he came through the door it was 8.15pm and Charlotte was just putting a delivery meal in the oven. "We decided on Chinese. That okay?" she asked.

"Great. Hope it's nothing like the stuff I get served up over there. I'm just off to get changed."

"You look like you saw a ghost, dude," said Gideon, drinking a can of lager.

By the time Rob had re-joined them, Charlotte was flicking through the TV stations to find something to watch while they had dinner. Just then his mobile rang. He looked at the screen; 'Shelby calling'.

"Hello? Rob?"

"Hi Shelby, what's up?"

"Hi Rob. I didn't know who else to call. My car's just died and I can't get it started again. I've tried over and over."

"Where are you?"

"Er... on the hard shoulder of the M11. Quite near the Cambridge slip road."

"Shit! Stay in the car, lock the doors, and I'll be there in about twenty minutes."

Exactly twenty five minutes later, Rob pulled up behind Shelby's car on the hard shoulder. He jumped out of the car and ran over to the driver's door. Shelby let the window down. "You'd better get into the passenger seat while I have a go at starting her," Rob said. After trying several times to start the car, he decided the battery was dead. "It's not gonna work. Have you got any jump leads?"

"I don't think so," said Shelby.

"Well they probably wouldn't help anyway. It's either your battery or your alternator."

"What does that mean?"

Rob and Shelby had become good friends over the last few weeks and he didn't hesitate with his offer. "It means you'd better come back to the flat with me and we'll call someone local to pick up the car. We can't leave it here all night."

When they got back, they found that Charlotte and Gideon hadn't started on the Chinese yet. So, with the introductions over, they all sat down together to tuck in. During the meal they decided that it would be best if Shelby slept on the sofa for the night and they'd get her back on the road in the morning. Having made that decision, they opened another bottle of wine and the conversation began to flow freely.

"By the way, Gideon, have you heard of the Bundesburg Group?" asked Rob, suddenly remembering the file in Mitch's safe.

"Do you mean the Bilderberg Group?" corrected Gideon.

"Er...yeah, probably."

"Of course I've heard of them. They're only the biggest bunch of Nazi's on the planet – hell bent on world domination. They're sort of like the Illuminati... or they are the Illuminati. I'm not really sure. Why do you ask?"

"I'm not sure you'd want to know." Rob was enjoying the moment.

"Don't tell me, they've asked you to join them at their next conference," laughed Gideon.

"Not exactly, but they've invited Mitch to attend."

The two girls stopped what they were doing and listened to the conversation.

"No way!" Gideon exclaimed. "How do you know?"

"I've seen the invite," Rob said with obvious pleasure.

"That's bull. They keep the arrangements secret up to the last minute."

"Well, suppose I told you that this year's conference is on 22nd August in London."

"Which Hotel?"

"I don't know, like you said – it's a secret," admitted Rob.

"Dude, this is cool. My contacts have been trying to get inside one of their conferences for years... and I might just be the one to do it," said Gideon excitedly.

"How you gonna do that? You don't know where it is."

"Grant me with some intelligence Robbie. I'll ring round every top hotel in London and try to book a room for that period. The one that says they're all booked up will be the one."

"What is it you do, Gideon?" enquired Shelby.

"Me? Er...I'm a peripheral visionary," Gideon replied.

"What does that mean?"

"I can see into the future, just way off to the side," laughed Gideon.

"Ignore him, Shelby. He's a prat," said Charlotte, shaking her head.

Rob and Charlotte decided to call it a day just after midnight and left Gideon and Shelby discussing the pros and cons of a single worldwide bank and tax system. The discussion was getting quite heated. "We're going up, - try and keep it down a bit. And try not to strangle each other," Rob said, as they started to climb the stairs to their bedroom.

When Shelby finally got to bed, she felt totally exhausted. Sleep came quickly and she began to dream:

She was leaving work and appeared to be the last one to go; as per usual. She surveyed the car park, which was empty of cars, and decided to walk home. She looked up at the skies and saw it was raining. Taking a coat off the coat-rack in the reception area, she set off across the car park. It was dark and still. The street seemed to stretch out before her like a runway. As the rain got heavier, she saw that large silvery objects were falling among the rain drops. She looked round for somewhere to shelter and saw a large white building, with pale green doors, just off to the side of the street. She looked down at her feet and saw a large fish land in front of her and start flapping. As she looked up, she realised what the silvery objects coming down with the rain were. She started to run towards the entrance of the building. Suddenly, she was standing on the edge of a motorway; cars flashing past in both directions, preventing her from reaching the building. She looked down and saw her mobile phone lying on the ground. It was full of water.

She awoke with a start. When she opened her eyes she saw that Gideon was standing over her. She sat bolt upright.

"Are you okay?" he asked, concerned. "I thought you were having a fit or something."

"I'm sorry. I mean, I'm fine. It was just a nightmare. It happens when I sleep in a strange place," she lied.

"Hey, you're shaking. Come here." Gideon knelt down beside the sofa and put his arms around her.

Rob was the first one up in the morning and he headed downstairs to the kitchen-diner to make some coffee. He stopped suddenly when he saw that the sofa was empty. He looked at his watch and thought to himself, *surely Shelby wouldn't have left already, it's only 9.30am.* The pillows and spare duvet were neatly folded on the arm. The mystery was solved half an hour later as Gideon and Shelby came through the front door together. "We were out of milk," said Gideon, waving two pints in the air.

"Gideon's offered to help me with the car this morning Rob. Thanks for your help last night and everything," Shelby gabbled, as she avoided eye contact with both of them and helped Gideon with the milk and coffee.

"Yeah, I thought I might join Shelby in St. Albans for the rest of the weekend and expand my knowledge of the local geography," added Gideon with a grin. "Give you guys a bit of a break, eh?"

"That's very thoughtful of you, Gideon," said Charlotte trying to suppress a smirk.

Give you two something to gossip about all weekend more like, thought Gideon.

Well that really was a surprise, thought Rob after they'd gone. *I'd have never imagined those two together. I hope Shelby knows what she's let herself in for.*

Two days later

Rob and Charlotte received a call from Gideon informing them that he was staying with Shelby for the next few weeks, while he looked for a job in London. He was quite full of himself as he explained that he'd tracked down the hotel where the Bilderberg Group were to meet, and that they were recruiting extra staff for an event planned for August. *I do hope Gideon's not going to cause trouble,* thought Rob, as he flicked over to the News at Ten:

"... *Presidents of the United States and Mexico and the Canadian Prime Minister signed an agreement earlier today to create a North American Union. Plans are in place to elect a single President in the next four months. Opponents rejected the agreement, stating that it was the end of American democracy. In other news, the body of a Cambridge astronomy student was discovered in his flat, apparently having taken a lethal overdose of ecstasy...*"

The significance of the second item was lost on Charlotte and Rob, but wouldn't have been lost on Gideon, had he been watching.

The Community Hall, North London, England

Gideon could barely contain his excitement as he disembarked the train. It was his first conspiracy theorist meeting since moving to St. Albans with Shelby. He'd met his contacts over the Internet, and regularly joined in with discussions, on-line meetings and blogs. This evening he would meet everyone in person for the first time.

He took a cab to the address that Stu Collins had provided. The old Community Hall had seen better days, but it was dry, warm and cheap. "You must be Gideon," said Stu, spotting Gideon looking a little lost in the main entrance hall. "I'm Stuart Collins, but everyone calls me Stu."

"Yeah, I'm Gideon Mycroft. Hi," replied Gideon. "Everyone calls me crazy," he added, laughing nervously.

"We're all a little crazy, Gideon. Wait until you meet the others. Love that stuff you posted on fluoride, by the way. It's on the agenda for discussion later. You can either present your findings to the others and we'll have a discussion at the end, or we can just throw it open to discussion straight away. It's entirely up to you," said Stu, leading Gideon to the meeting room.

The room was barely lit, possibly intentionally, as there was a PowerPoint projector set up opposite a tatty looking screen. Gideon sat down at one of the desks occupied by a couple of geeky-looking youths. He found out that they were the 'techies' who supplied the laptop and projector at these get-togethers. Their names went in one ear and out the other.

By the time Stu got the meeting underway, there were seven of them in total. *Not a great turn out*, thought Gideon. Stu started off by apologising for the poor attendance, stating that the meeting, which had been arranged a month ago, unfortunately clashed with a book signing in London. Apparently, some of the usual gang had decided to go and demonstrate outside the book shop.

Top of the agenda was the Bilderberg Group. They talked for a couple of hours about the Group's real intentions, alleged conspiracies that they had instigated, and that they were due to meet again, most likely in London, this year. They looked at several websites claiming to have proof of underhand dealings on the laptop projector. Stu finished by reminding everyone that as soon as they knew the location of this year's conference, he'd arrange a demonstration. "I'll co-ordinate with our friends in the US, Canada and Australia," he said. Gideon had to suppress a smile when he thought of the information about the Bilderberg meeting that had been handed to him on a plate.

They gradually made their way through the agenda; different attendees getting up to deliver mini-presentations on information they had researched or uncovered.

Gideon had prepared a datastick on the information he had been researching on fluoride, and when his turn came round he plugged it into the laptop. Stu introduced him, then left him to explain what he'd learnt. Unaccustomed to public speaking, Gideon decided to treat it as if he was explaining something to Rob and Charlotte, or even Shelby.

He took his position on the stage and began his presentation:

"Very few people, including dentists, realise that fluoride in the public water supply is actually industrial waste. It is, in fact, a waste product from the aluminium and phosphate industry," he began. "Yet, opposition to fluoride is treated like the Flat Earth Society, or being against the United Nations, or some shit. Did you know that fluoride is more poisonous than lead?" he continued, clicking through his slides. "Fluoride given to rats in the 1990's, in the US, had produced bone cancer and liver cancer, but the results were covered up. It has been linked to Attention Deficiency Disorder (ADD) and Hyperactivity...both covered up..."

He supported his findings with reports from dentists in the US, and continued further, "Not only is it a neuro-toxin, it has been used for mind control in the past. In 1954 Charles Eliot Perkins said, '*The real reason behind water fluoridation is not to benefit children's teeth... The real purpose behind water fluoridation is to reduce the resistance of the masses to domination and control and loss of liberty...*' in other words, mind control."

Gideon advanced the slide. As the presentation progressed, he found he was growing in confidence. He continued, "Perkins goes on to say, '*When the Nazis, under Hitler, decided to go into Poland ... the German General Staff and the Russian General Staff exchanged scientific and military ideas, plans and personnel and the scheme of mass control through water medication was seized upon by the Russian Communists because it fitted ideally into their plan to communise the world...*' Perkins was a scientist who spent nearly twenty years investigating the effects of fluoride. He concludes, '*any person who drinks artificially fluorinated water for a period of one year or more will never again be the same person, mentally or physically.*' And no-one is taking any notice."

Gideon finished his presentation to rapturous applause. *Wow, this is the best high I've ever had*, he told himself as he returned to his seat.

The last presentation was on a topic close to Gideon's heart. It was presented by one of the geeks from Gideon's table. "...according to recent literature, it is now possible to analyse human emotional EEG patterns, using supercomputers, and to replicate and store them on another computer. They can then be used to induce and change the emotional state in another human being..."

I knew it, thought Gideon. *Secret signals capable of controlling minds.*

"...Doctor Michael Persinger wrote an article stating, '*Contemporary neuroscience suggests the existence of fundamental algorithms by which all sensory transduction is translated into an intrinsic, brain specific code. Direct stimulation of these codes within the human temporal or limbic cortices by applied electromagnetic patterns may require energy levels which are within the range of both geomagnetic activity and contemporary communication networks.*' He goes on to conclude..." the geek continued, but Gideon had already switched off.

My God, I hope I didn't sound that dull, he thought.

After the presentations, the small gathering regrouped at a local pub. Gideon was still feeling pretty pleased with himself, particularly when the others insisted on buying him drinks. *You haven't seen anything yet, dudes. You wait until I get you the scoop from the Bilderberg Conference*, he told himself.

At King's Cross station, Gideon picked up a late edition of the Evening Standard to read on the journey back to St. Albans. He enjoyed reading the political sections most of all, particularly if he could find any inconsistencies. As he found a seat and unfolded the paper, the headline caught his eye.

"Another child goes missing."

Shit! That's gotta be the fifth or sixth kid that's gone missing in the last couple of months, he thought. He read on a little further.

> *"A police spokesperson said that a nationwide task force is being set up to investigate the disappearances. Police have yet to confirm that the seven cases across the country to date may be linked. The first child, Martin Foster, disappeared from a special needs school in Rochester last May. He was diagnosed with Attention Deficit Disorder (ADD) when he was 10 years old."*

There are some sick bastards out there, he told himself, and flicked to the political comment section on page fourteen.

CHAPTER THIRTEEN

Head Office of IDSys, Cambridge Science Park, England

Simon and Mitch were in Mitch's office discussing the results of the tests completed by DNATech. Apparently, they were a complete success. There were no side affects in either of the test batches and the design had full approval to go into production. "This is excellent news, Mitch. Time to start pushing Shackelford for a production schedule," grinned Simon.

"You're happy that China can cope with the predicted volumes?" enquired Mitch.

"That depends on the delivery schedule. If the Government set aggressive delivery times, we won't cope with our current capacity, but I've looked into some additional manufacturing sites in China." Simon paused to think. "We've always got Cheltenham as a fallback," he added.

"I noticed that the quality issues have been resolved. What's the long term reliability like, though?"

Simon drew a long breath. "Truth is, we don't know at the moment. Rob's doing some tests. Should have an answer for you in a day or so."

"I'll be at the Strand Hotel."

"Of course. It's your Bilderberg Conference. Good luck, buddy. That could bring in plenty of investment for the company. Then we'd easily be able to solve our capacity issues," said Simon, encouragingly.

Suddenly, Sarah burst into the room. "Oh my God, Mitch. Have you seen the news?"

Mitch flicked the TV on:

"*... early reports indicate that there may be thousands of fatalities. We can go over live to our reporter in Folkestone...*"

The picture changed to a shaky live image from the Channel Tunnel crossing in Folkestone. Clouds of dust (smoke?) appeared to be engulfing the entrance.

"What's going on?"

"They think there might have been a terrorist attack on the Channel Tunnel," replied Sarah.

"When did it happen?"

"About half an hour ago, apparently."

The live broadcast continued:

"*…no access from either end of the tunnel. Police are not ruling out a terrorist attack. Several witnesses reported hearing a series of loud explosions… two trains are believed to be trapped…*"

Head Office of DNATech, St. Albans, England

Shelby was reading the copy of the test report that had been sent to IDSys. There's no mention of the third batch, she pondered. The results from the third batch of mice had shown some startling effects. Firstly, their DNA pattern pre-insertion seemed to have some strange anomalies. At the end of the test their DNA had been altered slightly and their behaviours had been extremely passive – almost trance like. She had alerted Kim to her findings, but had been told that this batch was not related to the RFID chips and was for a different client. '*But clearly there has been some sort of change in the mice,'* she had protested. '*Not relevant,'* Kim had replied. '*This is not part of the IDSys trial.'* Consequently, the report had been sent out with no mention of that particular batch of mice. Shelby decided that she had no choice but to report the strange results to Runnels. She had never found Runnels particularly approachable, despite his avuncular demeanour. Whenever she was around him, she felt quite uncomfortable; not that he'd ever tried anything unprofessional. It was just something about the man.

As she left her lab to walk down the corridor to Runnels' office she noticed that the place seemed unusually empty. Normally there were at least three of the five labs in operation during the day. She could hear a TV in the small canteen at the other end of the corridor, but couldn't make out what was being broadcast.

When she got to Runnels' office she found the door open and the room empty. Had she seen him earlier, or was he out today? She approached his desk to see if his PC was switched on. The screensaver was bouncing the DNATech logo around the screen and there, on the desk, was her report. She picked up the folder and opened it. It was her report all right, but it was only the results for the mysterious third batch of mice. The report contained a letter from Runnels to a company called ORME Metals. It stated that the results had been found to be satisfactory and that all of the mice in the batch had reacted to the stimuli. *Why would a metals company be interested in the RFID chips? Were they trying different compounds for the casing? But this was just one trial – one specific test – and why was the DNA slightly different before the device was inserted?* The mice had since been removed from the lab, so she was unable to investigate the DNA further. She replaced the file and decided to talk it over with Rob when she got the chance.

She was about to enter her lab again, when she noticed that everyone still seemed to be in the canteen listening to the TV. Entering the room she realised why.

"... *the excessive heat appears to have weakened the internal structure of the tunnels and it is feared that they will collapse at any moment...*"

"Oh my God! What's happened?"

Head Office of IDSys, Cambridge Science Park, England
Everyone had crowded into Mitch's office to catch the breaking news.

"...*the Prime Minister is appealing for calm as reports claim that the Channel Tunnel Disaster was indeed a terrorist attack...*"

"It's unreal," someone said.

"...*immediate measures to ensure the security and safety of our citizens. An emergency bill will be passed in Parliament tonight to introduce Radio Frequency Identification Devices for everyone; young and old...*"

Simon and Mitch stared at each other, trying to suspend their disbelief.

PART TWO

"Three may keep a secret, if two of them are dead."
Benjamin Franklin

CHAPTER FOURTEEN

2nd Floor, Palace of Westminster, London, England

The phone on the antique desk began ringing and the occupant of the office waited two rings. The phone went quiet, then, seconds later starting ringing again.

"Hello?"

"Is that extension 333?"

"No, it's extension 322."

"Are you alone?"

"Yes."

"The bill has been passed by all sides of the house."

"Excellent."

"Are your people able to commence mass production?"

"Yes they are. The first devices will be ready in three weeks. Production will reach 100,000 a week in another two weeks. They will be at full production a month after that."

"How is it being rolled out?"

"We'll start with the over fifties, then over thirties. It is anticipated that over 80% of all adults will be chipped in three to four months time; children will be chipped as soon as programmes can be put in place in schools. Hospitals will begin chipping at birth from next month."

"The French are doing likewise. Germany has also indicated that it will introduce devices for their citizens as soon as possible."

"Have they found their own suppliers?"

"Yes, the designs from IDSys have been copied and circulated to the major governments in Europe and the near East. Our leaders are very satisfied."

CHAPTER FIFTEEN

Head Office of IDSys, Cambridge Science Park, England

All of the engineers and technicians had desks away from the main lab, which was often over-crowded with equipment and experimental set-ups. Rob was at his desk reviewing the manufacturing data from China.

The speed of the announcement by the Prime Minister had taken them all by surprise. Reports of the investigation into the Channel Tunnel Disaster had identified four terrorists; caught on CCTV cameras at Calais and Folkestone. There had been no survivors and 1,450 people had been reported missing or dead. It seemed that burning fuel ignited by the bombs had been responsible for weakening the tunnel's structure, and had led to its complete collapse. Mercifully, experts said that death would have been virtually instantaneous.

The terrorists had been working as train operating staff in both London and Paris. All evidence pointed to Islamic extremists, who had obtained false identity papers; copies of which had been discovered in their hotel rooms. Although no-one had claimed responsibility for the atrocity, both the CIA and MI5 had claimed the terrorists were known to them and that they had been only days away from tracking them down. Perhaps they had suspected that they were being closed in on and had carried out the attack before the trap could be sprung. The French Secret Service had concluded that they had entered France via Morocco and Spain. Two of them had then entered the UK under false passports and had obtained employment at the train company.

This evidence had led to an all party agreement for the introduction of RFIDs. Rob was experiencing mixed feelings. On the one hand, he wondered if lives would have been saved had the RFIDs been introduced earlier, but on the other, he felt a pang of guilt about the sudden introduction of such a controversial measure. In a matter of months, no-one would be able to use a bank, obtain social benefits, see a doctor, or travel overseas without an RFID chip. His thoughts were interrupted by the phone on his desk.

"Hi, Rob?" asked Shelby.

"Hi there. You sound rough."

"It's just flu. Been off work for two weeks," she sniffed.

"How's Gideon?"

"Oh, he's fine – he starts his job at the Strand Hotel next week."

"Of course, I nearly forgot. He called me the other week when he heard we'd got the contract for the RFIDs," Rob remembered.

"He's not very happy about it. Thinks the Government are using the terrorist attack as an excuse to force people to have these implants."

"You got the '*Borg*' speech, then?"

"You bet. Anyway, he's going to try and find some evidence to support his theory at the conference."

"Yeah, I know. He's not going to make a fool of himself at this Bilderberg meeting is he? My boss is going!"

"He said it's purely investigative research," she said, followed by a nasty sounding cough.

"You really don't sound too good," said Rob, a little concerned.

"It's nothing, really."

Rob didn't think she sounded too convincing. *Or was something else bothering her? Did Gideon know that she'd performed the tests on the RFIDs?*

"Does Gideon know about your part in the great RFID conspiracy?" He enquired.

"We don't go there. He knows we gave them a clean bill of health…"

"And…?"

"Fortunately, he hasn't been around much. He's been hanging out with a group of conspiracy activists he found through the Internet," added Shelby.

"Lucky for you."

"Well, there's something else… I've put off calling you about it, but I've drawn a complete blank on my own."

"What is it?" Rob asked, his curiosity getting the better of him.

"Have you ever heard of ORME Metals?"

"Can't say I have. Who or what are they?"

"I can't find out anything about the company, but I did find some stuff on ORME's."

"So what are they?" asked Rob, becoming interested.

"It stands for Orbitally Rearranged Monatomic Elements."

"Which are...?"

"They seem to be superconductors, but they also have some strange bio-interactive effects," Shelby replied, vaguely.

"Such as?"

"I haven't been able to find out much more," She admitted.

"Well, I can look them up and see if I can find anything out about their superconductor properties," offered Rob, "But, where did you discover this?"

Shelby wondered whether to continue. Rob would think that Gideon had turned her into another loony conspiracy theorist.

"I haven't told anyone else this. Not even Gideon," she continued.

"Told what?"

Here goes, she thought, "There was an additional RFID experiment that I was asked to perform on behalf of another client of DNATech."

Shelby told Rob the whole story, including the strange reactions of the mice with the unusual DNA, and the additional report that was prepared for ORME Metals.

"Are you saying that the RFIDs had an effect on this set of mice?" asked Rob, starting to feel uneasy about where this was going.

"Yes, I believe so. But these mice had something done to them before the chips were implanted."

"Like what?"

"That's what I don't know," Shelby said, sounding worried.

"Let me get this straight. The RFIDs have no effect on mice and their behaviour ordinarily, but on specially prepared mice they do?" asked Rob.

"That's what it looks like," she admitted.

"And you think this ORME material might have something to do with it?"

"I know, it sounds crazy." Shelby sounded almost apologetic.

"Can this stuff be ingested or something?"

"Worse than that. If I'm right, it can interfere at a DNA level."

"Bloody hell. Does this stuff occur naturally in humans?" gasped Rob.

"No, of course not. Not as far as I can tell, anyway."

Gideon's theory about fluoride suddenly sprung into Rob's mind. *What had he said? - 'They're putting fluoride into the water so that they can control our minds.' - Maybe not so far out after all, Gideon. What about this ORME material? Could it really be activated by the RFIDs to change people's behaviours?*

"Look, Shelby. Don't mention this to anyone. Especially not to Gideon. I'll do some digging on the superconductivity properties of these materials. See if you can find out anything else about the biological interactions." He wrote down 'ORME' on a post-it pad on his desk.

"So you do think something is weird then?"

"I don't really know, but let's keep it to ourselves for the moment. No point in involving other people for the time being."

When Shelby had hung up, Rob started scouring the Internet for information about ORME's. What he discovered made him extremely worried.

"Various researchers, working independently, have identified these materials in this different state of matter. They have arrived at many of the same observations. These m-state elements have been observed to exhibit the quantum physical behaviors of superconductivity, superfluidity, Josephson tunneling and magnetic levitation. It looks like these are an entirely new class of materials.

These m-state elements are also present in many biological systems. We believe that they may enhance energy flow along the acupuncture meridians and in the microtubules inside every living cell.

It appears that this state of certain of these elements has been known throughout history. Several of the procedures for extracting or making ORMUS have been adapted from ancient alchemical texts. We believe that the Philosopher's Stone and the Biblical manna may be variations on this state of matter."

Ancient alchemical texts? This sounds like Gideon's Sumerians all over again. He'd read somewhere that the Egyptian Pharaohs, or someone, had eaten a form of gold because it was thought to increase longevity. *Could it really have been ORME gold?*

Rob decided to contact ORME Metals and see if he could obtain some samples. It would be interesting to subject the material to the signals from his RFIDs and see whether it would be affected or not. He didn't like where this was going one little bit.

If he could prove that the signals from the RFIDs interacted with the ORME matter, and Shelby could confirm that this could have an influence on human behaviour, then what kind of Pandora's Box had they stumbled upon?

As he returned to his production report, Duncan stuck his head round the door. "Hey Rob, you want anything from the drinks machine? They got that new fizz that's supposed to help you concentrate."

"No thanks, Duncan. Charlotte's got a fridge full of the stuff and I can't stand it. I'll have a normal cola though; full fat with a pork pie for good measure."

"No problem."

Shelby's flat, St. Albans, England
Shelby had a restless night. No sooner had she drifted into REM sleep, than she began to dream:

She was leaving work and appeared to be the last one to go; as per usual. She surveyed the car park, which was empty of cars, and began to walk home. It was dark and still. The street seemed to stretch out before her like a runway. She felt the first spots of rain, and realised she wasn't wearing a coat; in fact she was dressed in only a short cotton nightdress. The rain was starting to get heavy and she felt the cold go right through her. As the rain intensified, she saw that large silvery objects were falling among the rain drops. She looked round for somewhere to shelter and saw a large white building, with pale green doors, just off to the side of the street. She looked down at her feet and saw a large fish land in front of her and start flapping. As she looked up, she realised what the silvery objects coming down with the rain were. She started to run towards the entrance of the building. The doors were open when she reached them and she stepped inside to take shelter. She found herself inside an elevator. She tried pressing several of the buttons, but nothing happened. Then, just as the panic began to well up inside her, the lift started to descend. The doors opened and she walked towards another set of doors in front of her. She opened the doors and saw a room full of workstations; rows and rows of workstations with people sitting at them. One looked up at her. He had plain, indistinguishable features, apart from the fact that he didn't have a mouth. The others began to look at her; not one of them had a mouth.

She woke up screaming.

"It's okay Shel. It was just a bad dream," soothed Gideon.

They got out of bed and went through to the kitchen. "Might as well have a coffee," said Shelby. "I don't know when I'll be able to get off to sleep again." She switched the kettle on and busied herself by rinsing out a couple of mugs.

"Maybe you haven't quite got over the flu yet," Gideon suggested.

"I've only just got back to work, Gideon. I can't take anymore time off."

"I know. I was just saying." Gideon averted his eyes. He didn't want to argue.

They took their coffees into the living room. Gideon was getting increasingly concerned about Shelby. *It wasn't just the flu; the dreams were becoming more frequent,* he thought. "Shel, you'd tell me if there was something wrong, wouldn't you?"

"Of course I would, you big dope. It's just that I've got so much to catch up on at work, and Kim's been hassling me for reports."

"Not that witch..." started Gideon, grateful that it was nothing to do with him.

"Kim's all right when you get to know her," Shelby interrupted. Despite the fact that she was over-critical of her work, Shelby had a soft spot for her.

Gideon leant across to the radio on top of the hi-fi cabinet and flicked the 'on' switch.

"No, Gideon, don't!"

Radio static burst from the speakers and Gideon quickly turned the volume down. "What? It's okay, it's just not tuned in." He started fiddling with the tuning dial, but all he found was more static. "It was working earlier." He looked back towards Shelby, who was shaking her head. "What is it?"

Shelby looked a little awkward. "That always happens after one of my nightmares," she said quietly.

"What do you mean?" Gideon took hold of her hand, which felt unusually warm.

"I don't know. Radios just seem to go a bit haywire when I'm around. It's like interference or something."

"How long does it last?"

"Not long. I mean, I've never actually tried to time it. What sort of a question is that?" laughed Shelby, starting to see the absurdity of the situation.

"Just trying to decide if I should let my weird girlfriend near any of *my* hi-fi equipment," Gideon replied, putting on one of his childish expressions. They sat together in silence for a couple of minutes. Finally, Gideon spoke. "How about if I make dinner tonight? You can put your feet up."

"Okay, that'll be nice. So long as it's not spaghetti bolognese again," she laughed. "Didn't Charlotte teach you any other recipes?"

Gideon feigned offence. "It was good enough for you the first few weeks we were together. I suppose that means the honeymoon's over," he winked.

Shelby's eyes widened suddenly. "Er...Gideon, have you got a picture of the hotel you're going to be working at?" she asked, feeling a little stupid.

"Yeah, of course. I printed one off the Internet. It's around here somewhere," he replied, as he rifled through some papers under the coffee table. "Here you go, the Strand Hotel."

Shelby looked at the picture and was visibly relieved that it looked nothing like the white building in her dreams.

"Okay? Is it respectable enough for you?" laughed Gideon.

"It looks simply wonderful," she laughed back.

Shelby was feeling better already. She knew that Gideon was trying his best to make her happy. *I just hope I'm worth it*, she thought to herself.

CHAPTER SIXTEEN

The Strand Hotel, London, England

Security at the Strand was of the highest level. Mitch had seen nothing like it. Roads were cordoned off and police lined the entrance in addition to the private security that most of the guests had brought with them. *I wonder who pays for this lot,* thought Mitch as his car was permitted entry to the reception bay of the hotel. As he got out of the car, he could hear demonstrators just beyond the perimeter fence. Many had telephoto cameras. Obviously trying to identify the members as they get out of their cars, he thought. One of the demonstrators had a megaphone to his mouth and was ranting in an American accent:

"...*we are not your slaves Bilderberg Group. Tell your reptilian masters that we will not be subdued. We know about your plans for the New World Order and domination, but we will fight for democracy and the sovereignty of our nations. Come outside and identify yourselves. If you've got nothing to hide, publish your agenda. Tell the people what you spend three days each year scheming about...*"

Mitch was discretely bundled into the lobby of the hotel by a line of security men. He had known that groups of demonstrators had begun to attend the conventions over the last few years, but he was still amazed at their numbers. Inside the hotel, it was eerily quiet. At the reception desk he was given his room number and keys and told his bags would be sent up. He was also given an invitation to join the other members in the Conference Hall for a welcome meeting, where the activities of the next few days would be explained in more detail.

The hotel was huge. Mitch had never been anywhere like it. I'm gonna need a map just to find my way to breakfast, he mused. To the side of the lobby were four huge pairs of elevator doors. Above them was the floor indicator showing that there were 38 floors. He looked at his room number again; 1248 on the twelfth floor. *Royalty only on the top few floors*, he guessed.

Gideon saw Mitch's arrival in the lobby and hurriedly busied himself with one of the other guest's baggage; loading them onto a trolley for the porter to take upstairs. As Mitch passed, he kept his head down and his back slightly turned. He wasn't sure if Mitch would remember him. He had attended last year's Christmas Party with Rob and Charlotte in the IDSys restaurant. Mitch had spent time visiting each of the tables during the event and they had chatted briefly. *Best not to take any chances*, thought Gideon.

He had been pretty annoyed with Rob when he'd learnt that IDSys were the company supplying the RFIDs, but soon realised that if it wasn't for that connection, he wouldn't be here now. Gideon had never believed in co-incidences and had discussed at length, with Stu, the possibility that the Channel Tunnel Disaster had been an inside job, designed to expedite the introduction of the ID chips.

The similarities between the Tunnel Disaster and the World Trade Centre had been startling. Stu had shown him some of the 'unanswered' questions surrounding 9-11 and they had compared the two atrocities. In both cases, the authorities had claimed that the ferocity of the fires had warped the metal structures resulting in their collapse. In both cases, scientists had questioned the feasibility that temperatures of 1,100 degrees Celsius, necessary to melt iron, could have been achieved. In both cases, witnesses had heard the sound of explosions, suggesting that there were *multiple* explosives involved. In the 9-11 case, the President was in no hurry to get out of Booker Elementary School and in the Tunnel Disaster, the Prime Minister appeared equally unconcerned, as he attended a school sports facility in Lambeth.

Gideon was determined to find a link between the Channel Tunnel attack and the introduction of the RFIDs, and he would start with Mitchell Webb. Like Stu had said: *'It is during times of great fear that personnel freedom suffers the most.'* It was after the underground bombings in 2005 that the Government introduced the 28 days detention limit for terrorist suspects. That had recently been increased to 60 days.

He knew a number of the demonstrators outside, but had not let them know that he had managed to secure a position inside the hotel. *Oh no, let them wait.* He would share his information with them when the conference was over.

Arriving in his room, Mitch tossed his briefcase on the bed and collapsed on a chair. The room was massive. It had a raised bed area, with an en suite off to the side. There was a lounge area, with two sofas and an armchair, and a dining area with a table and four chairs. Along one wall was a built-in wardrobe and there were two TVs. He went to the bar area and made himself a stiff drink, then phoned Sarah to let her have his room number. After describing his surroundings to his excitable PA, he called Simon to see how things were going. He knew that their production facilities were at breaking point, but the Government had increased their order in light of the terrorist attack, and it was up to Simon to find additional manufacturing sites. "Hi, Simon – how're you getting on?"

"Yeah, okay, Mitch. There are three more plants in China that should be suitable, and I'm switching the existing product from our Cheltenham site to accommodate the RFIDs. What's the situation like there?"

"Terrifying! I just know I'm gonna get quizzed by some seriously important Government people about our production figures."

"Well, we're not looking bad at the moment. I'll be running over the reliability figures with Rob later. I'll keep you posted. Have you met any of the bigwigs yet?"

"Not yet, I've got a welcoming committee in about half an hour. You should see the number of demonstrators outside the hotel. You'd think it was a meeting of the G8, or something. I wish it was you here to broker some deals, rather than me." Mitch popped a Tic-Tac into his mouth.

"You'll be fine, Mitch. Most of the activities are right up your street; golf, shooting, croquet..."

"Yeah, right. Don't suppose they'll want to play squash."

"I hear *line dancing* is very fashionable again," joked Simon.

"What? You know I don't know anything about Country and Western music. I used to think Boxcar Willie was a medical complaint," Mitch quipped.

Simon had known Mitch long enough to know that when he made lame jokes, he really was nervous. "Mitch, you're in the club by invitation. I don't think you'll need to sell to anyone. More likely, they'll be falling over themselves to come to you with cash for investment. Have you seen the latest reports from the Government? They're claiming a

67% reduction in illegal immigration as a result of the introduction of our devices already. So relax, buddy. This is one of the biggest success stories in recent history."

Mitch felt a bit better having spoken to Simon. Either that, or the vodka he had earlier was kicking in. *Simon is right though. We need investment for expansion,* he told himself. The Government had only put them in touch with a couple of suitable manufacturers over in China. *What was really needed was a new purpose-built manufacturing site over here, or in Europe, at least.*

The Steadman's House, Swindon, England

Albert Steadman read the letter from the Home Office one more time. *Had things really got so bad that it was necessary to 'tag' everyone in the Country? It's all down to those cowardly terrorists,* he thought. "It's definitely this afternoon, Enid," he called to his wife. "Three o'clock."

His wife came into the sitting room. "What are you saying? Oh, Albert! I told you about that dog and the furniture."

Albert signalled to the dog and he climbed off the sofa and sat down by his feet. Branston was a five year old, chocolate brown, Labrador. "I was just saying, dear, it's this afternoon that we have to get those tag things done."

"Yes dear, so you keep reminding me. They're not tags – they're Personal Identity Chips. Caroline said she'd pop over to make sure everything's all right. I've put the birth certificates, the driving licences, and our passports on the hall table. Is there anything else we need?"

Albert looked at the letter again. "National Insurance numbers and a recent bill from one of the Utilities."

"Dear God," muttered his wife. "It's a bit late for them to decide we don't belong here after all this time. Do they really think a bunch of seventy-year-olds are going to blow themselves up in a terrorist plot?"

The Security Forces were sending a mobile unit round to their area that afternoon to register and implant all the residents over fifty. Anyone not able to supply the correct documentation at that time had thirty days to present it to their local police station, where they would be implanted or forfeit their rights to benefits, medical treatment, and access to their bank accounts. *Even bloody Hitler couldn't introduce something that draconian,* grumbled Albert.

Albert and Enid, both seventy-two years of age, had lived in their three bedroom semi-detached for the last thirty-two years. Albert had worked for the Railways until his retirement in 1996. "I'm going to take the dog for a walk," he announced. Branston leapt to his feet and disappeared into the hall to fetch his lead.

"Okay dear. Make sure you're back by eleven – I need to pop out to the supermarket."

Albert put on his walking shoes and his waterproof coat. He didn't bother putting the lead on Branston, preferring to carry it with him; just in case it was busy over the field. "Come on then, Branston. Bring your ball with you," he said to the dog.

The two of them headed off up the street towards the communal field, where most of the other dog walkers took their pets for a good runabout. He'd only been out five minutes, when he spotted the owner of a King Charles Spaniel.

"Morning, Albert," said the man.

"Morning, Roy. How are you?"

"Oh, I'm right as rain. You?"

"Mustn't grumble. Thought I'd better walk the dog for a bit longer this morning. We've got the mobile clinic this afternoon. You know, those tag things... Don't know what time I'll be home," Albert replied. The two dogs finished sniffing each other and began to play a game of tig.

"They were round our way last week. Got my implant done. Didn't feel a thing. Look." Roy held out his right hand. Albert looked, but couldn't see anything. Roy laughed. "You can't really see it. Here, feel the back of my hand." Albert ran his finger over the back of the man's hand. "There! Did you feel that slight bump?"

"I believe I did," said Albert. "So you don't think there's anything wrong with being tagged then?"

"Oh, I didn't say that. Just that having one put in wasn't nowhere near as bad as I thought it was going to be. The way I see it, they've already got us under surveillance with those CCTV cameras, and they already know my National Insurance number and where I live. They got my picture on my damn driving licence. What difference does it make if they want to stick a little device in my hand? If they want to know what you're up to, they'll find a way. I told Betty. I said, so long as you've got nothing to hide, you got nothing to worry about. She looked at me as if I'd just accused her of having a fancy man," said Roy with a chuckle.

"Well, I just don't know what to make of it," Albert said solemnly. "It all sounds a bit like Communism to me."

"They gave us some free lemonade after they done it," said Roy. "You know - that new expensive stuff that's good for your digestion." He started laughing.

"What?" asked Albert.

"I was just remembering that bloke what's got the Border Collie. What's his name?"

"You mean the accountant chap? Er... Armstrong, I think," said Albert, rubbing his head, as if this would aid his memory.

"That's him," said Roy. "Well, he only went and fainted when they put his in. I mean, look. There's not even a mark now," he chuckled. "Lot of fuss over nothing if you ask me. I said to Betty. Betty, I said, if it meant they could catch those murdering B's before they blow something else up, I'd have 'made in the UK' tattooed on my forehead." Roy obviously thought this was the funniest thing he'd ever said, because he laughed so hard he brought tears to his eyes.

Maybe I'm just being a stubborn old fool, thought Albert. He'd given up staying abreast of technology about the time they brought out CD-ROM's. There were just too many acronyms to remember: DVD, DAB, WAP, GPS, GPRS, HDTV, DVR – the list was endless. Their daughter, Caroline, had tried to get them to swap their VHS recorder for a modern DVR, but Albert had told her they don't bother with it anymore. He looked over to see what Branston was doing. "Oh, that blooming dog has just burst his ball again. That's his third in as many months."

Roy had calmed back down. "I've given up with Barney. He can't keep a toy for more than five minutes, the little devil."

"Anyway, I suppose I'd better take him round the long way. See you soon," said Albert, as he bent down to re-tie one of his shoelaces which had come undone.

"Yeah, you take it easy, Albert. And don't worry about those stupid implants. You won't feel a thing. To be honest, I'd much rather have one of them chips in me hand than to be left without any access to me pension... or a doctor for that matter. I told the nurse, I said, stick one in me other hand while you're at it, in case this one breaks." Roy started laughing again. "Barney! Come on! We're going this way, you stupid mutt."

Albert picked up Branston's flat ball and started heading towards the side exit to the field.

When they got home, Enid was waiting in the sitting room with her coat on. "There you are. I told you not to be very long. I've got shopping to get."

"Okay dear, I'll get the car," said Albert wearily. *I wonder if those tag things come with a volume control,* he thought with a smile.

Later that day

The queue outside the mobile unit stretched half the length of the street. *Bloody typical,* thought Albert as they joined on the end. *If she hadn't taken so long to get ready...*

Caroline had come over – '*just to make sure everything goes okay.'*

"Afternoon, Albert, Enid, Caroline," said the man standing in the queue just in front of them.

"Afternoon, Wilfred," said Enid. Albert nodded his greeting.

"Hello, Mister Tomasz. I haven't seen you for a while," said Caroline.

"Well, you're all grown up now. But aren't you a little bit young for this malarkey?"

"I'm just here to make sure Mum and Dad are okay," replied Caroline, undeterred.

"Nice day for getting branded," said Wilfred, looking up at the clear blue sky.

"You don't think it'll be painful do you?" asked Enid, suddenly feeling concerned.

"No, no. I'm only joking. Didn't you read the FAQ's?"

"FAQ's?" asked Enid.

"The leaflet they sent – Frequently Asked Questions," Wilfred explained.

"Oh that. Not really."

"It's crazy when you think about it," said Wilfred. "My father had to go to a Nazi concentration camp to get his arm branded. And here we are having the modern version because it will protect us from terrorists. We're all just numbers to them."

"I don't think this is anything like what happened back then," said Caroline, indignantly.

"He's got a point," said Albert. "They're dehumanising us. It's not a million miles away from what Hitler had in mind."

"Oh, Dad. Honestly! Would you rather that your granddaughter was brought up in constant fear of a terrorist attack instead?" She shot

Wilfred a look that said: '*now look what you've done'*.

"I don't think he meant that, dear," said Enid, jumping to Albert's defence.

They stood in silence until it was Albert's turn to enter the mobile unit. "See you in a couple of minutes," he said to Enid.

"Here. Don't forget your paperwork, dear," she replied.

Wilfred was on his way out when Albert was going in. "Piece of cake," he said, clutching his free bottle of Vitality.

CHAPTER SEVENTEEN

Head Office of IDSys, Cambridge Science Park, England

The eighteen-wheeled transporter truck pulled over in a lay-by close to the entrance to the Science Park. The driver switched on his Bluetooth headset and reached over for his sandwich box. Opening a bottle of mineral water, he selected a cheese and pickle sandwich from the box and settled back to enjoy his snack.

Rob was in the main lab running tests on the RFID chips he had received from China. As part of their quality control procedure, he required a sample of each production batch for analysis. Yields had been pretty good from the Chinese plants and the device life tests were proving more than satisfactory. He had been concerned initially that the whole project could have been put into jeopardy if the overseas devices couldn't meet the MTBF (mean time between failures) requirements. *Let's face it, they were unpopular enough already. Imagine the outrage if people needed to have them replaced because they broke down.*

He had been unable to test the receiving side of the circuit originally, as the Government had kept the details under wraps, but now, with production volumes being produced, he had been given the frequencies and codes to fully test the devices. Because of the original secrecy, he had designed-in fuses between the transmitter and receiver halves of the device. This meant that he could blow the fuses remotely and render the receiver useless in case of problems. It wasn't part of the design requirement, but the fact that he didn't know how the receiver part worked, and wasn't sure how it would interact with his part of the design, meant that he wanted to be able to isolate the two halves. In that way, he could prove that any problem (should there be one) wasn't of his making. That safeguard now seemed redundant and he wondered if a redesign, removing these fuses, would help with production. He wondered how Mitch would react to a redesign at this stage. Would he go mad at him for designing in this safety feature in the first place, when it hadn't been part of the original specification?

He looked at his watch. *Time to call it a day.* Charlotte had been getting on at him lately for getting home so late. Since Gideon had taken up residence with Shelby in St. Albans, she had no-one to moan at until he got home. *Gideon and Shelby.* He shook his head. *I still can't get my head round that one,* he puzzled. Gideon had virtually dropped off the radar lately. The last time they'd spoken, he'd told him about his new gang of mates, who were collating all of the Government's cover-ups on a website, ready to go public with testimonies from witnesses, amateur video footage, and apparently, actual secret Government memos. Of course, Gideon was convinced that the Channel Tunnel Disaster – now referred to as 6-16 (16th June), was an inside job, as were 9-11 and 7-7. Gideon said they were trying to obtain evidence that the tunnels were pre-fitted with explosive charges, so the Government could blow the tunnel up in case of invasion or something similar. He claimed that this was how they'd been able to fake a terrorist attack. There would be no chance of determining the actual cause of the collapse, as the remains were buried under 50 metres of water. They'd both steered clear of the fact that over 40% of the population of Britain had been implanted with IDSys RFIDs already.

The red light over the door flashed on and off and Simon entered the lab. "Ah, Rob. Just the person I'm looking for," said Simon, looking a little stressed.

"Oh, hi Simon. What's up?"

"How are the reliability tests going?" he asked, putting his hand on Rob's shoulder.

"No problem. They're exceeding our MTBF requirements by a healthy margin," he reported.

"Excellent. I've got to bring another two manufacturing sites up to speed in China, but I've got a meeting in Cheltenham first thing in the morning."

"Are they switching RFID production to Cheltenham?" Rob enquired.

"Yeah. Mitch has asked me to send some information over to his hotel, but it's at his place, and my car's at the railway station. I wondered if I could borrow yours?"

Rob's heart missed a beat. *The hotel! It's the Bilderberg Conference. Had he run into Gideon? Nah, it can't be anything to do with Gideon, otherwise Mitch would've called himself.* "Sure. Don't mind the mess though; I haven't cleaned it out for a while," admitted Rob, feeling slightly embarrassed as he remembered the pile of empty packets and water bottles covering most of the passenger seat and rear floor space.

"No worries. Have her back in about... twenty minutes or so," Simon said, looking at this watch.

They went back to Rob's desk to get the keys and Rob pointed out where he'd parked. As Simon left, he picked up the phone to let Charlotte know that he'd been delayed (again). Looking out the window, he saw Simon get into his car. *I'll never get the seat back in the same position*, he thought. He remembered that Simon had a habit of locking himself out of his car. *Damn! Too late to remind him to be careful with the keys.* As Simon reversed the car out of the parking space, Rob noticed a dark blue Audi exit the car park and race down the entrance track towards the dual carriageway, ahead of him. It looked familiar and he wondered if Duncan or Sandra had mentioned getting a new car recently.

The truck driver's headset crackled and a voice said "Start her up!" Starting the engine, he engaged first gear and let off the handbrake, keeping the clutch depressed. A dark blue Audi exited the Science Park and turned onto the dual carriageway a few yards ahead of him. The driver's headset instructed, "Go! Now!" The truck jolted forward and began to gather speed. As it approached the exit from the Science Park it suddenly swerved left, blocking the road to the dual carriageway.

Simon was approaching the exit and accelerated slightly, gaining speed to filter onto the carriageway safely. Suddenly, there was a huge black shape in front of him. He slammed on the brakes as everything went into slow motion. Two thoughts went through his mind: *What the hell is a truck doing coming in that way?* and, *Rob's water bottle is emptying out all over my new phone.* Then blackness.

CHAPTER EIGHTEEN

The Strand Hotel, London, England

The unconventional conventionists were in the conference hall for a social gathering following the welcoming meeting earlier in the day. Gideon, taking a scheduled break, made his way up to Mitch's room with a pass key. Letting himself in, he quickly scanned the room. Mitch had left his briefcase and a conference pack on his bed. Gideon hurriedly began searching through the conference pack. He already had a list of guests from the hotel registration, so he looked for anything that might contain an agenda or something explaining what they were here to decide. Much of the information was meaningless, at least to Gideon, although there were a few meetings on free trade, globalisation, and cross-border agreements. Frustratingly for Gideon, most of the real business and decision making seemed to be going to take place in break-out sessions that were by invitation only.

Mitch was keeping himself in his comfort zone, mixing with other industrialists and a few of the parliamentarians that he already knew through Shackelford. It was mostly small talk, intermingled with spurious offers of *getting together later to chat through some proposals,* whatever that meant. People seemed to be passing out cards to one another with meeting room numbers and times written on the back. He had learnt very little from the welcome meeting, but it seemed that there would be a number of break-out sessions over the next couple of days, where interested parties would discuss, as yet unknown, topics and come to some sort of arrangement.

He'd already overheard the CEO of a global soft drinks company cementing deals with various foreign diplomats, and there seemed to be almost unanimous support for the further integration of the European Union. Several people had congratulated him on attaining the RFID contract, adding what a huge contribution he was making to the security of the European community. Several representatives of the Middle Eastern Nations had commented that they would be interested in conducting negotiations in the future and his pockets were beginning to brim with business cards. He had been asked by some if the RFID chips were compatible with GPS technology, to which he had replied, 'Given the right transmission frequency and codes, anything was possible.' This was, in fact, true. The design for the RFIDs had been taken from the existing vehicle tracking devices, which had earned Mitch and the company most of their revenue to date. These were all features that could easily be switched on, although Mitch did feel a pang of guilt about where this could be heading. He looked at his own implant; a small bump on his right hand indicating its position, and wondered just how much information could be stored on such a device. Rob would know, he thought.

He heard a polite cough at his side as he finished exchanging business cards with a Russian millionaire, who'd made it big in aluminium production. It was a hotel waitress. "Excuse me, Mister Webb, I have a message for you," she said, slipping him a folded piece of paper.

Mitch looked at the note and a wave of dread swept over him. It was from Sarah and simply read:

> "Mitch, ring the office ASAP. There's been a terrible accident. Sarah."

Mitch left the gathering in somewhat of a daze. As he found himself in the lobby, a hand grabbed his arm. "I'm terribly sorry about your news, Mister Webb," said the man, who Mitch vaguely recognised as one of the parliamentarians he'd been talking to earlier. "He was a fine young engineer," he added, as Mitch broke free and entered the lift that had just arrived.

Mitch was at bursting point when the lift finally reached the 12th floor. Somehow the inappropriate musak playing overhead seemed to make the whole situation seem even more surreal.

Gideon suddenly felt as if an electric shock had just been administered to his spine. "Those murdering bastards," he hissed, as he folded the sheet of paper he had just read, and jammed it into the back pocket of his uniform. He had just found information on a meeting to be held later today to discuss who should receive the contract for rebuilding the Channel Tunnel. The owners hadn't lost out; thanks to an extremely generous insurance policy, and there was now money to be made, by a privileged few, on the reconstruction project. *Follow the money*, he thought to himself, *and you find the real reason behind events.* He was about to leave when he heard someone outside trying to open the door with the electronic key card. Looking around the room, there was only one hiding place; obvious as it was, he had no choice.

Mitch finally got the speed and the direction of his key card right and the lock popped open on his door. He ran across to the phone by the bed, knocking his briefcase and various papers to the floor as he did so. He frantically punched in Sarah's office phone number.

"Sarah? It's me. Mitch. What's happened to Rob?"

"This is Police Constable Troughton. Who is calling please?"

"Mitchell Webb, CEO of IDSys."

"I have some very grave news for you, sir," continued the policeman, as if he'd been rehearsing what he was about to say. "There has been a fatal car accident involving one of your employees."

"Fatal? You mean R-Rob's dead?" stammered Mitch.

Gideon could hear Mitch's side of the conversation from his hiding place in the wardrobe. His impulse was to burst through the door and find out what was going on, but his mind told him to stay put. He had no way of explaining what he was doing in Mitch's room. Let alone in his wardrobe. *This can not be happening.* He had to get out of there and call Charlotte.

"I'm sorry, sir, I don't know where you got that information, but the deceased is a Mister Simon Rockwall."

"Simon? My God! What happened?"

Simon? Who's he? thought Gideon. *What about Rob? Is Rob all right?* Mitch was saying something about returning to Cambridge in the morning.

"His parents' details are on his personnel record. Is Sarah there?" Mitch asked the policeman.

"She has already been taken home. Everyone else has also left. It's just me and your security man, sir."

"Okay, I've got her home number. Is Rob all right?"

"No-one else was in the car at the time of the accident, sir. Fortunately, the driver of the truck survived and we are getting a statement from him as we speak."

"Sorry, did you say whether you have already informed Simon's parents or not?" asked Mitch, having difficulty absorbing what he was being told.

"We have sir, yes."

"Okay, I'll ring them too."

Mitch slowly replaced the phone. *What am I going to do? It's all my fault. I've been overworking Simon. Hell, I've been overworking all of them. I have to speak to Sarah, then I'll have to leave and head back to Cambridge. Why had I thought it was Rob that had been involved? That guy in the lobby. He'd said something about it being one of my engineers.* He flicked on the TV, as he looked for Sarah's home number on his mobile. There didn't seem to be anything on the news about it yet.

"Hi Sarah, it's Mitch."

"Oh, Mitch. Thank God."

"I've just heard. What happened?"

"Simon took Rob's car to fetch something and... and... there was an accident at the end of the track. He... he collided with a truck coming the wrong way."

"He was driving Rob's car?" Mitch's voice had shot up.

"Yes. His was at the station. It was terrible..."

Someone driving Rob's car was killed in a car accident, Gideon digested. *There's something not right about this. I've got to get in touch with Rob.* His leg was beginning to lose its feeling and it looked like Mitch was going to be on the phone for hours at this rate. He needed a distraction to get out of the wardrobe. *Wait a minute! If it's to do with those RFID chips, Shelby's been involved as well. This can't be happening. Not to us. Damn, my leg's killing me.* The X-Files theme tune began to emanate from Gideon's inside pocket.

The door to the wardrobe suddenly flew open and Mitchell Webb was staring down at Gideon, curled up in the bottom of his wardrobe.

CHAPTER NINETEEN

Head Office of DNATech, St. Albans, England

Shelby was working late. Her bout of flu had put several of her reports behind schedule and Kim had been berating her for days. *I guess a little time to myself won't hurt. Gideon's working long hours at the Strand, so there'll be no-one home until late anyway,* she justified to herself. She'd pick something up on the way home for them to eat.

It had been three months or so since she and Gideon had found themselves strangely attracted to each other. It had happened at Rob and Charlotte's flat, she reflected. Although nothing had actually happened that night, it was the start of their relationship. Gideon had helped to pick up her car and had expressed an interest in attending some meetings close to St. Albans. Before she'd realised what she was saying, she'd invited Gideon down to stay and the two of them had set off the very next day. She had a spare room at her flat, though she never really expected to use it. Now that Gideon had practically moved in with her, it felt much better than coming home to an empty flat, and he had fixed all of the annoying little things that the landlord never seemed to have time to get round to.

She eventually had to tell Gideon about the dreams; explaining that she'd had strange dreams, ever since she could remember. She showed him the paintings she'd done as a child. He nearly didn't believe the age she'd been when she'd painted them. '*Most people couldn't paint like that if they'd been painting ALL THEIR LIVES,*' he'd said. He couldn't understand why she didn't want them up on the walls. She hadn't told him that she thought of it as more of a curse than a blessing. Or that she actually thought she might be jinxed or something. *At least he hasn't brought up that freaky radio problem again.*

She had a strong belief that the people she got close to ended up getting harmed, or worse, and that it was her fault. She had lost a couple of close friends on a school trip when she was fourteen. She hadn't wanted to go, but her parents had insisted. She'd had bad dreams for a week before they went, but like the ones she was having now, she couldn't interpret them properly. They were on an orienteering trip in Scotland, when a falling tree had killed her two school friends and badly injured her. The trip supervisors had been found to be negligent, but ever since then, she had become a bit of a loner and had shied away from relationships for the most part. Although she couldn't recollect the dream, the memory of that day would always be with her.

Shelby and her two friends, Rachel and Clare, were very athletic and extremely competitive. They were the star players of the hockey team and admired by most of their classmates. Determined not to be outdone by the boys on the trip, they had set off enthusiastically, and had soon built up quite a distance between themselves and the rest of the class. They picked up branches from the ground and snapped of any offshoots to make sticks that they used to help them climb the rugged landscape. The weather had started off well enough, but dark clouds had been building up and the wind had increased from a light breeze to something approaching gale force. They decided they'd better double back and find the others. Barely able to hear each other over the gathering storm, they resorted to hand signals. Fallen leaves were whipping around them and the visibility was getting worse by the minute.

As they began to descend a small ridge, Shelby's stick snapped and she slipped backwards, twisting her ankle. She heard a loud crack above the general cacophony of the storm and was knocked further down the ridge by flailing branches. As she lay at the bottom of the ridge she realized that she couldn't move. Her ankle was badly sprained and she was sure that her left arm was broken. The top branches of the fallen tree had whipped across her face and she could feel blood on her cheek. There was no sign of the other two girls. It took nearly an hour and a half for the supervisors to locate them.

She learnt of the tragic fate of her two friends at the hospital four hours later. She had never quite been the same after that. Although no-one at school had blamed her for anything, she kept herself to herself; dropping out of the hockey team, preferring individual sports instead.

Now she was living with Gideon. Why couldn't she bring herself to discuss this ORME thing with him? She knew that Gideon was a keen conspiracy theorist, but she also knew that a lot of it was put on for effect. He had changed lately, though. He'd been trying to get hold of a mate of his from Cambridge, but he wasn't answering his calls or his e-mails. Apparently, he was a student of astronomy and was writing a Ph.D on the Asteroid Belt. Gideon had said that he'd found something wrong with it and was taking his findings to his Professor, but he'd never heard anything back. Finally, he'd contacted the University and been told that his friend had died from a drug overdose. Gideon had gone crazy. '*Alex never even took Ecstasy,*' he'd insisted. Now he was getting involved with some strange characters that he'd met through some website and had contacts as far away as the United States and Australia. Shelby thought of the old saying; *just because you're paranoid, doesn't mean they're not out to get you.*

She'd made a passing comment to Kim a couple of days ago, enquiring whether there would be any more analysis required on the *mystery* batch of mice from the RFID tests. Kim had made it quite clear that it was nothing to do with her and that the client was satisfied with the results that had been provided.

Her investigation into the effect of ORME's at a biological level had only thrown up some bizarre folklore on the Internet, and she doubted its provenance. She did find the following, however, from the Geocities site:

> "*...As is well known among those familiar with the lore of ORME's, unusual biological and psycho-interactive effects are frequently claimed for human ingestion of small quantities of materials. We have explored this to a very limited degree with respect to Ir and Rh precipitates. Results were extremely subjective, and out of the scope of this report.*
>
> *During the experimental phase of this project, we did not neglect looking into historical accounts of "strange matter" or matter exhibiting implausible behavior. Perhaps the closest corollary surround some of the lesser known claims of Dr. Wilhelm Reich, with respect to materials he referred to as Orene, Orite, Brownite, and Melanor. While lacking any known critical replication since their disclosure*

during the 1950s, Reich was quite specific in his accounts of these materials, said to be "pre-atomic." In particular, the white powder called Orene, found near vessels containing alkaline aqueous solutions, bears an interesting resemblance to the 'g-orme' of Hudson. Both materials have been said to produce strong bio-interactive effects. Nevertheless, until such a time as we can better verify such material's existence, as well as come up with a coherent model, there is little more we can do except note the resemblance and speculate."

It was an extract from a report by N. Reiter and Dr. S. P. Faile from 25th August 2004. She would love to get hold of some of the ORME material and test it on her mice's DNA. She wondered if Kim would have a contact number for the ORME Metals Company in her office. Everyone had gone home, and she knew Kim rarely locked her door.

Entering Kim's office, she felt a pang of guilt. It felt like she was violating the woman. Resolving only to look at relevant documents, she decided to continue. Kim was, as one might have suspected, a compulsive filer. Her desk was neat and tidy and had three in-trays: In, Out, and Pending. Both the 'In' and the 'Out' were empty. Flicking through the 'Pending' tray, Shelby came across a remittance advice note from ORME Metals. *Why would ORME Metals be paying Kim £50,000 for a report commissioned through DNATech?* she wondered. She had an address though, and a company registration number. She copied the advice note on Kim's photocopier and replaced the original where she'd found it. She wondered whether to take a look in Runnels' office, but decided she'd done enough snooping for one night. *Anyway, Runnels was bound to have locked his office door.*

When she got back to her lab, she saw that her phone was bleeping and displaying a 'low battery' warning. *Damn*, she thought, *I was going to ring Gideon.* She opened her phone and saw that she had seven missed calls and one message before the phone died on her completely.

CHAPTER TWENTY

Rob and Charlotte's flat, Cambridge, England

Rob had been given a lift home in one of the police cars. He was thoroughly stressed out by the whole incident. The police said they'd be back in the morning to take a statement from him. "If I hadn't lent my car to Simon, that would've been me on my way home," he told Charlotte. "I've got to call Mitch."

Charlotte was distraught, but managed to get Rob's version of events out of him. "Have you told the police about the Audi, Rob?"

"Not yet," he mumbled, still physically shaken.

"But what if it was you they were after?"

"Exactly what I was thinking. I've got to call Mitch."

Mitch's phone was switched off or out of range. *I'll ring Gideon*, he thought.

St. Albans City Hospital, St. Albans, England

Kim Denton sat in the out-patients' waiting room. She'd been going there twice a week for the past four months. She picked up a magazine and flicked absently through it, looking for something that might be of interest to her. She stopped suddenly at something which seemed vaguely familiar. It was an advertisement for 'White Powder Gold'. Under the picture of a bottle of this intriguing material, the advertisement read:

> *"The ancient Egyptians believed this substance would increase their life-span and cure numerous diseases. Our fantastic m-state product does just that.*
>
> *Our White Powder Gold has been tested by independent laboratories in Europe."*

This sounds a lot like the ORME material that Runnels provided for Shelby's RFID tests, she thought, as she continued to read:

> *"White powder gold is "astonishingly" similar to David Hudson's ormus. We have developed a completely new manufacturing process that is fast, efficient and safe. Naturally, our product is produced only from 100% gold."*

The advertisement continued with testimonials from some satisfied customers:

> *"I have used this white powder gold for over a year now. My skin is now smoother, softer and more resistant to bruising. My body and my joints no longer ache. The aging process appears to have been reversed. I now have the energy and strength of a thirty year old man."*

> *"I fed white powder gold to our cat. He used to sleep for most of the day and was listless and in general poor health. He started to cheer up within a day of his first dose and today looks and behaves as if he is a kitten. These days we only see him indoors when he wants to be fed!"*

Kim took a pen and a post-it sticker from her handbag and jotted down the contact details for the company supplying the white powder gold. She also jotted down two names: 'David Hudson' and 'Sir Laurence Gardner'.

The speaker in the ceiling burst to life, interrupting her thoughts.

"Kim Denton. Kim Denton. Please go through."

CHAPTER TWENTY-ONE

The Strand Hotel, London, England

Mitchell Webb stood over the figure of Gideon Mycroft, cowering in the bottom of his wardrobe, and looked like he was about to commit murder.

"It's for you... it's Rob," said Gideon, handing his mobile to Mitch, and looking as innocent as a new-born.

"What the fuck? Who the... hold on, I know you, don't I?" started Mitch, dragging Gideon out of the wardrobe by his collar.

"Wait! Yes. I mean, ...it's me, Gideon, ...Rob's mate from the Christmas Party," stammered Gideon.

"Yeah, I remember. You're the weirdo who thinks 9-11 was an inside job."

"Mitch?" It was Rob's voice, through the mobile in Mitch's hand. "Hello? Mitch? It's me, Rob."

"What the hell are you doing in my wardrobe?" Mitch said, raising the mobile to his ear.

"Wardrobe? It's me, Mitch. Rob," Rob repeated.

"Not you! Your ... your mate..."

"Gideon," Gideon offered.

Mitch shoved Gideon against the wall, then pointed to the armchair. Gideon obeyed and took a seat.

"Rob? What the hell is going on?" he demanded.

"I tried to get hold of you, but your mobile was switched off. Is Gideon with you?"

"Oh, yes. He's here all right. Are you okay? What happened today?" he added suddenly, remembering the accident.

"You heard about the accident and... and Simon?"

"Shit, yes. What happened?"

"I don't know. Simon borrowed my car and crashed into a delivery truck coming the wrong way into the Science Park. It doesn't make any sense."

"And what is your mate doing hiding in my wardrobe?" He gave Gideon a menacing look.

"I don't know. I rang him because I knew he was working at your hotel."

Mitch was feeling totally confused and totally drained. "Christ, Rob. This is like... I don't know what this is like," he admitted. He half expected the guy from *Candid Camera* to appear at any moment.

"Mr Webb? Can I say something?" It was Gideon.

"You? What are you, some sort of pervert, or a thief or something?"

"I think I can explain, but first I need to speak to Rob, then I've got to ring my girlfriend," Gideon replied.

Not knowing what to do, Mitch handed the phone to Gideon and went over to the bar to pour himself another drink. *Jesus, how many is that today?* he asked himself.

"Hi Rob, it's Gideon. Are you and Charlotte okay?"

"Not really, but..."

"Good, good. Now listen to what I have to say very carefully and do *exactly* as I tell you."

When Gideon had finished his conversation with Rob he hung up the phone and tried Shelby. No reply. He tried again and left a message this time.

"Okay young man, I think you've got some explaining to do," demanded Mitch, taking a seat on the sofa across from him.

With difficulty, Gideon explained what he had found out about the Bilderberg Group, and how he thought they were somehow responsible for the deaths of his friend, Alex, and now Simon – possibly mistaking him for Rob.

"You're totally insane aren't you?" accused Mitch.

"Look, I think it's all to do with the RFID chips," Gideon tried to explain.

"And how's your astronomer friend involved with them?"

"Well, that's something else. But related, I'm sure."

"Maybe it's *you* they want snuffed out," Mitch said, goading him.

"Mitch, I don't have all the answers yet, but..."

"Listen to me, you little creep. I've just found out that my best friend has been killed..."

"There! You said it yourself. 'Been killed'...as in, *murdered*," interrupted Gideon.

Mitch put his head in his hands and deliberated for several minutes. *This has to be the worst day of my life*, he thought. *What the hell am I doing here? I should never have got into this in the first place.*

"Give me a chance, Mitch, and I'll prove it," pleaded Gideon.

"Look, er...Gideon. I agree there seems to be more to this than meets the eye. But, I'm not one for conspiracies, or secret societies, or any of that crap. There's a reason for this, and it may not be 100% kosher, but *I do* intend to find out what, or who, is behind it."

"Will you let me help?" asked Gideon.

"What do you suggest we do?"

A few minutes later, Gideon was tearing up the A1 towards St. Albans in Mitch's BMW. It was a 7-series Sport, and was capable of 0 to 60 mph in less than 6 seconds. Mitch had agreed to stay on at the conference and find out what he could about the Bilderberg Group's intentions and how much they knew about the *accident* at IDSys.

Twenty five minutes later, Gideon screeched to a halt outside Shelby's flat and ran up the stairs. The flat was empty. Gideon looked at his watch: 7.45 pm. *She should be home by now.* Checking his phone, Gideon dialled Shelby's mobile again. *No answer. Dammit! Where are you?* He tried again and left another message.

CHAPTER TWENTY-TWO

2nd Floor, Palace of Westminster, London, England

The phone on the antique desk began ringing and the occupant of the office waited two rings. The phone went quiet, then, seconds later starting ringing again.

"Hello?"

"Is that extension 333?"

"No, it's extension 322."

"Are you alone?"

"Yes."

"We have a problem."

"What now?"

"Our people killed the wrong person at IDSys."

"How? It was definitely his car. I saw the report."

"It was the wrong driver!"

"Okay. Does he suspect anything?"

"We don't think so."

"We can track him on his RFID chip."

"He doesn't have one yet. Too young."

"Okay... we can track him on his mobile phone. I'll pass the information on to the team. There'll be no mistake this time."

"There had better not be. The girl has also become a problem."

"The DNA girl?"

"Yes. She knows something about the ORME material."

"Are you sure? This is getting a little too hot to handle. We can't have the department associated with Gellar Pharmaceuticals."

"Then use a contractor. She must be silenced – immediately!"

"She lives alone in North London, I think."

"Correct. That's why Runnels selected her."

"Okay, I know a man who can deal with her."

"Don't fail us, Minister. We are very close to our goal and failure will not be tolerated."

"I know. He can handle it."

CHAPTER TWENTY-THREE

Shelby's flat in St. Albans, England

Gideon was pacing the living room in Shelby's flat. It was a typical Victorian flat, built on a slight hill and situated in a quiet street. There were steps leading up to the front door, while the back was on the same level as the garden. Shelby had the use of the garden nearest the flat and upstairs had the far end. Although he had been interested in conspiracy theories for the last four or five years, Gideon had never really taken them too seriously. He liked to surprise people with his knowledge of certain conspiracy related events, but for the most part he only did it for effect. He enjoyed winding Rob up the most. *Never in a million years did I expect to be involved in something like this,* he told himself.

He looked at his watch again. *She must be at work,* he thought. *She wouldn't have gone anywhere else. She knew that tonight was the first night of the Bilderberg Conference.* Wandering into the kitchen, Gideon opened the larder fridge to see if there was anything to eat. It was nearly empty. *I'll pick her up,* he decided. He grabbed Mitch's car keys from the kitchen worksurface.

The door bell rang. *Got her arms full of shopping again,* thought Gideon, *and can't get her keys out to open the door.* He ran to the door and opened it. The man on the doorstep was taken aback, clearly not expecting to see Gideon.

This slight hesitation probably saved Gideon's life.

In the split second of confusion, Gideon saw that something was wrong. The man dropped the flowers he was carrying and tried to pull something from his coat pocket, but it caught in the lining. Gideon tried to slam the door shut, but the man had managed to get his arm free and had shoved it forward. The door slammed against the man's arm, trapping it against the doorframe, and Gideon saw that he had a syringe in his hand. He pushed with all of his weight against the door and heard the man scream in pain. He briefly opened the door a few inches, and the man withdrew his arm. Gideon tried to slam the door shut again. This time it clicked shut, but the man's head and arm smashed through the glass in the upper half of the door. He didn't wait to see what happened next. He turned and ran down the hall, through the kitchen, and out into the back garden.

Gideon scaled the wall between Shelby's flat and the neighbour's and ran through the side alley into the street. Without looking back, he ran to where he'd parked Mitch's BMW and jumped in. He started the engine, locked the doors, and was halfway down the road before he noticed he hadn't put any lights on.

Fifteen minutes later

Gideon drove straight to DNATech. As he pulled up in the car park his phone rang; 'Shelby calling'.

"Hi Gideon, I just got your message. My phone was flat. Rob rang..."

"Where are you?"

"Just leaving work. What's up?" she asked, sensing the concern in Gideon's voice.

"I'm right outside in a silver BMW. Come straight to the car and ditch the phone on your way."

CHAPTER TWENTY-FOUR

A flat in Cambridge, England

Rob sat in the dinghy flat with the lights down low. He'd sent Charlotte off to her mum's just as Gideon had told him. *Why would anyone want him dead? And why was Gideon so worried about Shelby? It must be to do with the RFID devices, but why? They had checked out. The design worked. There were no known risks to humans. They... wait! Shelby had performed the tests. Did someone know that they knew about the ORME trial? He'd tried to order some over the Internet. They hadn't replied, but had someone known what they were trying to prove? Shelby could be in danger as well.* He tried Shelby's mobile number. No answer; straight to voicemail. *Phone must be switched off. Where the hell are you Gideon?*

A dark Audi pulled into the quiet street and parked outside the second block of flats on the left. The mobile phone tracking device indicated a flat on the second floor overlooking the street. The car moved on a bit further and parked in a side street. Two men in dark clothing got out of the car and began to make their way back towards the entrance to the flats. It was drizzling with rain, which did nothing to improve their mood.

Over the patter of rain, Rob thought he heard a car pull up outside and went to the window to see if it was Gideon. He looked for Mitch's BMW in the street below, but couldn't see it.

There were some teenagers hanging around near the lifts, so the two men took the stairs; not wanting to be seen. They stopped at the 2nd floor. The device showed that the mobile phone was in flat 8. They approached the door and withdrew their weapons. There was the muffled sound of music coming from one of the flats, as they took their positions; ready to break down the door.

Rob heard a noise on the stairs outside the flat. *It must have been Gideon after all*, he thought, and approached the door.

One of the men charged the door, with the second poised and pointing his weapon into the room. The door crashed in with such force it nearly came off its hinges. "What the fu...?" Four teenagers were sitting on the floor, smoking cannabis and drinking beer from bottles.

Rob opened the door and there in front of him were Gideon and Shelby. All three went inside. Gideon was the first to speak, "I see you found the keys okay."

"Yeah, I picked them up from your mate's sister, just like you said," Rob responded, as he sank into an armchair.

"What did you do with Charlotte?"

"Charlotte's at her mum's," replied Rob. "Fortunately, her boss didn't ask too many questions when she told her she had a family crisis."

"What about your phone?"

"Gave it to a couple of teenagers hanging around the Off-Licence. I picked up a new pay-as-you-go, like you told me."

Gideon filled them in on his conversation with Mitch. The flat they were hiding in belonged to one of Gideon's activist mates. "We'll be quite safe here," he told them.

"Why do you think they're looking for me and Shelby? Is it the RFIDs?" asked Rob.

"I can't quite get my head round it. We *do know* that the 6-16 incident was an inside job and that led to the compulsory IDs. It doesn't explain why they'd want to come after you two."

Shelby shot Rob a glance. "There is something else, Gideon."

They apprised Gideon on everything they had found out about the ORME's.

"That's incredible. Why didn't you guys tell me sooner?" They both looked down. "Mitch said something about a metals guy attending the Bilderberg Conference. There're a lot of deals being set up behind the scenes. I just hope he can find out more," continued Gideon. "Which reminds me, I've got to head back down there, or my cover will be blown."

"You can't seriously consider going back," said Shelby, brushing what looked like crumbs off the threadbare sofa before sitting down. She wanted to say something about the dreams, but feared that Gideon and Rob would ridicule her.

"Look, we don't have anything yet. If we can at least link some of the Bilderberg Group to what's been going on, we have a chance of blowing the lid off it before it's too late. Rob, is there anyway of disabling these RFIDs?"

"Actually, there is. If I could send an RF signal on the right frequency, then I could take out the fuses to the receivers rendering them pretty much benign."

"Well do it then," said Gideon.

"It's not going to be that easy. The codes are in Mitch's safe at IDSys."

"Well, Mitch can get them for us," answered Gideon.

"Then I need to find a way of sending the signal across the whole damn country."

"Mobile phone masts?" offered Gideon?

"No, that won't work – too many different operators and carrier frequencies," Rob answered, shaking his head.

"Well how do you think these Bilderbergs were going to activate them?"

Rob thought for a few minutes then said "There is one thing that operates within the right set of frequencies across the whole country."

"What is it?" asked Gideon, hopefully.

"Digital TV. Most of the stations are running at low power at the moment, because the analogue signals haven't been switched off yet. If we could upload the correct signal, at the correct power level, then those fuses would fry. I've got a pal who works at one of the transmitter sites. You remember Jeff don't you, Gideon? If we could fake some sort of broadcast test and get them all to transmit the signal at full power; it wouldn't have to be for long, we could just about nail it. Anyone within range, which is pretty much every household, would be zapped."

"That's brilliant. Make it so, number one," said Gideon in his best Jean Luc Picard voice. He was starting to believe that they could actually pull this off.

"Aren't we missing something here?" It was Shelby.

"What?"

"Well, assuming we're right and the whole point of this is to ensure everyone with an RFID chip *also* has ingested ORME material, so they could control their behaviour, how do you think they intended to distribute it?" she continued.

"Does it matter? If they were planning to use the Digital TV signals to activate the chips – they can't have done it yet. Full switch over won't be complete until 2012," stated Rob.

"No, Shelby's right. We need to screw the devices *and* stop the distribution of the ORME's," Gideon countered.

"So how could it be distributed? In the water?" asked Rob.

"No, too diluted, too wasteful, and too unpredictable," replied Shelby. "You need to have the right concentration in your DNA at the time the chip is activated for the bio-interference to take place."

"Food!" said Gideon. "They'd put it in something like food. I'll check the list of attendees at the Bilderberg Conference to see who represents food manufacturers."

"Or drink," added Shelby. "And while you're doing that, see if you can find out anything about ORME Metals. If we can find a connection between ORME Metals and a food or drink manufacturer, we may be able to get it withdrawn on health grounds. I've got contacts that could make manufacturers recall their products as a health hazard. We could even close them down."

"Will you listen to yourselves? This is way too big for us. How can we three possibly pull off something like this?" asked Rob.

"We don't need to do it on our own. Mitch is going to help us. And I've got my contacts; they can do a lot of the digging for us. And ..." started, Gideon.

"And in the meantime, we've got some Government agency, or worse, trying to kill us," interrupted Rob.

"Right, you two need to keep under the radar, but you'll be perfectly safe here," said Gideon.

Shelby looked around the tiny flat. The walls looked like they hadn't seen a fresh coat of paint since Jesus was in shorts, and it smelt funny. She was about to complain, but thought better of it.

"They have no way of tracking you since you got rid of your phones," Gideon continued.

"But that's not the case with Mitch," said Rob, despairingly.

"I'll get him to change his phone too," Gideon replied.

"I mean he's chipped," said Rob.

"Shit! Can't you do something to his device?"

"I can, but only to the receiver. The transmitter will still work, so theoretically, they could still track him," replied Rob.

"He's going to need it cut out," said Shelby grimly. "I could do it, but I'll need a surgical scalpel and some antiseptic."

"I'll think about it," said Gideon. "Perhaps there's another way."

Charlotte's mum and dad's house, Cornwall, England
Charlotte arrived at her mum's home at about 6.30pm. She'd had a decent drive down from Cambridge, the roads not being too congested until she got into Devon. She had stopped only twice, once for a quick toilet break and a cup of what they called coffee at the Membrey Service Station, just outside Swindon, and again at Saltash in Devon, just before she crossed the toll-bridge. She had a lovely lunch in a little cafe she knew there, where they served great omelettes. Back on the road it didn't take her that long to get down to Helston, near to where her parents had a nice little bungalow. When Rob told her she would be safer in Devon, she was furious at first, but after talking to Gideon, she agreed, provided Rob would stay in touch via e-mail.

When she finally arrived, her mother was clearly pleased to see her. "Oh, Charlie", she said. "You must be exhausted. It's such a long drive down here. I'll get you a cup of tea, and I've got your favourite shepherd's pie with cheese on top of the potatoes, just the way you like it."

"Thanks Mum, it's great to be here. We don't get together very often nowadays, do we? What with the distance and work, and all the other little things that seem to get in the way."

She sank into one of the comfy old armchairs she remembered from the old house, and kicked off her shoes. Her mum and dad had moved down here when her dad retired. He had been a headmaster at a junior school in Bristol for many years, but at the end of his career he had found it almost unbearable. '*It's getting impossible to teach the children these days,*' he would say. '*For some reason they just don't want to learn. Most of them seem to want to spend the day being as disruptive as they can. There is no discipline anymore. It's not how it used to be, when kids were polite, and wanted to learn. It's breaking my heart,*' he had said. So when Charlotte's grandmother's legacy had come their way, the decision to quit had been that much easier to make.

"Where's Dad?" she asked, as her mum came into the room with a cup of steaming tea.

"He popped up to the garden centre about an hour ago. Something

105

about hoods to cover the fuchsias before the frosts start," her mother laughed. "He likes to be prepared. Now he'll spend the next couple of months watching the weather forecast, so that he can put those hoods on in good time, whether the fuchsias like it or not!"

"He hasn't changed much then. He always did like to have everything ready in time. Whether it was buying huge packs of lightbulbs or boxes of white candles, so we were never left in the dark, or his massive collection of things that were *two for the price of one*. Do you remember, Mum?"

"Remember! The cupboards are still full of them now!" replied her mum with a smile."

Charlotte picked up the local newspaper from the arm of the chair, where her father had left it.

"Isn't it terrible about those poor children?" said her mother. "There's another one gone missing from a school down this way," she added, nodding at the paper in Charlotte's hand.

Realising that her mother was referring to the newspaper, she unfolded the paper and looked at the headline.

"*Local child disappears from Special Needs School.*"

"That's very odd," she said. "There's recently been a spate of missing children up our way too."

"I said to your father, *I don't know what the world's coming to*," remarked her mother.

They sat and chatted for a while, then Charlotte's mum decided she'd better go and see how the dinner was getting on. Just as dinner was about to be served, Charlotte's dad came into the kitchen loaded up with green plastic frost-hoods.

"Charlie's here, Malcs," announced her mum. "But before you go rushing in there to see her, you can dump those outside somewhere. I'm not having them in here cluttering up the house for months!" Then, lowering her voice so Charlotte couldn't hear, she added, "She's not said anything, but I think she might have had a row with Rob. So be tactful."

Charlotte smiled to herself in the living room, things really hadn't changed. Her parents had been together for more than thirty-five years and Charlotte couldn't remember a really cross word between them. There would the odd gentle argument about various things over the years, but one or other would always give in and life would go on in a comfortable, loving way.

After dinner, they sat in the living room chatting until it was time for the news on TV. "I just want to see the weather forecast," Charlotte's dad said. Then looked stunned as both his wife and daughter went into fits of laughter. "What?" he asked.

"Don't take any notice of us, Dad," said Charlotte. "You know how women are. We laugh at any silly little thing!"

"Well, the weather is a very dodgy thing," said her father. "You just don't know when a sudden early frost or something might come along!"

At that, both women decided they'd better go and arrange a hot drink before bed, breaking into laughter again as soon as they reached the kitchen. "Oh, it's so good to be home," Charlotte said to her mum, once they had calmed down. "I hadn't realised how much I missed all this until now. This is how a home ought to be, happy and laughing and caring. Has Susan been down to visit recently?"

Susan was Charlotte's older sister and more like a second mother, being twenty years her senior. Charlotte had been a bit of an accident; born two months after her mother's fortieth birthday.

"Yes, Susan pops down three or four times a year. She and Graham usually bring the kids with them in the summer holidays. Are you all right, Charlotte?" her mother asked suddenly. "You seem a little emotional. Much as I'm thrilled that you're here, I've never noticed you being quite so appreciative of your home before."

"Yes, I'm fine Mum. Maybe it's living in a constantly changing world full of work, shopping, cooking, cleaning, more work, more shopping, more cleaning.... I suppose that sounds rather pathetic. Really, I'm okay. Just in need of a bit of a rest, I guess."

"Right, then as soon as you've drunk this tea, it's up to bed for you my girl. And I don't want you to get up in the morning until you've had a proper sleep."

"Thanks, Mum. I think that's just what I need," Charlotte smiled.

The next morning Charlotte didn't wake until around 9.30 which astonished her. *I must have been tired*, she thought. She slipped on her old dressing gown and wandered downstairs to see what was happening, and found her mum in the kitchen. "Oh, there you are, sweetheart," her mum greeted her. "Just in time for your breakfast. We had ours a bit earlier and your dad's out in the garden, making sure that nothing is where it shouldn't be," she smiled.

"Really, Mum, you shouldn't have gone to all this trouble," Charlotte said, seeing her place all set at the table, and the bacon, mushrooms, egg and toast her mother almost had ready for her.

"Nonsense! A good breakfast will set you up for the day. I have to go out at ten. I help out at the local charity shop a couple of days a week, but I'll be back about two and we can have a bit of lunch. Your father will be here though."

"Okay, I can have a chat with Dad. It seems absolutely ages since we sat down for a chinwag, so that will be good," Charlotte smiled.

After breakfast, having washed up her plate and mug, she had a shower and got dressed. Then she wandered out to the garden to find her father. He was picking off dead heads from flowers and, here and there, picking up leaves and bits and pieces that had fallen to the ground. "You look busy Dad," Charlotte said, as she got closer to him. His hearing wasn't quite what it used to be. "Do you want to have a cup of coffee with me and take a rest for a couple of minutes?"

"Super," he replied. "Then you can tell me why you've chosen this particular time to come down and what you've done with young Rob."

Charlotte laughed. "I haven't done anything with him," she said. "He's just really busy right now. He's been working in China for just about one month in every three. So I thought this would be a good time to come and see my mum and dad. Let's face it, I don't often make a visit, it really is a hell of a drive!"

"Yes, I know, dear girl," her father sighed. "But it's just so peaceful down here, and your mum and I are really settled now. We found it a bit difficult at first, what with retiring and then moving down here so soon after. For a while I kept feeling I should be doing something more, you know? It was very alien to me to just potter about the place. Then, gradually, I got used to this slower pace and your mum and I found a good tennis club and a friendly church. We've joined the local drama group, and I write the Panto each year. We've made a few friends. We do what we want, when we want. We're safe and warm, and comfortable ...and well fed. Your mother's started having the occasional coffee morning with the blue-rinse brigade. What more could we want?"

"I'm so glad you feel so good about this place," Charlotte said. "But don't you let mum hear you referring to them as the blue-rinse brigade, or you *will* be in trouble!"

They chatted on until Charlotte's mum came back and Charlotte helped her get a bit of lunch for the three of them.

"If you two don't mind, I think I'll go for a little drive round this afternoon," Charlotte said when lunch was over and she could see her dad's eyes struggling to stay open. *Too much wine always made him sleepy*, she remembered.

"Charlie, you do whatever you want to. It's your break, so you fill it as you wish," her mother said, smiling at her.

"I'll give you a hand with the washing up first, though."

"There really is no need dear. We do have a dishwasher. Technology has managed to find us, even down here," she laughed.

So that afternoon Charlotte drove down to Mullion Cove, her favourite place in the whole world – so far. She parked her car and walked down the road, past the little cottages on the left, behind the little brook. As she neared the bottom of the road she veered over to the right and made her way to the rocks. It was a beautiful day, quite warm for the time of year, and there weren't many people on this rocky side. Most were over on the left, where the beach was.

She climbed onto the rocks, found herself a seat and sat looking out, watching the sea crashing on the large rock just off the coast below her. She had been here several times before, at different times of the year and each time, whether it was winter or summer, the sea never changed. It came in, crashed against the huge rock, and then swirled around waiting for the next big wave. Although it looked really dangerous, the sound of the constant breaking of these large waves was particularly soothing.

As she sat there her mind wandered to the situation between herself and Rob. Apart from the fact she was worried about him, because of Simon's accident, she knew she was becoming a little insecure in her relationship with him. Oh, she was sure he loved her, but she felt there was a definite lack of commitment. It had been great fun in the early years; touring the bars, arriving home at all hours, then making cheese on toast and coffee, talking and laughing, before finally collapsing into bed. Rob and his three mates from university, Jeff, Ian and 'Gibbo', were great pals and even after they'd left Birmingham often got together for a weekend, either at Rob and Charlotte's, when Gideon was away, or occasionally, at one of their places.

Charlotte was always invited along; she was a good cook and was always around to come and rescue them when their escapades got out of hand. She knew that was why she was invited, but didn't mind. At least she could keep an eye on Rob and make sure he didn't get arrested. Although she got on reasonably well with Rob's old room mates, she had always been wary of Ian, who never really knew when enough was enough. She often felt that she came across as a bit of a prude whenever she told him off about his foul language.

She had to admit some of their ridiculous antics had been hilarious. Like the night the boys went off for a 'quick drink' before dinner, while they were staying at Rob and Charlotte's place. As usual, Charlotte was called to collect them, only to find them stripped to their underpants, with their shirts tied around their waists, *Morris dancing* with the aid of four snooker cues in a local square. Although she was laughing her head off, she knew they were lucky not to have been detained by the local constabulary.

They didn't meet up quite as often as they used to, and Charlotte had made her own friends from work. She'd tried to integrate them into Rob's world and she knew Gideon was quite keen on her friend from work, Sue. The problem was, as the years had passed, Charlotte had tired of this childish behaviour and was looking for something a little more stable, and a little more mature. Maybe buying their own place; nothing too fancy - perhaps an old house they could do up together - would be the answer. She realised that what she was really seeking was a hint of real commitment from Rob. Was it really asking too much, after they had been together for so long? What made her feel even more insecure was the risk that if she pushed Rob into further commitment, she may push him away altogether. And that was the last thing she wanted.

She realised that she had been sitting watching the waves for quite a while and the sun was beginning to drop low over the sea, so she climbed back down over the rocks and walked back up the street, stopping to get an ice-cream from the little cafe just above the rocky outcrop where she had been sitting. She ate this as she walked back up the hill to the car park, and decided to just enjoy this little break with her parents and put aside the niggling thoughts about her relationship, at least until she got back to Cambridge.

When she got back to her parents' house she noted the worry in both their eyes. She smiled at them cheerfully. "How do you both fancy a little drive down to the seal sanctuary at Gweek tomorrow?" she asked. "We'll take our macs and stand well back. I've been caught too many times by those seals throwing themselves about and splashing everyone within reach!"

CHAPTER TWENTY-FIVE

The Strand Hotel, London, England

Gideon arrived back at the Strand in time for the start of his shift. He looked a little crumpled, having slept in the back of Mitch's car. He really needed to find somewhere to stay now Shelby's flat was out of bounds. He left a package for Mitch at reception and went to find the duty roster.

It had taken Mitch some time to recollect his thoughts after Gideon left yesterday evening. He'd rung Simon's parents and given his commiserations, and he'd made a personal vow to himself to find out who was behind it. The story had appeared on the late news. Apparently the driver was lost after ten hours of driving and had pulled into the Science Park to ask for directions. He hadn't noticed he had turned into the wrong entrance. The police were going to throw the book at him, but he'd probably get away with a '*death by dangerous driving*' charge rather than manslaughter. His company admitted that he had exceeded the guidelines for driving hours, and were taking their share of the blame. Mitch had made a mental note to discover which freight company had been involved.

He'd rung Sarah again and told her to contact everyone and tell them that the company was closing for the next few days, at least until after the funeral. He made an excuse for why he wasn't returning straight away, and added that he'd like to see her on Monday; without the others. He didn't mention anything about Rob, though he wondered what she would think when she found she couldn't contact him.

Alone in his room, he admitted to himself that he'd had an uneasy feeling about this contract from the start. He wondered how much Shackelford knew about the latest developments. He decided to pump the parliamentarian who had stopped him by the lifts for information. He'd have to be careful though, he didn't want anyone to suspect anything. The first thing he wanted to know was how he knew what was in the note. He looked through some of the business cards he'd collected last night. One stuck out: Mark Runnels, Director of Gellar Pharmaceuticals. *The name rings a bell, but the company doesn't.* He tried to entice his memory to associate a face or a location with the name, but he couldn't.

By the time he'd steadied himself and rejoined the other attendees downstairs, everyone knew about the accident. They were all '*terribly sorry,*' offering all sorts of help; '*if there's anything I can do, just let me know.*' The parliamentarian had told him that he'd overheard the message from Sarah when the receptionist took the call. He knew that to be a lie, because the message had simply said to call the office as there'd been an accident. So, if Gideon was right, and Mitch was slowly coming round to the fact that he might be, he may be able to catch a few people off guard, particularly if the accident was supposed to involve Rob and not Simon. He'd stopped drinking several hours ago, but continued to act as if he was getting a little drunk to throw people off their guard. After a couple of hours, he decided he was getting nowhere and was about to retire. Then he saw him. Runnels! *I recognise the face, but...* Runnels was already on his way over.

"Hi Mitchell. Terribly sorry about your news."

"Thanks... er...Martin..."

"Mark Runnels. Gellar Pharmaceuticals. But, you'll know me from DNATech."

Of course, thought Mitch. He'd never actually been to DNATech; it had mainly been Rob and Duncan. "Of course. It was the company name that threw me." Mitch felt a bit stupid. *These guys are bound to be on more than one board of directors,* he berated himself. The handshake was damp and limp, and Mitch took an instant dislike to the man.

"Oh, I'm on the board of several organisations – it just depends which business cards I remember to bring with me," beamed Runnels. "The reason I sought you out, old chap, was because we've been having all sorts of trouble with our delivery vans. Animal rights activists, you know. That sort of thing. Thought your vehicle tracking system might come in handy."

"Well, I'm sure we can come to some arrangement... Mark. St. Albans isn't it?"

"Indeed. I can usually be found there at least two or three days a week."

"That's great. I'll give you a bell."

After a few more pleasantries, Mitch managed to extricate himself from the gathering and went to bed.

The next morning, most of the guests were taking in some recreational activities in the hotel gardens. *Anyone for croquet?* A few of the others were popping into the countryside for a spot of shooting. Mitch had made his excuses and decided to spend the morning in his room. He needed to catch up with Gideon.

Gideon finally rang on the hotel phone at 9.30am.

"Hi Mitch, it's me, Gideon."

"How'd you get on? Are Rob, Charlotte and your girlfriend okay?"

"Yeah, fine. Can't talk now. Order breakfast or something for 10.00. Oh, and ask if you've any messages. I'll bring them up for you."

Gideon knocked on Mitch's door at 10.12am. He quickly ran through the events of the previous evening, including the ORME material and Rob's idea to disable the RFIDs. He had some news about Shelby's visitor too, having sent one of his mates round to check on the flat. The story from Shelby's neighbour was that a flower deliveryman had interrupted a burglary and got the door slammed in his face for his trouble. He was recovering in hospital, having needed fifteen stitches to his face and arm. "The landlord's changed the locks and boarded up the broken glass in the door," Gideon said.

Mitch wasn't really listening. "So the little bugger designed in fuses, eh?" he grinned. "He wasn't asked to." He popped a Tic-Tac into his mouth.

"Lucky he did," replied Gideon, lowering himself onto the sofa.

"I think we've been going about this all wrong, Gideon."

"What do you mean?" asked Gideon, nervously.

"Attendance of the Bilderberg Conference doesn't implicate anyone. I mean, I'm here aren't I? No, we have to find something that links these guys to something outside of the Bilderberg Group."

"I'm not following you." Gideon busied himself with the dish of boiled sweets on Mitch's coffee table.

"Let me explain," said Mitch, joining Gideon on the other sofa. "These guys are pretty senior to people like you and me, but they're following orders from much bigger fish. It's kinda like a pyramid and these guys are fourth or third tier at best. Any scandal with this lot and they'd be replaced overnight with other willing participants. We need to find out who they're working for."

"But, some of them are Royalty," said Gideon.

"Still not major players in the scheme of things. Sure, they can make you connections. Hell, I could be running a multi-national enterprise in no time thanks to these guys, but the only thing they've got in common is greed, and the *same people* pulling their strings."

"So what are you saying? We've risked our necks for nothing? We should take the money and just give up?" Gideon was beginning to doubt that Mitch was really on their side after all.

"Hey, buddy, who's offered *you* any money?" Mitch could see Gideon was offended, and he knew it wasn't to do with the money. "Okay, I never said they're not gonna be useful to us. I've got names and I've got companies. If we can start connecting these guys, we may find out who they're really working for."

Mitch opened his laptop and connected to the Internet over the hotel's wi-fi system. He'd showed Gideon a website where reports on directors could be purchased. "Check this out," he told Gideon.

He entered '*Mark Runnels*' and clicked on 'search'. The results page showed four Mark Runnels and the option to buy reports on each of them.

"This isn't going to work; we don't know which Mark Runnels he is," said Mitch, scratching his head.

He entered '*Gellar Pharmaceuticals*' in the company search box and clicked on 'search': One result.

"That's better," Gideon said, getting interested.

Mitch clicked on 'available reports', then selected director reports. The screen told him he could purchase the director report for £27.00 as a PDF download. Entering his credit card details, Mitch bought the report.

"Now we have a list of all the directors of Gellar Pharmaceuticals and look, here's Runnels and his pals. All we have to do is download director reports from the companies that these guys represent and look to see if any names come up on more than one board. Then we'll be getting closer to the real power."

"You mean all *you* have to do," said Gideon. "At twenty seven quid a report and over 100 companies, that's like... nearly three grand."

"Plus VAT," added Mitch. "It's gotta be done. I'll meet you after your shift. This should only take me a few hours to collate."

"Oh, I nearly forgot," said Gideon. "Add this company to your list." He handed Mitch the information on ORME Metals that Shelby had taken from DNATech. "And this package came for you."

Mitch opened the package and saw it contained a pay-as-you-go phone. "No fucking way. All my numbers are on my SIM card."

"They can trace you through it, Mitch. Keep it switched off if you're not going to bin it. Use the PAYG phone for everything."

Mitch looked at the details on the piece of paper that Gideon had just given him. "Who are they?" he asked.

"They're the company that got your missing RFID test report."

"Okay. I'll crack on with this. We'll catch up later. Oh, chuck us a can of that new fizz - I'll need all the concentration I can get."

Gideon opened the fridge and pulled out a can. As he flicked the ring pull, he suddenly stopped in his tracks. "What is this stuff, Mitch?"

"Oh, we've had it at the office for months. It's that new health drink that *aids concentration and enables your digestion*," he said, mimicking the advertisement. "They were giving away free samples when I had my chip implanted."

"Don't drink anymore of this shite!"

"What?"

"I don't know! But check out *this* company on your Fancy Dan website first, and see if any of the Bilderberg lot are on *its* board of directors."

Mitch went as white as a sheet. "I *know* they are. I've already met the guy."

"Fuck! We need to check out your DNA for this ORME shit."

"You don't mean...? How the fuck are we gonna do that, Einstein?"

"I hate to say it, but Shelby's got to go back to work," said Gideon, looking concerned. "There's something else..."

"What's that?"

"She's going to have to cut your chip out too," replied Gideon. "She's got all the necessary equipment in her lab."

Mitch looked at the small bump on the back of his hand and said, "I hope she knows what she's doing."

CHAPTER TWENTY-SIX

A flat in Cambridge, England

Shelby was pacing the floor of the dingy little flat. Rob was sat on the sunken sofa, wondering how he had got involved in all of this. Neither of them had slept well the previous night; the beds were uncomfortable and the less said about the linen the better. "Rob, I can't stay cooped up in here any longer. It stinks of wet cat, ...or something worse."

"Shelby, we can't go anywhere. They're looking for us, for Christ's sake," Rob reminded her.

"But what about my belongings?" she asked.

"I don't know. I assume someone called the police, or something, and they took them into custody."

"Typical man! I've got nothing to wear. All my stuff's in the flat...I mean personal things and everything. Gideon dragged me straight up here from work," Shelby fumed.

"Look. Why don't you ring your neighbour, or someone, and have them go round to collect some of your things and we'll work out how to pick them up later."

Shelby seemed to cheer up a bit. "Okay. Good idea."

She rang her neighbour on the new pay-as-you-go phone Gideon had given her. Apparently, the news was that a flower deliveryman had interrupted a burglar at her flat and had got himself badly cut in the process. The landlord had boarded up the door, changed the locks and left a spare key with her neighbour, who was also a tenant of his. "Right then, we should be able to nip down there and grab some of my things," she said.

"But we don't have a car," Rob tried to explain.

"We could hire one. I've got my cards with me."

"Hold on. Simon's car is at the railway station and I know where he leaves a spare set of keys," Rob suddenly remembered. "He's always locking himself out of the car."

"Well, let's go. This place is disgusting," said Shelby, wrinkling her nose again.

They took a cab to the railway station and Rob started searching the car park for Simon's white MR2. After fifteen minutes of fruitless searching, he decided the Police had probably towed it away. "Now what?" he said to Shelby, looking exasperated.

"Well, we're at the station. Let's get a train."

They travelled from Cambridge to St. Albans by train, changing three times – by necessity, not choice! The journey took a little over two hours. On the way, Shelby got a call from Gideon.

"Hi hon, how you doing?"

"I'm fine. How about you?"

"Sweet, I got back to the hotel okay, and me and Mitch are hatching a plan." He made it sound like Mitch and he were old friends.

"Are you sure it's safe down there?"

"Yeah, yeah. It's you guys I'm worried about. Is Rob there?"

"Yeah. We're on our way to pick up some things," Shelby started to explain.

"On your way where? I told you to stay in the flat."

"I'm going to *my* flat to get *my* things. I rang the neighbour and everything's fine. We'll be straight in and out."

"Bloody hell, Shelby. I've already had the flat situation checked out and the police and everyone think it was a botched up burglary or something," said Gideon, exasperated.

"So, if we don't want them to know we're on to them, I've got to do the normal thing and get my stuff."

"Well... it *is* unlikely they'll try anything at the flat for a while," said Gideon, as an opportunity came into his head.

"Good. So you agree?"

"Look hon, it might also be cool if you rang work and told them that you've been burgled and won't be coming in today. That would really confuse them, assuming they're involved." Gideon fought back a feeling of guilt.

"Right! And should I also tell them that I hope to be back on Monday?" she asked sarcastically.

"I know, I know. But honestly, that might be the best thing to do.

If they think you're coming back, they're not going to waste time looking for you, are they?"

"What's he saying?" It was Rob.

"Oh, only that I should ring work and tell them I'll be back Monday."

"Good idea. It'll buy us some time," agreed Rob.

"Fine. I'll do it then, but once I've got my stuff we're finding a hotel to stay in. I'm not spending another night in one of Gideon's mate's dingy old squats."

They travelled most of the rest of the way in silence. Rob was sorely tempted to ring Charlotte, but Gideon had impressed upon him the importance of 'radio silence' for the time being. With the prospect of a long boring journey ahead, he started the crossword in a newspaper someone had left on the seat opposite. Meanwhile, Shelby made the call to Kim Denton. As he readjusted his newspaper, Rob noticed the headline in inch high bold type. *Holy shit! They think another kid's been abducted. Kids aren't even safe in school these days,* he lamented.

When they finally arrived at St. Albans Station, Shelby drew some money out of the cashpoint for cab fares.

Kim Denton's house, St. Albans, England

Kim went home to rest after her treatment. The chemo made her feel so tired and a bit nauseous. Still, she'd been lucky so far, her hair was as thick and curly as ever. She had told no-one about her illness except Mark Runnels. She had to tell him, as it would be necessary for her to have time off every so often for her chemotherapy. He'd been very good about it, telling her to take as much time as she needed. He knew she was a workaholic and would be back at her desk as soon as she could. Everyone who knew Kim, knew she would rather be at her desk than just about anywhere else.

Kim made herself a cup of tea, put on her favourite music and lay down on the sofa. She tried to relax but the fears were still there. Would the chemo shrink the tumour sufficiently, would she need surgery and if so, how much, a full hysterectomy? Would she get through all this? She resolved to look up Sir Laurence Gardner and David Hudson on the Internet later and find out as much as she could about the white powder gold. She might also have a word with her boss to see if he had any idea how this could be used as a possible cure for cancer. She felt sure that the ORME material and this white powder gold were the same, or certainly very similar. Just now though, she felt so horribly tired.

I must relax, she told herself, trying yet again to do so. She knew all the relaxing exercises but, somehow, they just didn't seem to work for her. She had always been so healthy and active that she was generally able to have a warm bath, a warm drink and go to bed to sleep with no trouble at all.

Right, she thought, *let's try again. Tighten your toes then let go, tighten your knees and then let go, tighten your thighs and let go. Oh, for God's sake, this just isn't working.* She got up and got herself some warm milk and a couple of Hob Nobs and relaxed back into the cushions again. It was at times like this she wished she had a really close friend she could ring. One who would come running over to listen to her worries and assure her that *everything was going to be just fine.* But Kim didn't *'do'* friends. She allowed absolutely no-one to get close to her. For many years she had thought she needed nobody. And indeed, up until now, she hadn't. That was probably why she could empathise with Shelby. But Shelby had a boyfriend now – *stupid little slut*, she thought. It crossed her mind that it would be nice to have her mother to call but quickly brushed that thought away. Her father had died two years earlier and her mother, now eighty-five, lived in sheltered accommodation. Sadly, she'd ruined her relationship with her parents many years ago with that *'bit of business'* she'd had.

Her mind drifted back to that summer over twenty years ago. She had just left school, having got four 'A' levels and was waiting to go to her university of choice. She'd had no real friends at school either. Kim was what the other kids called a 'swot' and a 'weirdo'. She worked hard at all her subjects in order to get the highest pass she could, because she knew it would please her parents. They considered a good education the most important thing in anyone's life. They had been in their early forties when Kim had come along. Her father was the local bank manager in the small Welsh town where they lived, and her mother did a lot of voluntary work at the local hospital and in one of the local charity shops. Completely unused to children they had brought her up very much as they had been brought up. Very strictly, *for her own good*. Even then, she had to be in at ten, though she was heading for her eighteenth birthday.

Then she met Kieran and her life changed. She had seen him around, usually with a group of lads his own age, laughing and watching

119

the girls go by, as most young lads did at that age. Then one day, he had wandered over to her as she walked back from the library and chatted to her and made her laugh. He asked if he could see her again. Maybe go to the pictures or something? She had been thrilled and scared in equal measure but said that maybe they could. And so began her romance. They went to the cinema on a Saturday afternoon and then for a coffee in the local cafe, so that she could be home on time. Or for a walk early in the evening, ending up in a coffee bar for a drink; to listen to all the latest music, which was played non-stop. Then he would kiss her goodnight at the end of her road and arrange to see her again.

One warm evening they went for the usual walk, strolling along holding hands and chatting, when Kieran suddenly stopped and drew her to him and kissed her. This was no goodnight kiss but a kiss that seemed to go right through her. Then he kissed her neck, her eyes, her cheeks and she realised that he was drawing her down to the ground. She was so scared, yet so totally overcome with senses she had never before known, that she went with him. After they had made love, he held her in his arms, talking gently to her and she felt that this was all she would ever want. Then he lifted her up and they walked back towards her home. So it became their ritual, their secret love, for a few months of that wonderful, warm summer. Until she suddenly became unwell. It wasn't much, just a general feeling of nausea, probably to do with her period she thought. Then it hit her, she hadn't had a period this month, or come to think about it, last month either. She didn't know a lot about life but she did know what nausea and lack of periods meant!

Kim was petrified and not sure what to do but she knew she should see a doctor. She made an appointment for that afternoon and sat in the waiting room, shaking slightly, until her name was called. The doctor gave her an examination and asked her to produce a urine sample. She had to go out of the doctor's surgery to the toilet along the corridor and return with the sample bottle in her hand. Walking past the people still waiting outside the doctor's door, her face scarlet, she felt sure that everyone sitting there knew what was wrong with her. When the doctor confirmed her worst fears, she felt numb, lost, almost unreal. She stumbled out of the doctor's room and out into the bright sunshine, which almost blinded her. She had no idea what to do next, but she was sure Kieran would. So that evening she told him she was pregnant. She watched the colour drain from his face as he stepped back from her, almost as if she had told him she had the plague.

"How could that happen?" he gasped. "I though you were on the pill!"

"What pill?" Kim was confused.

"Dear God, every girl in the country's on the pill – except you! How could you be so bloody stupid?"

"Kieran, please don't shout at me," she begged. "I thought you might be able to decide what to do."

"Yes, well, look, let me think about it for a couple of days and then we'll look at the options, yeah?"

"Okay," she replied. "I do love you, Kieran, you know that don't you?"

"Yeah, sure, 'course I do. Look, I'll see you in a couple of days okay?" and with a quick kiss on her cheek, he was gone.

Kim wandered home trying to think what they would do. Would she still be able to go to University, or would that have to be postponed? Where would they live? *They could get jobs*, she thought. She was a clever girl; she could get quite a good job with her 'A' level results. She suddenly realised that she had no idea what qualifications Kieran had, or what kind of job he would be able to get. *Still, they could sort that out shortly.*

She entered the house and strolled into the living room to be met by her stony-faced parents. Her mother had tears in her eyes and her father just stared at her as though he had never met her in his life.

"How could you?" her father roared; his face white with fury. "I never thought I'd raise a little slut. My name's good in this village. So's your mother's...with her good works at the hospital and everything...and now this. Destroyed by a wanton little whore!"

Kim collapsed onto a chair. They knew, how did they know? She had only just found out herself.

"Oh, Kim," her mother whispered. "How could you do this to us? I always trusted you. I thought you were such a good girl. Dear God, what are we going to do?"

Still Kim remained silent. She was totally confused. What was all this shouting for? Why were they so concerned about what she'd done to them – what had she done to them? Surely this was about her. Her problem. Shouldn't they be thinking how they could help her?

"I know exactly what we're gong to do," her father said, his voice quieter now. "She's going to get rid of it, that's what's going to happen. And the sooner the better, before she starts to show!"

"How do you know?" asked Kim, suddenly finding her voice. "I only found out this afternoon".

"Doctor Dawkins is a good friend of ours, you stupid girl. He rang me as soon as you'd left his surgery. He felt we should know".

"He can't do that, can he?" asked Kim. "Isn't he supposed to keep patients' problems to himself? Isn't there some oath or something that says he can't do that?"

"You're underage, Kim", her mother said. "He felt he had no choice but to tell us."

"I'm nearly eighteen," Kim replied. "I'm fairly sure that under sixteen is *underage* these days."

"I don't give a damn if you're sixteen, eighteen or twenty-eight," roared her father. "You will get rid of it! And fast! Now get up to your bed and out of my sight!"

Kim left the room and climbed the stairs to her room. She curled up on her bed, trying to be as small as possible. If she got really small perhaps they would leave her alone, she thought, or maybe if she got small enough they might forget about her altogether. There was a small knock on the door. It was her mother. "I've brought you some supper. You still need to eat. You're father is gong to arrange something for you tomorrow, and then we can forget this little bit of business and get back to normal," she announced.

"Thank you," Kim answered politely. She took the tray and her mother left the room.

A couple of days later, Kim went to look for Kieran but couldn't find him in any of the usual places. She did bump into Tommy Logan though; who she knew was Kieran's best mate. "Any idea where Kieran is?" Kim asked him.

"Gone away," he replied.

"Gone away? Gone away where, when?" gasped Kim.

"Gone to visit his Gran in Ireland. Went last night apparently." He stuck his hands in his trouser pockets.

Kim just stared at him. "Are you sure?" she asked.

"Yep, just been round for him. His mum told me. Won't be back 'til the end of September she said," Tommy replied.

Kim walked away. *So that was that then.* Kieran was gone out of her life, so it would seem. So much for her romantic dreams. She suddenly realised what a fool she had been to trust this boy. She had fallen in love with him, but she was just a bit of fun to him. So he'd ducked out and she was left to pick up the pieces. Well, that would be the last time she'd ever trust a boy again, of that she was certain.

So it was that three days later she checked into the clinic her father and Doctor Dawkins had arranged for her. She was on her own, as both her mother and father were afraid to be seen in 'such a place' in case they were recognised.

She was shown straight into a cubicle to get changed into a hospital gown and from there into the operating surgery. She remembered seeing the massive white light above the operating table and the rows of knives and scalpels and things, which looked to her like instruments of torture. Then she was given an injection in her hand and all the lights disappeared.

When she came round she was in a little ward on her own. She let out a scream of pain. Someone was sticking a spear through her stomach to her back. *Oh God, I can't stand this*, she thought. *Oh, please somebody help me.* A nurse came in and spoke to her gently. "Bad, is it?" she asked. When Kim nodded she said, "I'll get you something for the pain, love, and then when it eases, we'll get a taxi to take you home. We'll give you some painkillers to take with you as well, as it may be a bit uncomfortable for a day or so."

The nurse returned and gave Kim an injection, which did help to ease the pain, then when the taxi arrived, she got in it and went home with her painkillers. When she got in, her mother asked her if she was all right. Kim nodded and went straight upstairs to her room. There she curled up on her bed and tried to sleep. She awoke sobbing and praying that the pain would soon pass. This was a pain she had never come across before and she didn't know how to deal with it. One minute it was in her stomach, then it was in her back, then her legs and then everywhere at once. Also, she was still bleeding quite heavily. *Dear God,* she thought, *why isn't anyone helping me?* She took her painkillers and, though they dimmed it for a while, it wasn't too long before it was back again. It felt as though it would envelop her completely. She had refused anything to eat from her mother but had accepted a warm drink of milk and a hot-water-bottle to help ease the pain. Her mother had said *'goodnight,'* and she was sure the pain would be much better in the morning. *'Then we can put this little bit of business behind us.'* She was alone again, with no-one to hold her hand, or talk to her, or listen to her as she lay there crying late into the night. Eventually the tears stopped and, as she lay there in the darkness, she renewed her vow never to trust a boy again. Not only that but, with the total lack of care from her parents, never to trust anyone again.

Within a couple of months she started at university and, although she made a few friends, no-one ever got really close to her, or she to them. She went home for the weekend a couple of times, but the atmosphere was so strained that, after the second visit, she didn't repeat the process. As the years passed she sent birthday cards and a Christmas card to her parents and received similar in return. However, she never returned home again. Eventually, she gained her honours degree in Physics and Chemistry and was offered a job at DNATech in St. Albans.

Lying on her sofa, with the soothing music playing in the background, she thought to herself, with a bitter little smile, *my 'little bit of business' would have been in his or her mid-twenties now.* Fighting back a few tears, she got up to get herself a snack and another warm drink.

CHAPTER TWENTY-SEVEN

2nd Floor, Palace of Westminster, London, England

The phone on the antique desk began ringing and the occupant of the office waited two rings. The phone went quiet, then, seconds later starting ringing again.

"Hello?"

"Is that extension 333?"

"No, it's extension 333."

"Okay, you have company. I'll ring back in ten."

"No, twenty."

Twenty minutes later the phone rang and the usual ritual was re-enacted.

"It seems that we underestimated the intelligence of our engineering friend. He offloaded his mobile phone and ran us a merry goose chase," the Minister admitted.

"Has he surfaced yet?"

"No, but if he's using a new phone it's only a matter of time before we cross reference the numbers he's called on this one with his previous one, and we'll be able to track him again."

"There's some good news on the girl. She doesn't suspect a thing. She rang work to tell them she had been burgled and would be back at DNATech on Monday."

"Good, we'll deal with her there. I'll call off the surveillance on her flat."

"We need to make it look like an accident. Runnels will have returned from the Bilderberg Conference by then. He can deal with any questions."

"The Bilderberg Conference seems to be going well. Webb seems to be playing ball, despite the unfortunate accident with his friend."

"Webb's just a temporary necessity at the moment. Once we've secured his company, he's expendable."

CHAPTER TWENTY-EIGHT

The Strand Hotel, London, England

Gideon took the lift to Mitch's room at 7.45pm. Mitch had spent the morning cross referencing directors of companies and had come up with some surprising results. Of the 115 companies represented at the Bilderberg Conference, there were 28 directors who were on more than one board, all of whom were the directors of seven companies within the group. *In other words*, thought Mitch, *these twenty eight people were sitting at the top of seven of the most powerful companies in Europe.* They included international financiers, royalty and a few European dynastic families.

In the afternoon, Mitch attended a couple of break-out sessions that he'd been invited to. They didn't seem to be that important; commitment to globalisation, single currency, single banking system, single tax system - Mitch had heard it all before. He did hear something that caused him some concern though. As he was refilling his coffee cup from one of the urn's in the corridor, he overheard two of the guests discussing '*the problem of over-population of the planet*'. He couldn't see who they were, as they were standing just inside the doorway of one of the rooms.

"I'd a say a forty percent reduction was required myself. In most of the highly populated areas, people live like peasants anyway," said one of the men.

"Precisely. The problem is, everyone wants modern technology these days and the fastest developing Third World countries are using up most of the resources," replied the second man.

"I'd happily see two-to-three billion of them wiped off the planet's surface for good," continued the first man.

"Rather them than us," laughed the other.

Gideon knocked on the door of room 1412. There was no answer. He let himself into the room with his pass key. The room was quite a bit bigger than Mitch's. All right for some, he thought. After a quick look around, he saw the laptop on the table. He wiggled the mouse and the screen came to life, displaying the DNATech logo and a password entry box. *Oh well, it was worth a try,* he told himself. He poked around for a while, looking to see if Runnels had left any useful documentation lying around. He felt through the pockets of the jackets hanging up in the wardrobe. Inside one of them he found a list of names on a faxed sheet of paper. There were thirty five names in all. Deciding he couldn't take it with him, in case Runnels noticed it was missing, he started to copy the names down on a sheet of the Hotel's paper. He got as far as number ten on the list, then decided it would take far too long. *This'll have to do for now,* he told himself. He was just about to leave, having returned the faxed sheet to Runnels' jacket pocket, when he spotted a folded sheet of paper in the bottom of the wastepaper bin. He retrieved it, unfolded it and read it. It looked to be in Runnels' own handwriting, but what was it about?

"Monday Gellar !
Security - clear building. Denton. Animals.
Still missing."

He recognised the name of Shelby's supervisor – Kim Denton. Gellar obviously meant Gellar Pharmaceuticals. *What animals? Who's still missing?* he wondered. *Shelby? Rob, possibly? Clear building? What building?* As he debated with himself whether to pocket the piece of paper or put it back where he found it, he heard the lock being activated. *Oh crap, not again,* he said under his breath. Stuffing the piece of paper in his back pocket, he crossed the room and opened the cupboard containing the Mini Bar.

When Mitch returned to his room he knew something was amiss immediately. He charged to the wardrobe and nearly wrenched the door off its hinges, his fists balled, ready for action. There was no-one there. He calmed his breathing. He knew someone had tried to access his laptop, because he always left the mouse on top of the lid and now it was next to it. Looking around, he had the feeling that, although things had been rifled through, someone had gone to a lot of trouble to try and put things back just as he'd left them.

Meanwhile, two floors up, Runnels entered his room and said: "Can I help you, young man?"

Gideon put on his best smile and replied, "Just checking your Mini Bar, sir. Is there anything I can get you? Anything you've run out of?"

"Er... no thanks. Everything's fine," Runnels said, checking his laptop.

"Then I'll leave you in peace sir," Gideon said, making his way to the door.

"Wait a minute! Aren't you forgetting something?"

Gideon turned round nervously.

"Here." Runnels shoved a five pound note into Gideon's hand.

"Er... thank you very much sir," he said in surprise.

As he left Runnels room, Gideon thought he heard him say, 'scruffy little twerp.' Entering the lift, he thought to himself, *So that's the fearsome Runnels, eh? My money would be on Mitch any day.*

There was a tap at the door. When Mitch opened it, Gideon was standing there; still in his uniform. Mitch grabbed him and threw him across the room. "You're a bit too fond of snooping around in people's rooms, sunshine!"

"What?" gasped Gideon.

"I know someone's been in here while I was in a meeting this afternoon."

"Well it wasn't me. I've been searching Runnels' room, actually – This is the first chance I've had to come back." Gideon said, picking himself up off the floor.

Mitch took a couple of deep breaths and decided Gideon was telling the truth. He wouldn't be stupid enough to jerk him around again. Particularly when his girlfriend's life was at stake. "Okay buddy, I'm sorry. This whole thing is making me paranoid," apologised Mitch.

"What do you mean someone's been in here? Have they taken anything?"

"No. My laptop's password protected, but they've opened it up and tried," Mitch replied.

"Do you think they're on to you?"

"Probably just being careful. Anyway, I've got some news for you."

Mitch told Gideon what he'd discovered, and said he'd give him a list of directors for his mates in the US and Australia to cross reference with American and Australian companies.

128

"The ORME Metals lead is a blind alley; they simply supply the raw materials. It looks like someone has been trying to cover their tracks or divert attention from themselves. But guess who they supply material to - Gellar Pharmaceuticals; whose directors are also on the boards of Vitality Health Drinks, Colbrite Toothpaste and a cayenne pepper manufacturer in the Far East. They also have connections with The Federal Reserve Bank in America. In short, the same directors are on the boards of DNATech, Worldlink Transport, EuroSat, Euro-Continental Films, Clearwater Energy and DigitalTV UK Ltd, among others."

"EuroSat? Do they make Sat Navs?" asked Gideon; his spider senses tingling.

"No. Satellites for NASA and the European Space Agency," answered Mitch. "Why?"

"No reason," replied Gideon, feeling slightly foolish. "So what does it tell us?"

"It tells us that there are a very small number of people at the top of a large number of multi-national companies," announced Mitch, with a feeling of satisfaction. "*And* it establishes a link between our ORME producers and the food chain. What's more, some of the minor players that came up are not entirely unknown to us: Runnels and Shackelford, for example. But the big one - Maxwell Lindburg – also happens to be at this very conference. He's the current Bilderberg chairman, no less. There are also several international bankers and some pretty old European families, but I think we'd better start with the ones that we can reach."

"I don't get it, Mitch. This thing has to be bigger than just the UK and America. You do know that the current President of the US and the current Prime Minister both attended Bilderberg Conferences prior to holding office?"

"Actually, I didn't. But, it doesn't prove that the Bilderberg Group are behind some secret plan for world domination. Look at the people involved." Mitch passed the list to Gideon. "They just don't have the clout. There would have to be some other organisation behind them, and I just can't subscribe to the notion that there is some global conspiracy taking place. It's more likely some scheme to make even more money for the international bankers." He could see disappointment written all over Gideon's face. "Look, it doesn't mean that I'm not going to do my best to screw up Lindburg's plans for our RFIDs, and whatever they're intending to do with that ORME stuff," he conceded.

Apart from Runnels and a couple of the bankers, the names meant nothing to Gideon. He pulled the sheet of paper he'd written on earlier from his back pocket. "I found these names in Runnels' room. Mean anything to you?"

"They're nothing to do with the Bilderberg Group or their financiers, as far as I can tell. None of these names came up during my searches. Who are they?"

"I don't know. I was hoping you'd recognise some of them," said Gideon. "What about this note?" He handed the screwed up piece of paper over.

Mitch looked at the handwritten note. "Gellar Pharmaceuticals, clear building. Animals? Who's still missing?"

"I don't know. Do you think he means Shelby or Rob?" asked Gideon. "Denton's Shelby's supervisor at DNATech," he added.

"Haven't a clue what it's about," said Mitch, shaking his head. "But that reminds me. Did you discuss your girlfriend's return to work with her?" he asked.

"Er...sort of. She's going to ring them and tell them she'll be back on Monday."

"Okay, that gives us the weekend to convince her she'll be quite safe."

"She will?" asked Gideon, not entirely convinced himself.

"Of course. *I'm* going to be there." Mitch walked over to the phone by the bed and tapped in a number. "Hi Mark, it's Mitch."

"Mitch, yes. How are you, old boy?"

"I'm much better thanks. I was thinking, since I'm in London for the weekend, I might call in at your place in St. Albans on Monday - on my way back to Cambridge. Take a look at what you do."

"Well, that would be fine, but I'm not there on Monday. Could we, say..."

"No problem, Mark. Does that pretty young girl who did our testing still work there? Perhaps she could show me round – a guided tour, so to speak."

"Er... I don't know."

"What? You don't know if she still works there, or if it'll be all right?" challenged Mitch, winking at Gideon.

"No... I mean... of course she still works there. I don't know if she'll

130

be there on Monday... I mean, they're always on holiday these days aren't they?"

"Well, I'll get my secretary to contact her and set it up."

"I can give you the name of my assistant: Kim Denton. She'll ..."

"No problem. Look forward to chatting to you about your vehicles when you return. Thanks Mark, and bye," interrupted Mitch, hanging up before Runnels could say anything else. "Right. That's done then. Your girlfriend..."

"Shelby," corrected Gideon.

"Right. *Shelby* is going to check my DNA on Monday. Now, I don't know about you, but I'm starving. I'll order us some room service, if you don't mind hiding in the wardrobe when they deliver it," laughed Mitch.

"Very funny, Mitch. I bet Runnels is a better tipper than you," he said cryptically.

"What?"

"Nothing. Got anything decent to drink?" asked Gideon, opening the Mini Bar.

CHAPTER TWENTY-NINE

The Abbey Hotel, St. Albans, England

Rob and Shelby booked into the hotel in separate rooms. Shelby was on the first floor in a double room with en-suite and balcony, while Rob took a twin room on the second floor overlooking the road.

They had collected a suitcase full of Shelby's clothes, shoes and makeup from her flat without incident. The neighbour had said that the landlord wanted to talk to her about the cost of repairs, but Shelby told him she didn't have a number he could contact her on at the moment, but that she'd call him from work on Monday. The first thing Shelby did when she got to her room was take a long, luxurious bath.

Rob had used his IDSys company card to pay for the rooms, knowing that he'd be able to square it with Mitch later. He was worried about using his personal cards in case he could be traced. While he waited for news from Mitch and Gideon, he decided to get to work on his plan to disable the receivers in the RFID chips. The actual fuse ratings were in his head, all he had to do was calculate the signal power required to blow them. Altogether there were eighty-five Digital TV Transmitters; including Scotland, Wales and Northern Ireland. Four of them were in East Anglia, and he had a friend from University who was a test engineer at the Sandy Heath Transmitter near Bedford. That would be the place to test his theory. He decided to ring his friend to see if he could show him round the facility. It took him a while to find the number, but he eventually got put through.

"Hello?"

"Jeff? It's Rob"

"Wasssupp?"

"Yeah, okay mate. Long time no see," said Rob, feeling a little guilty for leaving it so long.

"You're only up the road in Cambridge. How come you've not been over? Charlie won't let you out these days, eh?"

"Well, funnily enough, that's why I'm calling. Wondered what you're up to next week."

"She's kicked you out, hasn't she?"

"No, no, nothing like that. Just felt like catching up with some of my old buds. You still working at Sandy Heath?" Rob asked, hopefully.

"Yep. Digital switchover's first of April 2011 for our region. Can you believe it? April fucking fool's day."

"Ha ha. I can believe anything these days. Hey, don't suppose there's a chance you could show me round the place? Never been in a Transmitter Station before," Rob said, trying to sound casual.

"No problemo. When do you fancy coming over?"

Arrangements made, Rob still had one problem: he needed the receiver codes and some equipment from IDSys, not to mention a handful of RFIDs from the lab.

Shelby sat in her room wondering what she was going to do. Her impulse was to leave the area and stay with relatives up in Scotland until all of this blew over. But Gideon and Rob needed her help. The *country* needed her help. Forget that; all of Europe needed her help. She'd stumbled across a multi-national scheme to manipulate people's DNA for mind control for chrissake. She looked down and saw that her leg was shaking uncontrollably. *I can't do this,* she thought. Maybe if she rang Kim and explained what was happening, *she* would do something to expose the plot. *Okay, Kim had received payment from ORME Metals for the test report, but was that just a one-off back-hander or was she more deeply involved? Or was Mark Runnels a better option? What if he didn't know anything about Kim's involvement with ORME Metals?*

Try as she might, she couldn't imagine Kim being involved in anything as serious as the mass manipulation of human DNA, and definitely not attempted murder. When she'd spoken to her earlier in the day to explain about the burglary and to say she'd be back on Monday, Kim seemed genuinely concerned. If only she could make sense of the dreams she'd been having. She decided to take a look on the Internet to see if there was anything about dream interpretations. Connecting her laptop to the room's Internet port, she typed in 'dream interpretation' and hit 'search'. Surprisingly, she found a site that had an A-Z of dreams and their interpretations.

She looked up *Fish*. The site said '*to dream of fish signified insights from your unconscious mind.*' She looked up *Rain*. The site said '*to dream that you get wet from rain signifies that you will soon be cleansed from your troubles and problems.*' Okay, she thought, and looked up *Building*. The site said '*to see a building in your dream represents the self and the body. To see a building in ruins means that your approach to a relationship or situation is all wrong.*'

Oh this is just mumbo jumbo, she thought. *I need to try and understand what my dream is trying to tell me specifically.* At the start of the dreams, she was at DNATech, she felt sure. But when she went out in the rain, it was somewhere quite different. *The fish falling from the sky could definitely mean that my sub-conscious is trying to get through to me. Perhaps a warning?* she considered. She felt sure that the white building was an actual place, rather than some symbolic icon for her relationship with Gideon. *But where was it and why was it so important to her?* Maybe part of the dream meant that she should confide in Gideon. *Oh, I just don't know.*

Later:

Shelby had a restless night. No sooner had she drifted off, than she began to dream:

She was leaving work and appeared to be the last one to go; as per usual. She surveyed the car park, which was empty of cars, and began to walk home. It was dark and still. The street seemed to stretch out before her like a runway. She felt the first spots of rain, and realized she wasn't wearing a coat; in fact she was dressed in only a short cotton nightdress. The rain was starting to get heavy and she felt the cold go right through her. As the rain got heavier, she saw that large silvery objects were falling among the rain drops. She looked round for somewhere to shelter and saw a large white building, with pale green doors, just off to the side of the street. She looked down and saw a huge snowball land at her feet. As she looked around, she saw that the snowballs were getting larger. They were crashing into trees and splitting their trunks apart. They were leaving huge craters in the ground around her. She ran towards the building but, as she looked ahead of her, it was struck by a large snowball and burst into flames. The heavens turned black, and dust filled the air and her lungs.

She woke up choking and screaming. She was suddenly terrified that something would happen to Gideon. *Why couldn't she make sense of the dreams? The white building wasn't IDSys – she'd been there. She knew it wasn't the Strand Hotel either.* "Damn, shit and disaster," she said out loud.

PART THREE

"A man cannot be too careful in the choice of his enemies."
Oscar Wilde

CHAPTER THIRTY

The Strand Hotel, London, England

Mitch picked up the empty plates and piled them on the room service tray. He'd ordered a 16oz steak with an extra side portion of chips, so he and Gideon could share. He didn't want it to appear obvious that two of them had eaten. He flopped down on one of the sofas. He was beginning to get to like Gideon, despite some of his outrageous ideas. *He's a little screwed up, but generally trustworthy*, he thought. *Don't suppose he can be too bad if he's a mate of Rob's.*

"How do you feel like leaving Runnels a little surprise?" he asked Gideon out of the blue.

"What do you mean?"

Mitch opened his briefcase and pulled out one of his vehicle tracking devices. "What say we put this little baby in his car?"

"Sweet. Will you be able to track his movements?"

"I will when I get back to the lab at IDSys," beamed Mitch. "Can you check the booking form on reception and find his car registration number?"

"Better than that, dude. I can pick his car keys up from valet parking."

Mitch looked at his watch – 11.45pm. "Okay, I'll meet you in the car park in half an hour."

It was a simple matter of connecting the device to Runnels car battery, once Gideon had popped the hood of Runnels' silver Mercedes. It was an ad hoc installation, but it should hold for a few days, thought Mitch.

"Better not be seen entering the hotel together," he told Gideon. "I'll go first. You return the keys and come up later."

The next morning Gideon woke up suddenly, and for a split second he didn't know where he was. Mitch and he had chatted until early in the morning. Finally, Mitch had offered him one of the sofas to sleep on. *'And for God's sake put that uniform through the trouser press in the morning,'* he had said. *'If you worked for me, I'd have sacked your ass by now.'*

It was the last day of the Bilderberg Conference and they were planning on meeting up with Shelby and Rob later, to discuss their next steps. Shelby had texted him the name of the hotel in St. Albans where they were staying.

Gideon was about to go into the bathroom to answer a call of nature, when he heard a noise at the door. He froze where he was. Nothing happened. As Gideon approached the door, wearing just his boxers, he saw that a note had been shoved under it. It was addressed to Mitch.

"What is it?" enquired Mitch, waking up fully alert as usual.

"It's a note for you."

"What does it say?"

Gideon felt pleased that Mitch trusted him with something that could be important "Erm... *'Meet me in the coffee lounge at 10.00am.'* Signed, Maxwell Lindburg."

Mitch looked at the LED clock next to the bed; 8.00am. "Now that *is* a surprise. Okay Gideon, as soon as you're showered and dressed, you'd better let yourself out and clock on downstairs. I'll give you a shout when I'm leaving. I guess it's your last day today as well."

"Yeah," said Gideon in deep thought. "It might be better if I left earlier and got your car. I can pick you up when you're ready," offered Gideon.

"My car? Where is it?"

"Relax! It's parked a few streets from here. I could hardly turn up for work in it yesterday, now could I?"

"No. Good thinking. Okay, you wait in the car when you're ready. I should be leaving by lunchtime," confirmed Mitch.

When Mitch arrived in the coffee lounge he found it deserted apart from the immaculately dressed figure of Maxwell Lindburg. Two security men let him through. They didn't look like the other hotel security guards, so Mitch suspected that they were in Lindburg's employ. The coffee lounge was tastefully decorated and laid out with little groups of sofas and armchairs, in an attempt to create an informal atmosphere.

Next to each sofa was a low table and table lamp. It reminded Mitch of the mocked up display lounges at Ikea.

"Mitch, you got my note. Do you take it black or with milk?"

"Black will be fine," replied Mitch, extending his hand in greeting.

The two men shook and seated themselves in two of the sofas facing each other.

"I imagine it has been quite an experience for you, Mitch," Lindburg started.

"It's not the sort of thing I attend often," Mitch replied guardedly.

"But I'm sure you've made some valuable contacts."

"I have, yes," Mitch agreed.

"The reason I asked to see you before you left is twofold, really. Firstly, I wanted to remind you that anything that was discussed here is strictly between the Group and is not to be repeated outside of this hotel."

"Of course. That's understood," said Mitch, picking up a biscuit to dunk in his coffee.

"Good. You strike me as an intelligent man, Mitch. A man who knows what he wants. Which brings me to my second point: a man in your position, doing important work for the security of the nation, needs backing. I don't just mean financial backing, Mitch. I mean friends. I'm sure your recent loss has reminded you of the value of friendship. But I'm not talking about ordinary friends, Mitch. I'm talking about friends in positions of power. Friends that can help you to get where you want to go. And with friends like these, Mitch, what don't you need?"

Enemies? thought Mitch, staying silent.

Not waiting for an answer, Lindburg continued, "You don't need to do anything to upset them, Mitch."

Mitch was experiencing mixed feelings: anger and insecurity. This was a very powerful man, with a lot of very powerful friends, and he was trying to intimidate him. He was also succeeding. "I wouldn't dream of it," Mitch replied, trying to sound casual.

"Do you mind telling me what you were doing in the car park last night?"

Fuck! Was I spotted with Gideon? Did they know about Runnels' car? Mitch felt the hairs on the back of his neck stand on end. "I often take a stroll when I can't get to sleep at night," he answered slowly. "I didn't know it was against the rules to get some air." Mitch tried to force

141

a smile, but his cheek muscle started twitching. He hoped Lindburg hadn't noticed.

"Now you see, Mitch, I knew there'd be a reasonable explanation. It's called trust, Mitch. We do a lot of good work as a group, Mitch. Some people don't always see the bigger picture, but I think you can. Work with us, Mitch. The rewards are there."

They didn't see anything, Mitch thought to himself. He wondered how much longer this bastard was going to lecture him. He was beginning to get annoyed with the man's over-use of his Christian name. "Well... I look forward to being invited to the next get-together," he smiled.

Lindburg narrowed his eyes, trying to decide if Mitch was being sincere or had just given him the bird. "Take care of yourself, Mitch. We appreciate your...co-operation. I'll be in touch if there's anything you can help us with."

Before Mitch could reply, Lindburg ended the meeting by getting up and leaving the room without as much as a second glance. The two goons followed him out. Mitch sat there feeling small. *I must be off my head getting involved with this lot,* he thought to himself. He'd felt quite good about things last night, particularly when he'd got one over on Runnels. Now he came back down to earth with a bump. *These people don't know the meaning of the word 'difficult'. Anything they don't have, they simply go out and buy it,* he concluded.

Quickshop Supermarket, Swindon, England

Albert Steadman and his wife were in the dog food aisle of the small local supermarket. As usual, Albert was checking the *'special offers'* shelf. Like most convenience stores, the prices were slightly higher than the large out-of-town supermarkets, but Albert preferred them because they saved time. They also had a less comprehensive range, which meant Enid couldn't fill the trolley up with things they didn't really need. Grabbing a large economy pack of dog food, Albert turned to put them into the half-full trolley.

"Oh, Albert. Put those back, it's a false economy. You know Branston hates that make," said Enid warily. "We've still got three tins of it in the understairs cupboard at home."

"Bloody dog used to eat anything we gave him until you introduced him to those prime select chunks," mumbled Albert, putting the tins of dog food his wife had just passed to him into the shopping trolley instead. "Is that it? Have we finished?"

Enid checked her list. "Yes, dear. That's the lot, unless there's anything you need."

Albert rolled his eyes. "Right, let's get out of here. We've wasted most of the morning already."

They headed out of the dog food aisle towards the line of checkouts. "This one will do," said Albert, joining the end of a small queue at the nearest till.

As he began to place their shopping onto the conveyor belt, a young shop assistant came up and said, "It's all right, sir, we've got a special service till for people like you."

"People like me?" Albert enquired indignantly. "You mean *old* people?"

The assistant looked embarrassed. "No sir. I didn't mean that. I meant that we have a special checkout for people that have been chipped. I mean, you *have* been chipped haven't you?"

"Of course I've been chipped. What's that got to do with anything?"

"Here let me help you," the assistant continued, as she began putting Albert's shopping back into his trolley. "Over here, sir." She led the couple to a checkout closer to the door. "This is our express till for our chipped customers," she smiled.

Albert was about to continue arguing when he felt his wife's hand on his arm. "That's very considerate of you," she said to the young assistant. "Isn't that helpful, Albert?"

Albert grunted and started loading the conveyor belt again. When the assistant had moved away, he turned to his wife and said, "This is getting ridiculous. I don't know why they don't just make us wear bloody great badges with *'I've been chipped'* printed all over them."

Enid began packing the shopping into their bags, while Albert checked the correct price for each item was displayed on the till monitor.

"That'll be fifty-six pounds and seventy-nine pence, please sir," the checkout operator announced.

Albert handed over his debit card.

"Any cashback?"

"No thank you."

"Enter your PIN...Thank you...Now, can I just swipe your chip?"

"I beg your pardon?"

143

"I just need to swipe your implant with this." The checkout operator waved a wand-like device in front of him.

"What on earth..." began Albert, but it was already done.

"Thank you, sir. Have a nice day."

Before Albert could remonstrate further, they were distracted by a commotion a few tills away. Voices were raised, and two security guards approached the disgruntled customer. Albert couldn't hear what was being said, but the man was clearly annoyed about something. Moments later the security guards marched him off through a door marked 'staff only'.

Albert turned to the checkout operator that had just served him. "It's okay, sir. It happens from time to time. Someone tries to use a debit card without the proper ID," the young man explained. Albert continued to look at him blankly. The operator shook his head. "No implant. If you should have been chipped and you try to use your credit or debit card, payment is rejected. That's why I had to scan yours." He smiled and put the till receipt into one of the shopping bags.

Albert was about to ask what would happen to the man, when Enid grabbed his arm. "Albert!" she warned. "This lady is waiting to be served."

On the way back to the car, Albert remembered Roy's comment about asking to have a chip put in his other hand in case the first one failed. *I've got to pick up my repeat prescription from the doctor's next week,* he thought. *What's the betting he's got one of those wand things too?* Enid was surprisingly quiet on the drive back home and Albert realised that the incident at the supermarket had affected her more than she had admitted. He couldn't help wondering what would happen to all those people that had refused to have RFIDs implanted.

CHAPTER THIRTY-ONE

Underground cavern, somewhere on Mars

Enlil was monitoring the progress of the NASA satellite, Dawn. His people had set up a colony on Mars some 400,000 Earth years ago. Their own planet had been destroyed millions of years earlier. With too few ships and too little fuel to go round, it was a difficult choice to decide who should evacuate and who should remain. Those who were lucky enough to get selected included engineers, builders, chemists, biologists, astronomers, physicists and medical doctors. They were put into a form of aquatic stasis to make the journey into deep space; a long elliptical orbit that wouldn't bring them back to this part of the galaxy until 400,000 years ago. Originally there had been 5,000 of them in a flotilla of ships, but only 300 of them had survived the journey back to where their homeworld had once been. The calamity which had befallen their own planet had not been foreseen soon enough to prevent its occurrence.

Things had gone reasonably well when they'd first settled on Mars. There was a breathable atmosphere, and there were enough minerals and indigenous plant life to sustain them. They had of course brought equipment for building shelters, canals, and for the cultivation of whatever crops their biologists could adapt to grow in the red planet's soil and waterways. As conditions worsened on Mars; it grew colder and the atmosphere thinned, they quickly established underground caverns, for protection, as well as for climate control purposes. They built huge pyramids above their underground caverns to defend themselves from the devastating solar storms that occasionally swept over the surface of the planet.

Soon after settling on Mars, Enlil ordered a reconnaissance mission to evaluate the damage to their homeworld and the near planets.

The crew of the spaceship reported that, Tiamat, their homeworld had been split into two pieces: most of the land mass had been shattered into small pieces that were trapped in an orbit around the Sun between Mars and Jupiter. The portion containing the most water had been propelled into a new orbit between Venus and Mars. Mars itself had suffered a lot of surface damage and had gained two moons, but it was the remains of their homeworld, in its new orbit, which interested them the most.

When they had first returned to the original location of their homeworld, they only had enough fuel and life-support to reach their target destination – Mars, but with the establishment of a base, it would soon be possible for them to explore the remains of their former planet. Fuel production and mining had already begun on Mars, and the riches of the inner core were being exploited by the new inhabitants.

Early reports from missions to their former homeworld indicated a planet still ravaged by volcanic activity and ice ages. It was deemed an unsafe environment for the time being. Time wasn't really an issue for the Tiamatan race, they had long ago mastered DNA manipulation, and using mono-state atomic particles, they were able to prolong their lives almost indefinitely. Often growing to heights of seven or eight feet tall, the Tiamatans were a formidable race. Finally, some 80,000 years ago the first explorers from the Martian colony set foot back on the remains of their homeworld. Before they had set off on their epic journey into space, the Tiamatans had stored frozen eggs and the genetic code for as many life-forms as they could manage, in preparation for the re-population of a new planet.

After several exploratory trips, a group of Tiamatans decided that they wanted to set up a colony on their old world. There were valuable minerals and crops that could be genetically modified and cultivated back on Mars in their underground 'greenhouses'. It was agreed that Enlil's brother Enki would lead the mission.

The returning Tiamatans were highly successful in establishing a colony on their former homeworld. They soon set about cloning the DNA that they had stored to see which species could survive in this new environment. Disappointingly, most of the indigenous creatures from their original planet failed to adapt to the new environmental conditions, including the dinosaurs. But they had some success with the smaller reptiles, birds and insects, and mammals; in particular, the apes and the hominids. These creatures thrived in the lush conditions they found themselves in, whereas they had struggled on the old planet.

Over the next 20,000 years, most of the successful new species had adapted and evolved into many different varieties. But, the Tiamatans needed workers. There were too few of them to complete the tasks before them, both on

146

Earth and on Mars. So they decided to create a race of slaves. They mixed their DNA with several of the other species in an experiment to find a suitable combination that they could 'breed' for manual labour. Many of their grotesque creations were destroyed as soon as they were 'born'. Others either escaped, or were cast out to roam the planet. One particular species proved highly successful – this was the product of *hominid* and Tiamatan DNA. The resulting *humans* were extremely adaptable and made excellent slaves. The first generation of humans exceeded their expectations by a long way. They were both physically strong and relatively intelligent. They were keen to learn about their environment, including the stars. They wanted to know how they had come into being and what their purpose was. Many of the Tiamatans formed a kind of mentor relationship with their favourite slaves. Unfortunately, this thirst for knowledge was to be their downfall. The humans that were better educated than the rest began to exercise control over the others. They saw themselves as superior beings and wanted more and more privileges. The Tiamatans eventually became disenchanted with their greed and cast them out of the colonies to fend for themselves. Enki then commanded that future humans should have limited access to their technologies and their teachings.

It was a harsh environment for the Tiamatans, though; being much closer to the Sun than their original homeworld. So the Tiamatans orchestrated the building of huge pyramids to protect them from the harmful Sun's rays; teaching their slaves how to construct these monuments from solid stone blocks using highly advanced Tiamatan technology. They were coated in white marble to reflect the Sun. Inside these massive buildings, the Tiamatans installed equipment to chart the positions of the stars; making the trip between Earth and Mars easier to navigate.

Later, the Earth-based Tiamatans began building underground caverns beneath the pyramids, as they had on Mars. They installed special 'greenhouses' for the cultivation of crops, and vast laboratories for their DNA experiments. The natural lifespan of the new creations was around nine-hundred years, but the Tiamatans had not foreseen how quickly they would multiply. Within a few generations of their introduction, the humans they had cast out of the colony quickly spread across the planet.

Those that were left on Mars disapproved of the experiments being conducted on the new planet and relations between the brothers became strained. Eventually, the two colonies grew apart and visits between the two planets became less and less. The next generation of Tiamatans living on the re-born homeworld began mating with the species they had created, and soon there was a new species. This hybrid species looked more like the humans they had created than their Tiamatan forebears, and they set up kingdoms across the land, ruling over their followers. The hybrid masters were often fiercely competitive with each other, as they sought to discover new riches and new lands.

After several thousands of years, there were three distinct groups of survivors from the original world: the underground colony on Mars, the underground colony on Earth and the many hybrids with their human slaves.

As the humans spread further across the planet, it became harder for the hybrids to remain in control and eventually, they too became ineffective masters of a species that was out of control.

A few thousand years later, relations between the hybrids had disintegrated to the point of war. Fearing that the hybrids would destroy the planet with their powerful weapons and technology, the Tiamatans on Earth made peace with their brothers on Mars, and jointly decided to take action to regain control. To ensure that none of the hybrid technology and weapons would survive, they conspired to flood the entire land mass of the planet. Leaving Earth in their spacecraft, they fired their weapons through the Earth's crust; creating huge cracks and fissures, which released the high pressure subterranean water up through the ground. The land was engulfed by two to three hundred foot tsunamis, destroying everything in their wake. But Enki hadn't wanted his handiwork to be completely destroyed. So he went behind Enlil's back and instructed his favourite hybrid, Atrahasis, to take all of the DNA and frozen egg samples from his laboratory, including that of the humans, and store them safely in one of his ships. When the floods came, Atrahasis, his wife, their three sons and their wives, weathered out the storms in Enki's ship.

The great deluge took place approximately 4,400 years ago.

When the Tiamatans returned after the floods had subsided, they saw that the fissures they had created in the Earth's crust had forced the land masses apart, creating huge continents.

When Enlil learned of Enki's treason, he was furious at first, but soon accepted his brother's explanation that they needed slaves for their continued survival. This time, under the watchful eye of Enlil, the new humans (and the resulting hybrids) were created with inherent flaws. The Tiamatan scientists modified their DNA; shortening their life-span to around one hundred and twenty years, and restricted their brain capacity to about 12%; to prevent them from becoming as widespread and as powerful as they had in the past. All but Atrahasis, who Enki rewarded by bestowing on him the secret of the Tiamatan's

148

immortality. They selected which of the former species from their homeworld they wanted to re-create from the original DNA codes, and cloned only those most suitable to survive in the new environment. Only these few survivors retained the ancient knowledge.

The Tiamatans now controlled the planet from their underground caverns on Earth and Mars, using hybrid generation after hybrid generation as their rulers on the surface. (Many of these hybrid rulers have made their way into human history, religious texts and legends: Goliath, Hercules, Alexander the Great, and Caesar Augustus, to name but a few).

For a time, the new race of hybrids copied their forebears and had giant pyramids constructed as places of worship and as burial chambers; in places as far apart as South America, Egypt, India and China. Learning from their previous mistakes, the Tiamatans jealously guarded their knowledge, allowing their offspring only limited access to their ancient technology. Progress was very slow, and the Tiamatans were content to let the hybrids and the humans get on with their lives, so long as they kept them well provided for.

But, once again, the Tiamatans and their hybrid offspring failed to control the human population and just under 80 years ago, the Tiamatan rulers decided it was time to take action again. As in previous times, the people of the planet had fragmented into individual societies and there were different leaders for each land. The Tiamatans put their trust in a hybrid named *Adolph Hitler*. He was to unite Europe and Asia, and reduce the population of humans on the planet to a controllable number. They provided him with technology in the form of rockets and airships, and they were to have shown his people how to create the ultimate weapon; an atomic bomb. However, they had underestimated the resolve of the British, Australian and American peoples. They hadn't anticipated the defection of German scientists to the United States, who developed the atom bomb ahead of Hitler's own scientists.

After the failure of Hitler, journeys between the planets increased again, as the colony on Mars required more and more raw materials and plant specimens for their continued survival. These flights were conducted as covertly as possible, but were witnessed occasionally by a few of the human population.

With resources becoming scarce both on Mars and, once more, on Earth, the Tiamatan race has been preparing to re-take control of the planet. A programme of desensitisation of humans to alien beings has been taking place since the early fifties. Disinformation about the very origins of the human species has been planted to cause confusion, yet create the acceptance of a higher being (or beings). The threat of the destruction of the planet by asteroids, or other means, from outer space has been popularised in films and other media. The prophecies of doom in Sumerian, Akkadian, Mayan and contemporary religious texts has prepared the human race for some extraordinary revelations at the end of the era.

Now, the New World Order was marching on, under the guiding hands of their hybrid offspring, and the countries of the planet will once more be united under one leader, one religion, one bank, and one army. And that leader will be Tiamatan.

Now was the time for the Tiamatans on Mars to return to their homeworld; to join their brothers - already re-awakening in their underground caverns. Now was the time to complete the greatest conspiracy in the history of the Universe. They were coming home.

CHAPTER THIRTY-TWO

The Strand Hotel, London, England

Gideon pulled the silver BMW up to the reception bay, where two security guards helped Mitch into his car after securing his luggage in the boot.

"Where to, Kemo Sahbee?"

Mitch wasn't in the mood to play along. "St. Albans," he grunted.

Gideon gunned the car. They still had the gauntlet of activists to navigate. Mr Megaphone was still there:

"...*That's right, go back to your reptilian masters and tell them your plans. We're not your slaves, Lindburg. You don't own us, Queen Beatrix...*"

Reptiles, thought Mitch, *that guy sounds like a fully paid up member of the David Icke fan club.* Gideon could see him in the rear-view mirror. He looked tired and defeated.

"Hey, Mitch old buddy – you okay?"

"I'm fine, Gideon, just a little tired. Do you mind if we don't talk until we get there?" he replied, popping a Tic-Tac into his mouth.

"You're the boss," shrugged Gideon.

The journey to St. Albans took nearly an hour in the heavy traffic. It was a glorious sunny afternoon by the time they arrived, so the four met in the hotel garden out back.

Mitch filled them in on his experiences with the Bilderberg Group, including his meeting with Lindburg. They joked about Gideon hiding in the wardrobe and for a moment they forgot about the situation they were in. When Mitch returned from the bar with another round of drinks and saw the looks on the faces of the three friends, he felt he had the weight of the world on his shoulders. They trusted him completely and believed wholeheartedly that he would sort everything out. The moment of frivolity had passed.

They needed a plan. What was worse was that Simon's funeral was planned for Wednesday. Mitch felt that he had had a limb amputated as the reality of Simon's death washed over him in the cold light of day. *Who could they trust? The trouble with hanging around with conspiracy theorists is that you become paranoid,* he thought. But this was no conspiracy *theory;* this was conspiracy *fact,* and the deeper they scratched, the more absurd the facts seemed to be.

Taking a deep breath Mitch said, "Shelby, I need you to go to DNATech on Monday. Can you do that for me?"

Shelby felt herself shake involuntarily.

"I'll be there, you'll be perfectly safe," he added.

"I know...I mean, yes, I can be there."

Mitch pulled a can of 'pop' from his pocket. "And can we analyse what's in this stuff?"

Thinking about the analysis process had a strange calming effect on Shelby. "We can indeed. I'll need to read up on how we test for ORME's - I gather it isn't easy to detect from what I've read so far."

"Okay, and what do you need from me to check out my DNA?"

"A blood sample would be best. I can do that in the lab. Just a little prick."

Whether it was nervous tension or Gideon's infectious laughter, they all fell about.

"Umm, we also need you take out Mitch's RFID chip, Shelb," said Gideon finally.

"I've got everything I need in the lab, but it might hurt a bit," replied Shelby, looking a little uncertain.

"That's okay, Shelby, I'm sure you'll do your best," said Mitch, trying not to think about it. "Okay, Rob. Finish up your beer. We've got to get back to IDSys tonight and get you set up with whatever you need to deactivate these little bastards," he continued.

"But Mitch, I've got a room booked here," protested Rob. "Can't we start in the morning?"

"Don't worry Rob, it's only money. I assume you booked it to the company, anyway."

Thirty minutes later, after Rob had collected his things from his room, Mitch and Rob were driving up the M11. They dropped Gideon off at DNATech to collect Shelby's car on the way. When Gideon returned, he and Shelby had dinner in the hotel restaurant. Gideon was starving and chose his favourite dish: cheese filled organic breast of chicken, wrapped in Parma ham, and served with fine green beans, broccoli, baby carrots and saffron potatoes. Shelby went for the lemon sole. They rounded off the evening with a few drinks in the bar, before retiring to bed early.

A dark blue Audi pulled into the little car park of the Abbey Hotel and two men in dark suits got out. The two men went into the Hotel reception and while one approached the small desk, the other went into the bar.

"Do you wish to check in, sir?" asked the receptionist, with a smile.

"Er...my friend and I are not from around here, and I was wondering if you had something like a local guide?" answered the man. He was joined by his friend, who shook his head almost imperceptibly.

"We should have a leaflet here somewhere, sir," the friendly receptionist was saying, as she turned to look under the counter behind her.

The second man quickly ran his finger down the hotel register.

"What are those over there?" said the other, pointing to a pile of printed leaflets and distracting the receptionist.

"Oh no, they're nothing," she said, continuing her search. "Here you are," she declared a moment later, and handed the two men a leaflet printed by the local tourist board.

The two men thanked her and went into the bar to look through the leaflet.

"Room 205," said the second man.

"Wait until the receptionist has gone and we'll pay our little friend a visit," said the first.

Like most small hotels, the receptionist had more than one responsibility and fairly soon, she left the desk unattended to take some dirty plates through to the kitchen. She stopped by the two men on her way and asked if they wanted anything to eat from the bar menu. They both politely declined.

As soon as she was out of sight, they made their way through reception towards the stairs. Reaching the second floor, they followed the signs to room 205. The first man pulled something out of his pocket that looked like a credit card and slid it into the door lock. The light immediately turned from red to green and they opened the door; drawing their weapons as they entered.

The room was empty. One of the men checked the en-suite

bathroom and came out shaking his head. "Looks like he checked out," he said.

"He's proving to be an elusive little runt," said the other.

"I wonder what he's doing in St. Albans."

"He checked in with the girl," replied the other.

"What room is she in?"

"109. Shall we pay her a visit?"

"No. She'll be dealt with on Monday. Runnels already has plans set in motion. We don't want to spook her. He'll use his company credit card again soon and we'll pick up his trail."

Rob and Mitch stopped for a bite to eat at the same service station that Shelby had on her first trip to Cambridge, before driving to the Science Park. Rob was lying on the back seat of Mitch's BMW with a blanket covering him.

"I can get you ten minutes max, Rob. So get in, grab your toolkit, get the codes from my safe and hide in the lab," instructed Mitch. "And don't forget to remove the bulb from over the door."

The red light over the lab door was to let people know that the lab was occupied. A Health and Safety requirement for people working alone, remembered Rob. "What about my bags?" he asked.

"I'll look after them. You get the work done for your trip to Bedford next week."

"But Mitch, I've got no change of clothes or anything. How am I supposed to stay holed up in the lab for three days?"

"I'll be back tomorrow. I'll smuggle some things in for you then." Mitch knew that the details of their plan hadn't been thought through fully, but they were running out of time. He had to have a majority of the RFID chips disabled as soon as possible.

"What if I need the bathroom?"

"Here, take five of these," said Mitch, tossing a packet of Imodium onto the back seat. "I read somewhere that the SAS use these when they're on a stake-out," he added.

CHAPTER THIRTY-THREE

Head Office of IDSys, Cambridge Science Park, England

When they reached the entrance to the Science Park, Mitch shook his head. *How could that truck driver have missed this and tried to enter through the exit instead?* He drove up to the entrance of IDSys and parked in the first space; the one marked 'M. Webb – CEO'. Mitch surveyed the car park. There was only one other car and that belonged to Cliff, the security guard. *Good. We're not being watched,* he satisfied himself. Rob stayed hidden in the car as Mitch entered the building. Two minutes later, Mitch came out with the security guard and they both started walking down the stretch of road that led to the place where Simon had had his accident. A soon as they were out of sight, Rob leapt out of the car and let himself into the building with his pass.

First stop; Mitch's office, he thought to himself. After removing the file containing the codes from Mitch's safe, Rob headed for his own desk on the first floor. He took his toolkit and some schematics, plus a handful of RFIDs that he'd finished reliability testing last week. Making his way to the lab door, he stopped and pulled a screwdriver from his toolkit. Standing on tiptoes he tried to reach the light above the door. *No good, it's too high.* He grabbed a chair from the office next to the lab and climbed up on it to unscrew the cover and remove the red lightbulb. He had just replaced the cover, and was tightening up the second screw, when he heard the main doors open downstairs. He jumped off the chair, moved it out of the way and entered the door code. As the door opened he could hear Mitch talking to the security guard downstairs. Looking up, he saw the security camera pointing directly at the lab door. He grabbed his things and shut the door again, as softly as he could.

The guard talking to Mitch had his back to the row of security monitors on his desk. Mitch saw the door to the lab close on one of the monitors, and noticed the chair immediately. "Thanks Cliff, er... I don't suppose you could do me a favour could you? I've got to make an important call from my office and I've left a couple of bags in the boot of my car. You couldn't fetch them up for me, could you? I'm in a terrible rush tonight," he said, improvising.

"No problem, Mister Webb. Where do you want them?"

"Could you leave them in Sarah's office for me? Just pop the car keys on her desk. Thanks again, Cliff."

As the guard headed out to Mitch's car, he headed up to the lab and slid the chair back into the office next door. One of the screws in the light cover was only partially screwed in. *Sod it. It'll have to do*, he told himself. When he got to his office he saw that there was a message on his desk from Alan Porter; his Finance Director. It read:

"Tried to ring you. Your phone's switched off. Need to talk to you urgently. Ring me ASAP. Alan."

He fumbled in his jacket pocket and found his phone. He was about to turn it on, when he remembered Gideon's warning. Taking out the PAYG phone Gideon had given him, he looked for Alan's mobile number in his address book. "Hi Alan, it's Mitch. Sorry for ringing so late. I just got your message."

"Mitch, thank God. I'm really sorry about Simon...we're all going to miss him."

"I know. I'm keeping the office closed until after the funeral on Wednesday," Mitch informed him, as he sat down on one of his sofas.

"Are you there now?"

"Yeah."

"Take a look at the share price on your PC."

Now what? Mitch went over to his desk and clicked on the list of favourite sites he had stored on MS Explorer. The IDSys share price came up. "Jesus! The stock is up nearly 400 per cent," exclaimed Mitch.

"Yep, the company is valued at £125 million," confirmed Alan. "But there's some bad news too."

"What's that?"

"While you were away, we received notification of a hostile take-over bid. We were powerless to stop them. They bought up 60% of our stock, including Simon's 15%, which he had left to his sister. They now have controlling interest over the company. They've already invested over £90 million."

"Who are they?" asked Mitch, suddenly feeling sick.

"All I know is that they are an investment company going by the name of The Starbright Partnership."

Mitch recognised the name immediately and pulled up the company director reports he'd bought online yesterday. "Maxwell Lindburg," he said out loud. "That bastard made his play while I was tied up at his stupid conference."

"I'm sorry Mitch. I don't think I can continue in this role, so I'll be selling my shares and standing down as CFO. You should consider selling yours too – they should be worth around £44 million at today's price. They've called an EGM for next week to vote in a new board of directors."

"Thanks for letting me know Alan. Take care. I'll be touch."

In other circumstances, Mitch would have been pleased with that kind of growth. Instead, he sat with his head in his hands trying to make sense out of what had happened to his company. He looked at the list of directors again and saw another couple of names that made his blood boil: Mark Runnels and Preston Shackleford. *They sold me out completely,* he thought to himself. *I've been a complete fool. They've run rings round me from the start.* It was absolutely incredible. Before he'd attended the Bilderberg Conference his company had been valued at around £35 million; with his own stake worth £12 million. Now he had £44 million in shares, but had lost control of his company. The company that *he* had set up and run successfully for the last six years.

Had Lindburg planned Simon's accident to get hold of his shares or had he just spotted an opportunity and acted? He remembered that he still had to find out who was involved with the haulage company that had caused Simon's crash. A few clicks later and he had the information he wanted. The company was a subsidiary of Gellar Pharmaceuticals - Runnels again. That was one co-incident too many. An idea started to form in his mind.

On his way out, he collected Rob's bags from Sarah's office and dropped them off in the lab, where Rob had already started his tests. After making sure Rob had everything he needed, he decided he'd done everything he could for one night.

"You off now, Mister Webb?" asked Cliff, as Mitch came down the stairs.

"Yeah. I'll be back tomorrow. By the way Cliff, don't go into the lab upstairs when you make your rounds, I've left some equipment running – don't want you being subjected to any stray microwaves."

That was enough for Cliff. "Don't you worry, Mister Webb, I won't be going near any of that sort of thing. You never know what they can do to you, eh?"

Mitch went straight home, made a few calls; including one to Sarah, and went to work off some of the tension he was feeling in his home gym. He had a range of free weights, in addition to a bench press, punch bag and rowing machine. After a thirty minute work-out, he put his gloves on, taking extra care to bandage up his cut hand. He began hammering the punch bag; imagining first Runnels, then Shackelford and finally, Lindburg.

Eventually, feeling exhausted, he collapsed in his bed. *It's nice to be back in my own bed again,* he thought as he drifted off.

CHAPTER THIRTY-FOUR

The Abbey Hotel, St. Albans, England

It was Sunday morning and Shelby started looking further into the connection between ORME's and DNA. Gideon was going over to Shelby's flat to pick up some of *his* things. They both figured that it was safe enough for the time being.

After trying various search terms, she came up with the following information on FemaleFirst.co.uk:

"In the May 1995 issue of Scientific American, the effect of the platinum group metal ruthenium was discussed in relation to human DNA. It was pointed out that when single ruthenium atoms are placed at each end of a short strand of DNA, the strand becomes 10,000 times more conductive. It becomes, in effect, a superconductor. For some time, chemists had suspected that the double helix might create a highly conductive path along the axis of the molecule, and here was confirmation of the fact.

Similarly, the Platinum Metals Review has featured regular articles concerning the use of platinum, iridium and ruthenium in the treatment of cancers (which are caused through the abnormal and uncontrolled division of body cells). When a DNA state is altered (as in the case of a cancer), the application of a platinum compound will resonate with the deformed cell, causing the DNA to relax and become corrected. Such treatment involves no surgery; it does not destroy surrounding tissue with radiation nor kill the immune system, as does radiotherapy or chemotherapy.

The medical profession entered the high-spin arena when the biomedical research division of the pharmaceutical company Bristol-Myers Squibb announced that ruthenium atoms interact with DNA, correcting the malformation in cancer cells. (Monatomic gold and platinum metals are in effect "stealth atoms", and it has now been ascertained that body cells communicate with each other by way of stealth atoms through a system of light waves.) What the new science determines is that monatomic ruthenium resonates with the DNA, dismantles the short-length helix and rebuilds it correctly—just as one might dismantle and resurrect a dilapidated building.

It is known that both iridium and rhodium have anti-ageing properties, while ruthenium and platinum compounds interact with the DNA and the cellular body. It is also known that gold and the platinum metals, in their monatomic high-spin state, can activate the endocrinal glandular system in a way that heightens awareness, perception and aptitude to extraordinary levels. In this regard, it is considered that the high-spin powder of gold has a distinct effect upon the pineal gland, increasing melatonin production. Likewise, the monatomic powder of iridium has a similar effect on the serotonin production of the pituitary gland, and would appear to reactivate the body's "junk DNA" along with the under-used and unused parts of the brain."[2]

This told Shelby all she needed to know to confirm the presence of monatomic particles in the health drink and in Mitch's DNA.

When Gideon returned she showed him the article.

"Wow, this is amazing," he said. "So this stuff could actually be put to good use, as well as what whoever's behind all this is planning?"

"It appears so. But it's in the interest of governments and pharmaceutical companies not to let the world know that there is a potential cure for cancer. Imagine what would happen if the population at large learnt that not only was there a cure for cancer, but that the ageing process could be slowed down, or even arrested altogether. They wouldn't be able to sell any of their other drugs. The Government would

[2]http://www.femalefirst.co.uk/board/about78920.html

lose billions in pension benefits."

"Do you think you can get enough evidence together to have the drinks company recall their product?"

"If it contains monatomic elements, I'm sure my contacts at the Food Standards Agency could get it withdrawn on health grounds. I mean, who knows what effects it could have on people; good or bad. There are strict tests that they should have performed before the public at large is allowed to drink it."

"I'd like to get this information over to my buddies to see what they make of it," said Gideon.

"I think we should wait until we've met with Mitch tomorrow. He'll know when the time is right to go public with this."

Mitch arrived later that evening and arranged to take over Rob's room, since it was already paid for. He'd been back to IDSys and left him some food and drink. They discussed their plans for the next day. Mitch would meet Shelby at DNATech at 10.00am. That left her on her own for an hour, but she felt comfortable enough with that arrangement. "Anyway," she told him, "I need time to set up my lab equipment." They would get the tests over with, then Shelby would leave with Mitch. That way he could ensure her safety.

Mitch was up bright and early Monday morning and, as he ate breakfast in his room, he watched the early news.

"...Now for some business news. IDSys, the company behind the identity chip has a new owner from close of play Friday. The Starbright Partnership has a 60% stake in the company and has promised a huge investment to complete the roll out of identification devices by the end of the year. Over the next couple of months, 18 – 30 year olds are required to contact their doctors to receive implants. They have until the end of November to get chipped. After that, they will be unable to access their bank accounts or claim benefits ...The company's stock was up around 400% on Friday and further rises are expected today. The CEO was unavailable for comment..."

Mitch smiled. All in good time. All in good time, he thought.

"...In other news, the Bilderberg Group finished its annual meeting in London on Saturday. The Group meets every year, but refuses to talk about, or publish, what was discussed. Its chairman, Maxwell Lindburg, did confirm that the meeting had been a success. Maxwell Lindburg is best known as the chairman of Euro-Continental Films, who brought us *such classics as 'Alien Contact' and 'Asteroid: the Aftermath'. There were the usual chaotic scenes as crowds of protestors waved banners and shouted their disapproval of the secret meeting..."*

Mitch flicked the TV off.

CHAPTER THIRTY-FIVE

Underground cavern, somewhere on Mars

Enlil summoned his chief scientist, Nabu.

"How is the graviton experiment proceeding, Nabu?"

"We have reformed a portion of the Asteroid Belt into a sizeable body that can be directed towards Earth at your command," he replied.

"How long can we maintain its orbit?"

"Our graviton device has reached equilibrium. We can maintain its current attitude for as long as is necessary."

"The Earth probe will be in range in another few weeks. We can then start transmitting images to it."

"The images are complete. Their scientists will have no doubt that a huge astral body has entered the Solar System and is currently passing Neptune and Uranus on a collision course with Earth."

"Is the jamming equipment in place to block the signals from Voyagers 1 and 2 and the Hubble Telescope?"

"As you requested."

"I will be in contact with my brother again very soon. By the end of the year, he expects to have created the North American Union, the Extended European Union and the African Union. Unfortunately, the South Pacific Union is taking too long to resolve. We may have to adjust our plans slightly," Enlil conceded. "Our return to the homeworld is close, Nabu. Very close."

CHAPTER THIRTY-SIX

The Head Office of DNATech, St. Albans, England

Shelby arrived at DNATech at 9.00am on the dot. Entering the building she saw Kim coming towards her. *Okay. Here goes*, she encouraged herself, as she used her pass to open the turnstile barrier.

"Shelby! How are you? We were worried about you. Especially when we saw that you'd left your car here overnight."

"I'm fine thanks, Kim. Apparently it was a flower deliveryman who got injured. It was lucky I was working late, I guess," she smiled.

"A nasty business indeed. I'm glad you're back. Mark rang me to let me know that we have a visitor from IDSys coming this morning; a Mister Webb. He has asked for you to show him round. Unfortunately Mark won't be in today, so if you need anything, let me know."

"Oh, okay. Does he get the full tour of the labs?"

"Mark wants him to get the works. He should be arriving in just under an hour. I'm sorry it's such short notice. Will you be all right?" Kim asked.

"Yeah, I'll be fine. I've met him at IDSys before." Shelby thought about telling Kim about the health drink, but Mitch had been quite insistent.

She made her way upstairs to her lab. She felt relieved that Runnels was out of the office and began setting up her equipment. Placing the can of 'pop' on the workbench next to her, she started preparing test samples.

Mitch arrived slightly late at 10.15am, and the security guard paged Shelby.

"I suppose I should stick my head round the door and say '*Hi*' to Kim. We don't want her getting suspicious," he said, as they went upstairs.

"I'll take you past her office. It's on the way," agreed Shelby.

With the pleasantries over, Mitch and Shelby entered the airlock to Shelby's lab, where they donned their protective clothing. Once inside, Shelby took a blood sample from Mitch and put it in her analysis equipment.

"It will take a while to run, shall I show you around?"

"Why not?" said Mitch.

"Keep your protectives in this bag," she said, handing him a plastic pouch. "You'll need to put them on again for each lab we visit."

The full tour took a little over an hour. As they sat in the canteen drinking coffee, Shelby checked her watch. "The results should be available in half an hour or so. It's a bit early for lunch, but I wouldn't mind escaping for a while. We need to keep away from Kim, or she'll wonder why you're still here," she told Mitch.

"Okay, let's tell her we're popping out and we'll be back later to finish up."

They told Kim they were taking an early lunch. *My treat*, Mitch had told her. Kim was okay with that, but she reminded Shelby that she needed to be back promptly. '*There are reports that are way behind schedule*,' she'd complained. She suggested that Shelby might like to stay on a little later that evening to catch up.

After a light lunch, Mitch took Shelby back to the Offices. Kim wasn't around, so they went straight into Shelby's lab. Mitch took a seat while Shelby prepared to remove his RFID chip. She placed a surgical scalpel, bandages and antiseptic on the table next to Mitch, before she found some freeze spray and a needle and sutures. "Okay, Mitch, this will hurt a little – I'm sorry, I've only got freeze spray," she said.

Mitch gritted his teeth and looked away, as Shelby made a small, neat incision and carefully removed the device. She cleaned and sutured the wound before covering it with a small plaster. She cleaned off the device and gave it to Mitch, who put it in his pocket.

Having cleared up, Shelby began printing off the analysis results. "I'm afraid this confirms that the ORME particles have attached themselves to your DNA, Mitch," she said, looking worried.

"Are they harmful, now my implant's been removed?"

"I don't think so ... er... the mice that were affected didn't show any problems until after the RFID was activated. From what I've managed to ascertain, they seem to have an influence on the pineal gland in the brain, which releases melatonin. High levels of melatonin increases one's state of cosmic awareness and psychic ability. Low levels can have the opposite affect, reducing one's sense of being, and I think this is how they are able to influence human behaviour. During my research, I discovered that the brain has naturally occurring high spin iridium atoms anyway. So it's the combination of whatever they're transmitting through the RFIDs, together with the presence of these particular ORME's that's the problem."

"Okay, you've lost me," said Mitch, feeling only slightly reassured. "But you can confirm that the source of these particular ORME's is definitely the drink?"

"Yes."

"Right, we'll need copies of the analysis."

Shelby printed off two more copies and Mitch put them in his briefcase. "I'll head down and sign out. Meet me outside in ten minutes. We need to get you out of here," he told Shelby.

"Don't worry. I don't intend to spend a minute more than necessary," she replied.

Mitch left the lab, stopping to say goodbye to Kim on his way. She had returned from lunch and was back in her office. "I hope Shelby showed you everything you wanted to see," she enquired.

"Oh yes. It was very interesting," confirmed Mitch. "Would you tell Mark, when he gets back, that I'll be in touch?" he added, keeping his injured hand in his trouser pocket.

Kim agreed and escorted him out of the building. She was just returning to her office, when Shelby came out of her lab. "Shelby, can I see you for a minute?" Kim asked.

"Er, yeah. Sure. In your office?"

"No, in your lab please."

Shelby's heart missed a beat. *Had Kim seen the tests they had been performing earlier? Damn! They shouldn't have left the lab unattended.* Shelby entered the airlock and put her keys and phone down on the changing bench. She was about to enquire what Kim wanted, when the door slammed shut and she heard a code being entered on the electronic keypad. The door was locked from the outside. She banged on the door but it was useless. All of the labs had an emergency 'lock down' code in case of contamination. Kim switched the lights in the airlock off. No-one passing could see or hear her. Shelby could see from the light coming through from the hall that her phone had been taken. "Kim," she screamed after her. "What the hell is going on? For chrissake open this door."

But Kim was long gone, and no-one else could hear her through the sound proof door. The silence was eerie.

"I can't believe this," she said out loud. "Where are you, Mitch?"

She looked around for some kind of inspiration. *I must be able to break the door down, surely,* she thought, then realised that would probably be beyond her slight frame. *Damn,* she muttered. *How did I get into this mess? Okay, so Kim had locked her in the lab. What was the next move?* It was the uncertainty that was so frightening.

"Shit, damn and disaster," she screamed in total fury.

She sat down on the bench to think. *I mustn't panic,* she told herself. *Yeah, right!* She was locked in her own lab, with no phone, and no way out. Now Shelby was really getting scared.

Mitch sat in his car with the engine running. *Where was she?* It had been over ten minutes. Mitch gave it another couple of minutes then he got out of the car and re-entered the building. The security guard wouldn't let him pass.

"Who do you wish to see, sir," he asked.

"Shelby Taylor."

The guard paged Shelby but there was no reply. "Sorry sir, she's not responding to her page."

"Look I've got to get back in, I've left something upstairs," Mitch bluffed.

"I'm sorry sir, but you need to be escorted. Can I call someone else?"

Mitch thought for a second, then decided to give it a shot. "Kim Denton."

"I'm sorry again, sir. Kim says she's unable to come down at the moment; she's in a meeting," said the security guard, replacing the phone. "Maybe you could come back tomorrow."

"Tomorrow? That's ridiculous. What time does everyone finish?"

"Usually, around five o'clock, sir."

Mitch looked at his watch; it was 3.20pm. What could he do? He couldn't afford to make a scene. He didn't want Runnels to know that Shelby and he were more than just casual acquaintances. Not yet anyway. This had not turned out the way he had expected it. He headed back to his car and drove out of the car park and parked up on the street a short distance away. From there he could see the entrance and would notice if Shelby, or anyone else, left the building.

The Abbey Hotel, St. Albans, England
Gideon was alone in the hotel room. After channel hopping on the small TV for several minutes, he decided that he might as well do a little more research. *Daytime TV really sucks*, he thought. *It's either programmes made for, and featuring, trailer trash, or tedious chat shows with tired old 'has beens' trying to revive their flagging television careers.* He went over to Shelby's laptop and established an Internet connection. He knew he wouldn't be able to understand the technical information about ORME's like Shelby, so he typed in '*David Hudson*'and hit search. To his surprise, he found the Hudson story quite fascinating.

David Hudson was an agricultural farmer from Phoenix Arizona. In 1975 he began to collect soil samples from his farm for analysis. It was essential when farming in those difficult conditions to ensure that the soil didn't contain too much sodium, which could lead to a condition called '*black alkali*'. David Hudson and his workers were bringing back truck loads of 95% sulphuric acid, from nearby copper mines, and injecting thirty tons to the acre into the soil. This had the effect of converting the black alkali into white alkali, which water could penetrate and, in which, crops could grow. In addition, it was important to have the right nutrients in the soil. It was whilst performing the analysis of the soil that they discovered some strange materials that they couldn't identify. They traced this material to a particular area on the land and decided to perform some chemical tests on it.

They were able to produce a black powder precipitate from the material, which they put in a funnel and left to dry in the hot Arizona sun. When the material dried, it exploded in a blinding white light, leaving no trace of the material whatsoever. David Hudson repeated the process, only this time, he stood a pencil up on end next to the drying precipitate. Again the material exploded, burning about 30% through the pencil, but without knocking it over. Hudson concluded that it was not really an explosion, nor an implosion, but more like a massive release of light energy.

When the material was dried without sunlight, it didn't explode. Hudson took some of this dried material and performed a crucible reduction. Elements that were lighter than lead would float out, leaving the heavier elements in the lead. They found elements that were heavier than the lead. Normally they would be gold and silver. When they had it analysed, it *was* gold and silver. Yet this material wasn't soft like gold and silver. When it was struck by a hammer, it shattered like glass. Hudson then separated the gold and silver out and was left with a black substance. He eventually found someone at Cornell, who had the right equipment to analyse it, and was told it was iron silica aluminium. They removed the iron and the silicon and the aluminium. They were left with 98% of the material, which was still unidentifiable. The PhD's at Cornell couldn't help him further.

After making enquiries, Hudson finally found a spectroscopist who had trained in West Germany. They began their own analysis of the black substance using a modified spectroscope. After fifteen seconds, they read iron, silicon and aluminium, then nothing. After fifty-five, sixty, sixty-five seconds – still nothing. Then at seventy seconds, they read palladium. Then platinum, then rhodium, then ruthenium, then iridium, then osmium. All of which are extremely rare and extremely valuable. Hudson and his spectroscopist repeated these tests regularly for a period of about two years.

Eventually, Hudson introduced the material to more scientists and they worked on it from 1983 to 1989. He contracted a company to make fuel cells from the material and evaluate them. They were very successful, so in March 1988 Hudson filed for a patent, calling the material Orbitally Rearranged Monatomic Elements – ORME's. But to complete the patent, they required more technical information about the white powder.

One of the first problems he encountered was when they tried to weigh the material. They heated the material at 1.2 degrees Celsius per minute, then cooled it at 2 degrees per minute. Oxidization increased the weight by 2%. Hydro-reduction increased the weight by 3%. But when the material was annealed and turned snow white, it weighed only 56% of its original weight. Even stranger, when it was heated to the point that it turned black, all the weight was regained. Successive cycles of heating and cooling the material, resulted in weight increases from three to four hundred percent all the way down to *less than zero*, but it would always return to 56% of the original weight. Hudson had remarked that if the material was in a pan, the pan would weigh less with the material in it than it did when empty.

When they tried to measure the electrical conductivity of the material, they found it didn't conduct at all. However, when they used a radio frequency transmitter and resonated a wire next to the material, it acted just like a superconductor. With no resistance whatsoever, it would run like a perpetual motion machine. Energy could be put into it, left for an indefinite period of time, and it would still be there with no losses.

When Hudson involved a scientist, who was working on a new theory of gravity, they made an even more astounding discovery. When the material is in the state where it weighs only 56% of its original weight, it is actually bending space and time the scientist told him. The material was actually resonating in two dimensions. At the point where the material weighs less than zero, the scientist concluded that it had actually left our three dimensions altogether. The material appeared to be the key to controlling gravity and space/time.

In 1991 Hudson read a book called *Secrets of the Alchemists*, that described a white powder gold. He immediately recognised it as the material he had discovered on his farm in Phoenix. He read research by Bristol-Myers-Squib that showed that the material inter-reacted with DNA, correcting damaged DNA.

Becoming intrigued with this new discovery, Hudson gave some of his material to a Golden Retriever that was suffering from tick fever, valley fever and a huge abscess on his side. No veterinarians had been able to help the dog. After one week of medication, the dog was completely cured. The doctor that Hudson was working with, administered the material to a terminally ill AIDs patient and another with skin cancer. Both apparently made a full recovery.

Gideon read on. There were many similar cases. *So how come this stuff isn't more widely available?* he thought. He soon found his answer.

David Hudson's patent had to be approved by the US Department of Defense, because of its strategic importance. The Defense Department wanted the technology, but because Hudson wouldn't give them what they wanted, they turned down his patent application. Having spent $540,000 trying to secure the patent, Hudson had to finally give up.

Gideon's mobile started to play the theme from the X-Files.

Head Office DNATech, St. Albans, England
Mitch had called Gideon from his car.
"Hi Gideon, it's me Mitch."
"Hi Mitch. How'd it go? Shelby with you?"

"Er... that's why I'm calling," said Mitch, cautiously.

"What do you mean? What the fuck's happened?"

"She was supposed to leave with me, but I can't get back into the building. Look, you get in a cab and get round here. You'll be able to act like *the concerned boyfriend*, and get someone to talk to you. I don't want to tip off Runnels."

"For chrissake Mitch. If anything happens to her..." Gideon blustered.

"I'll keep an eye on the place until you get here," reassured Mitch.

Gideon had trouble getting a cab at that time of day and eventually arrived at 4.50pm. The cab pulled up behind Mitch's BMW. Gideon got out looking like he meant business. He was dressed in a camouflage jacket with black jeans and heavy boots. He signalled Mitch to wind the window down. "Anything happened?" he asked, breathlessly.

"Get in," ordered Mitch.

Gideon climbed into the passenger seat. "What do you think they're doing in there?" he asked.

"I don't know – I don't think they'll try anything with the other staff still in there."

"Why didn't she come out?"

"I don't know. Maybe Denton held her up. She wanted her to work late tonight."

"No way. I'm going over there." He reached for the door handle.

"Gideon! Wait until the others have left," said Mitch, grabbing Gideon's jacket. "If she doesn't come out with them, then it'll be easier for you to persuade the guard to let you look for her." He waited until he was sure Gideon wasn't going to do anything rash, then released his grip.

They didn't have to wait long. At 4.58pm they started filing out of the building. One by one they left in their cars, but there was still no sign of Shelby or Kim Denton.

Gideon had waited long enough. He jumped out of the car and marched up to the front entrance. The guard opened the door as soon as he saw Gideon approaching. "You're early," he said, taking Gideon by surprise. "They've only just left. Where are the others?"

"Er... they're right behind me... be about another five minutes," he bluffed. If the guard was going to let him in, he didn't care who he thought he was.

As they entered the building together, the guard said, "Right, I suppose you'd better lock me in that cupboard. Here, take my keys and my pass. You'd better take the tape out of the CCTV recorder as well. I thought you'd be wearing balaclavas."

Gideon did as he was instructed without saying a word. Once he'd locked the guard in the cupboard, he went back to the front door and signalled for Mitch to come over. Mitch started the car and drove up to the front entrance. "What's going on? Where's the guard?"

"Case of mistaken identity, I think. He's locked up in that cupboard," Gideon said and shrugged.

"What?"

"I'll tell you later. Let's find Shelby and get the fuck out of here."

Mitch led the way up to Shelby's lab. As they passed Kim's office, they saw that she was still in there. Together, they overpowered her and forced her to sit down in her chair. "Where's Shelby?" demanded Gideon.

"You're too late," she spat. "They'll be here in a minute."

"Leave her," said Mitch. "She's probably in the lab. We'll lock this one in here and look around."

After ripping out her phone and trashing her mobile, they took Kim's keys and locked her in her office. They immediately saw that the keypad to Shelby's lab had been set to 'lock down'. *She must be in here,* thought Mitch and he flicked the light switch back on. They could see Shelby sat on the changing bench. She looked up and saw them through the small window. Gideon signalled to her to stand back and began kicking at the doors with his heavy boots. It took a few minutes, but they were soon able to prise the doors apart and get her out.

"That bitch Kim locked me in," Shelby explained. "I think she's on to us."

"Well now she knows what it feels like," said Gideon, indicating Kim's locked office door.

"I don't know what's going down," said Mitch, "But I think we'd better get out of here, fast."

They ran down the stairs towards the front doors together. As they climbed into the BMW, Mitch started the engine. He'd just reversed the car back a few feet, when there was a squeal of tyres and they all looked to the source. A large black transit van had entered the car park and had pulled up a few yards in front of them. The doors opened and three men, wearing balaclavas and carrying baseball bats, jumped out.

"Friends of yours?" asked Mitch.

"DRIVE!" screamed Gideon.

Mitch revved the BMW; more to warn the men to get out of his way than anything else, and lurched forward. Two of the men leapt aside, while the third swung his bat at the car. Mitch swerved and bounced the car off the side of the van just as the bat connected and the passenger side window shattered, spraying them with tiny cubes of glass. The car continued forward and Mitch managed to gain control and squeeze the car through the car park gates and into the street, losing the driver's side mirror and half of his front bumper in the process.

Gideon wiped some specks of blood off his cheek and said, "Who the fuck were they?"

They drove back to the hotel to get their things and decided it was time to get as far away from St. Albans as possible. Before they left for Cambridge, Mitch decided that the BMW was too conspicuous and, checking it into a garage for repairs, hired a Land Rover Discovery on his credit card. Much to their relief, they had an uneventful journey back to the Science Park.

Mitch told the other two to wait in the car when they arrived at IDSys. He went into the building and three minutes later came out with Cliff, the security guard. Cliff got straight in his car and drove off. Once he'd collected Rob and the four of them were back on the road, Mitch explained that he'd told Cliff that his services were no longer required now that they were under new management. He'd be re-assigned by his company in a couple of days, but Mitch promised to pay him up to the end of the week anyway. "He's also carrying my RFID chip in his coat pocket," he added with a wink.

CHAPTER THIRTY-SEVEN

Mitch's house, Cambridge, England

Mitch's house was a large seventies detached property on a quiet estate. It had a double garage out front and to the rear was an enclosed garden and swimming pool. Most of his neighbours kept themselves to themselves and generally paid little attention to the comings and goings of other residents.

All four of them climbed out of Mitch's new Discovery and by the time they'd settled down in the lounge, they were quite exhausted from the day's activities. Poor Rob had been sleeping in the lab for the last two nights, and made straight for the bathroom. The lounge was almost as sparse as Mitch's office, Shelby noticed. *This place could definitely do with a woman's touch,* she thought. When Rob returned, they filled him in on the events at DNATech.

Not being much of a cook, Mitch ordered a delivery Chinese and they tried to unwind with a bottle or two of his finest wine from the cellar.

By the time they'd finished eating, it was 10.00pm. Mitch put the news on.

"*... In breaking news tonight,*" the presenter was saying, "*we're getting reports of what appears to have been an attack on a research laboratory by animal rights activists in St. Albans...*"

"So that's their game," interrupted Gideon.

"*...Police fear two dead, whilst a security guard is recovering in hospital...*"

"What did they do to the guard? He was in on it for Christsake," Gideon protested.

"Shhh, Gideon. They said two dead," Shelby warned.

"*...The two missing, presumed dead, are both employees of the* *research laboratory and are assumed to have been working on the first floor, which was completely gutted by fire..."*

"Oh my God, they killed Kim. We should never have left her in there," gasped Shelby.

"It wasn't our fault," said Mitch. "It was Runnels. They weren't animal rights activists; they were Runnels' men. Remember that note you found Gideon?"

"We're dealing with a very dangerous enemy," added Rob. "I think it might be time to get the police involved."

"Dude, we can't be sure they're not involved," argued Gideon.

"We're not going to the police. Not yet anyway," instructed Mitch.

At the first sound of gunfire, Gideon dived for cover, closely followed by Rob. Mitch stared at Shelby as the hailstones continued to crash into the lounge window and the conservatory roof. Shelby remembered her dream from the hotel in St. Albans. *Whatever was going to happen, it was getting close.* Gideon and Rob climbed sheepishly back onto the sofa, when they realised what the noise was. There was an awkward silence for what seemed like an age, then they burst into fits of uncontrollable laughter.

"I don't know about Global Warming," said Mitch. "This is more like Global Freezing!"

They watched the spectacular hailstorm display for several minutes, while Mitch made everyone a hot toddy. Gradually, they all relaxed again.

"Okay guys. Time to talk tactics before we hit the sack," said Mitch. "Rob, you'll be heading over to Bedford tomorrow to meet your TV Station buddy. Gideon and Shelby, I'll get you some transport first thing in the morning so you can meet with your friends in the Food Standards Agency. The press will release your name tomorrow or Wednesday, Shelby, so try and get her to agree to do something ASAP." Remembering the other companies that Lindburg and Runnels were associated with, he added, "Try and get them to look into that new toothpaste and that cayenne pepper company, if possible."

"We can stop on the way and pick up some samples that they can test," suggested Gideon.

Mitch pulled out the list of companies that he and Gideon had downloaded at the Strand. "Here, take this. It's got the company names and addresses. And here's a copy of Shelby's analysis from the lab."

"What will you be doing?" asked Rob.

"I've got some arrangements to take care of, then I've got a funeral to attend on Wednesday. I need you to have disabled those frigging devices by Thursday at the latest Rob, if my plan is to have any chance of success."

"You got a plan?" asked Gideon, hopefully.

"The less you three know, the better," said Mitch. He went over to his safe and pulled out some cash. Sharing it among the three of them, he said, "Here, you'll need this. Don't go using any credit cards – we've already seen how effective they are at tracking us. Which reminds me, don't meet up back here when you're finished – they might have the place under surveillance once they discover I'm no longer chipped. Here're the details of how to get to my boat. It's moored in Lode." He passed a set of keys to Gideon. "You can get in with these. Now let's get some sleep. There're five bedrooms upstairs. Take your pick, but the front one's mine."

Once the others had gone to bed, Mitch made a phone call; just for appearance's sake.

"Mark, Hi. It's Mitch. Sorry for ringing so late, but I just saw the news."

Runnels sounded half asleep, "Mitch? Oh, yes. Terrible business. Bloody animal rights activists!"

"I was only there a few hours earlier, myself."

"Yes. It's a dreadful shame. I'm sorry to say, it looks like Kim and er... Shelby were caught in the crossfire. The police found their cars still in the car park."

"Like I said, I'm really sorry," said Mitch.

"Thank you, old boy. Really appreciate it. She'll be sadly missed."

That did it for Mitch. He knew exactly who Runnels was referring to, and it wasn't Shelby.

CHAPTER THIRTY-EIGHT

2nd Floor, Palace of Westminster, London, England

The phone on the antique desk began ringing and the occupant of the office waited two rings. The phone went quiet, then, seconds later starting ringing again.

"Hello?"

"Is that extension 333?"

"No, it's extension 322."

"Are you alone?"

"Yes."

"The girl is dead."

"At last."

"Any sign of the engineer?"

"It's just a matter of time. He can't stay hidden for ever. We are cross-referencing phone numbers and should have his new number anytime now. We're also checking CCTV images at Railway Stations."

"Good. We have control of the RFID company. In another three months we can switch on the transmission signal from the first of the TV Stations, and soon after we will have complete control."

"How is distribution going?"

"The drinks are selling well, and we are getting good figures for the toothpaste. Our operation in the Far East has reported excellent penetration. Our leaders are very pleased, Minister."

CHAPTER THIRTY-NINE

Rob set off for Bedford in Mitch's other car; a Mercedes CLK class cabriolet. Although the roof could be lowered in seconds, Rob decided that anonymity was the name of the game. He had arranged to meet Jeff Harrison at 8.00am. Jeff was working the 2.00am – 10.00am shift, so that gave them a full two hours before he finished. He pulled into the Station's car park at 7.45am and waited in reception for Jeff. Shortly afterwards, they were sitting at Jeff's work station.

"So, bud, you want the full tour or just the highlights?" asked Jeff, handing him a coffee.

Rob had been thinking about how to broach the subject of transmitter tests on the drive up. "How about you show me the transmitter control area and we'll take it from there?"

"No problemo. Hey, I've got a surprise for you when we're finished here," grinned Jeff.

"Yeah?"

"You'll never guess who's coming over for lunch and a few beers?"

Rob racked his brain, trying to remember who else was working in the vicinity. "Not Gibbo?"

"Getting warm."

"Not..."

"You got it! The Megatron!"

Ian Megarry was a university legend. A six-foot-two Welshman, who had run riot on campus. Built like a second row rugby player, his antics were part of Birmingham folklore.

"I thought he worked in Reading," said Rob, in amazement.

"He's taken the day off to join us."

Robin Kirk, Jeff Harrison, Shane Gibbs and Ian Megarry had shared accommodation at Birmingham University's halls of residence, which had quickly earned the nickname of *'the animal house'*. Megarry was big on nicknames, and had coined his own; the Megatron. Rob's was *'Captain'* (obviously), Jeff's was *'George'*, and Shane's was *'Gibbo'*.

Understandably, Charlotte couldn't abide the place and rarely stayed over. Rob would stay at Charlotte's whenever a *night of passion* was on the cards. When he did stay at his own accommodation, the lads used to tease him about getting *'time off for good behaviour.'* Nonetheless, he had been a part of many of their escapades; like the time they broke onto nearby Aston University's halls of residence, one Saturday night, and stole a frozen turkey for their Sunday lunch. They'd nearly all got frost bite carrying the thing home.

Seeing the expression on Rob's face, Jeff laughed. "Told you it was a surprise. Now, what do you want to know about the black art of digital broadcasting?"

Rob quickly understood the way the Station operated, and decided to chance his luck, when they returned to Jeff's desk. "So, Jeff, if someone wanted to broadcast a test signal on some side-band or other, is it easy to set up?"

"Depends what it is, but, yeah."

"How about something on these frequencies?" Rob asked, sliding his calculations across to Jeff.

"Not only possible, matey, we actually do transmit on these wavelengths from time to time during routine testing. At a low power though," he added.

"Could you increase the power a few notches?"

"Yeah, but why? Where did you get those frequencies from anyway? They're not part of the normal TV signal."

Deciding it wasn't the right time to fill Jeff in, Rob bluffed, "Just interested... from an interference perspective."

"Now that's what we were told was the reason for running these tests in the first place. Can't go interfering with people's phones, or their wi-fi connections, can we?"

Having completed the tour, and Jeff's shift, they set off to Jeff's house to drop off their cars, and head to the pub.

"Nice wheels, Rob. They must be paying you too much. What is it you do over there?" asked Jeff, admiring Mitch's car, as Rob tried to squeeze it into a parking space outside the house.

"Oh, you know. Vehicle tracking systems. Pretty boring stuff really." *I hope this thing will still have its wheels on when we get back,* he thought, eyeing the neighbourhood.

"So that's why you wanted to know about our transmissions. We've not been screwing up your locators have we?"

Rob saw an opportunity and pounced. "There's no fooling you, Jeff. You're right. We do have a few concerns that we may be getting some interference from the TV Stations, yeah."

"But the Government allocates the frequencies. You shouldn't have any problems," said Jeff, pointing out the way to the pub. "It's just a short walk up this way. It's an old real ale house, just behind the college."

As they walked, Rob decided to see how flexible Jeff was prepared to be. "Don't suppose you could 'up the power' a bit and check it out for me. I mean, what's the worst that can happen?"

"You could lose a few trucks I suppose," laughed Jeff, struggling to keep up with Rob's pace. "Slow down a bit, dude. The pub's open all day."

They reached the pub, which was full of students drinking halves of bitter and playing pool. It was an *olde worlde* style establishment; dark wood, brown walls and bench seats. The tables were various shapes and sizes, and were covered in scratches and chips. The whole place looked like it hadn't been cleaned properly since it had opened however many centuries ago.

Ordering two pints, Rob tried to press home his advantage. "So could you do something?"

"Oh, we're still on that topic are we? I'd have to get the changes sent out by my boss, so the other transmitter stations would do the same. I could always talk to him about it; say it was a legitimate concern to a local business and all."

This wasn't going to be as easy as Rob had hoped. Jeff used to be up for anything in the old days, particularly if it was bordering on the illegal. They found a table near the back of the bar; away from the pool-cue touting freshers.

The front door opened and was immediately filled by the frame of the Megatron. "There you are Captain! What do you two girls want to drink?" he called across in a broad Welsh accent, as he made his way to the bar. "A pint of your special and the same again for those two, lovely," he said to the young barmaid.

Putting three pints and three packets of cheese and onion crisps on the table, Megarry dumped himself in the seat between the two friends. Grabbing them both round their necks with his thick arms he growled, "Waaasssuuuppp," before adding, "Now what entertainment have you lined up for us today, George?"

After a few moments catching up on each other's latest gossip, the conversation switched and they re-lived some of their greatest antics. With each retelling, the exaggerations got bigger and bigger. "Do you guys remember the time Gibbo brought that minger from the Geography Society back to his room?" laughed the Megatron.

"Yeah, and we sang our own version of the Phil Collins classic, 'in the air tonight' outside his door," added Jeff, sniggering.

They all joined in with a somewhat flat rendition of the song – incorporating their own words, naturally.

Building up to a crescendo, they continued with an impersonation of the famous drum intro; each of them banging on an invisible drum kit: "Duh-doo, duh-doo, duh-doo, duh-doo, doo doo!" before falling into helpless fits of laughter.

"Then Gibbo came out and told us all to *'fuck off*,'" spluttered Rob, when he'd got his breath back.

"And Mega came out with the immortal line: *'I hope you're going to wash that now, boyo'*," roared Jeff, much to the amusement of the others.

Several rounds later, the Megatron surveyed the terrain, mischievously. "I bet we could kick their asses at pool," he challenged.

Two young girls tried to squeeze their way past the table on their way to the 'ladies'.

"Hmmm, nice legs. What time do they open, lovely?" leered the Megatron, bursting into fits of laughter.

Rob shook his head. He wondered if Megarry had ever got lucky with his awful one-liners.

Outside, a dark blue Audi pulled up next to the pub. The passenger checked the device he held in his hand and nodded. There was nowhere to park out front, so the car cruised up the road and turned into a small side street where it came to a stop. Two men in dark suits got out of the car and started walking back towards the pub entrance.

"We'll take a look and check he's in there," said the first man. "No rough stuff; we don't want to make a scene. If he's there, we'll pick him up when he leaves."

The three friends agreed that the clientele were a bit young for them after all, and decided to pick up some fried chicken and chips on the way back to Jeff's, where they could watch a movie and chill out for the rest of the afternoon.

"I'm off for a dump," announced the Megatron, rising from the table.

Rob and Jeff were deep in conversation and didn't notice the two men enter the pub and settle themselves down on a couple of stools by the bar.

"Look out, it's a bust," laughed one of the pool players, nodding towards the two men.

Rob looked up and felt icy fingers clutch at his heart. The two men stood out like a huddle of penguins on an Iberian beach. *Shit! How could they have traced me? Dammit! They must have worked out what phone I've been using,* he realised. *Well, they don't look that threatening,* he decided. *Perhaps I can give them the slip.*

"Two halves of bitter, please," said the first man to the barmaid.

"Okay, he's here. What's the plan?" whispered the second man to his colleague.

"We wait until he leaves, and we follow him."

"That might be ages. In the meantime, we're drawing too much attention to ourselves."

"Okay, look, he's going to the loo. You follow him in there and persuade him he's leaving with us, right now. I'll keep an eye on his mate."

Rob told Jeff he was going to take a leak. *There must be a back way out of here,* he thought to himself. On his way he saw the fire exit, but it was in plain view of the two men at the bar. *I can't risk it,* he thought, *they'd catch me before I even got 100 yards.* He went into the 'gents'. It was empty apart from one cubicle. He dumped the SIM card from his PAYG phone in the bin and splashed water on his face to clear his head. He checked the windows. *No way out!*

The door behind him opened and he saw it was one of the men from the bar. The man walked up to Rob and grabbed him by the arm. "Okay sweetheart, you're leaving with us. Right now," he said, menacingly. Rob tried to resist, but the man was far too strong.

A toilet flushed and the Megatron exited the cubicle, waving his hand in front of his face. "I'd leave it ten minutes if I were you boys," he said, walking towards the wash basins. "Who's the perve?" he asked, jerking a thumb at the man holding Rob's arm.

"Fuck off Taffy! It doesn't concern you. Me and..."

He never finished his sentence. In one smooth motion, the Megatron took a step forward and head-butted him on the bridge of the nose. Blood spurted out over the man's shirt and involuntary tears filled his eyes, temporarily blinding him. Megarry grabbed the man by his lapels and shoved him backwards into the tiled wall with the force of a charging bull. The man collapsed as if someone had just removed his skeleton. Megarry opened the man's jacket, to look for some sort of ID.

"Fucking hell Rob, he's packing! He's not the police is he?"

"No, but there's another one sat at the bar," Rob replied weakly.

"You got some explaining to do, boyo. Get yourself out the back way, I'll cause a diversion. See you back at Jeff's."

The man at the bar was getting anxious. His colleague should be back by now. The door to the 'gents' opened and the Megatron headed straight to the bar without giving Jeff a glance. *Must have been waiting for this guy to leave,* the man told himself.

"Pint please, lovely" said Megarry, putting on a slight slur and swaying a little next to the seated man. He looked at the man in the dark suit and grinned disarmingly.

The girl put the pint down in front of the Megatron, who knocked it straight over into the man's lap. The man leapt to his feet, wiping at his soaked trousers.

"Did you see that? You spilt my beer, you clumsy bastard," said Megarry in a loud voice, attracting the attention of the pool crowd.

Before the man could reply the Megatron punched him in the stomach and he doubled over, gasping for breath. Rob, who was standing in the doorway, saw his chance and ran through the rear fire exit, setting off the alarm. Megarry grabbed the bent-over man by the back of his jacket and slammed him into the now vacant bar stool, as if he weighed no more than a few pounds. Jeff jumped out of his seat in total surprise. The man crashed to the floor motionless.

"Oi! Less of that! You're barred," shouted the barman, lifting the bar hatch. "Who set that alarm off?"

"We were just leaving," Megarry called back, as he ran out the front door with Jeff close on his heels.

Rob didn't stop running until he reached Jeff's house. The door was locked, so he crouched behind the hedge in the front garden. About half an hour later, he heard Jeff and the Megatron laughing and chatting as they came down the street.

"Where the fuck have you been?" he said, popping his head up over the hedge.

"We had to stop on the way to get these," replied the Megatron holding up two bargain buckets.

"Christ, Mega, I thought you were going to kill those two bastards," said Rob in awe.

"Who me, boyo? Nah, they'll live. Probably broke a few bones though," he replied, thoughtfully. "Now are you going to tell us what the fuck has been going on?"

Once they were safely inside the house and munching their way through the Colonel's finest, Rob told them his story; leaving out the ORME details, but including the Government designed receivers. The friends sat in silence as they digested what Rob had just told them.

"You stupid fuck," said Megarry finally. "Why would you want to be involved in designing those electronic tags in the first place?"

"I just kind of fell into it," said Rob, lamely.

"Well, I'm not gonna have one of them put in me," said Megarry, defiantly.

"Me either," agreed Jeff.

"Look, I can disable the receivers, if you'll help me, Jeff," pleaded Rob.

"I don't want to get involved," said Jeff, remembering the two guys in the bar.

"You are involved, boyo. It's your transmitters that are carrying the signals to them. Jesus, what a pair of fuckwits!"

With the Megatron's assistance, they devised a plan to disable the RFID receivers. Testing usually occurred at 4.00am. When Jeff's shift started at 2.00am, he would send an e-mail from his boss's PC, advising the other stations of the changes to the test transmission. Rob was sure that a thirty second burst, at the power setting he specified, would be sufficient to blow the fuses. Jeff was confident that most of the transmitter stations would perform the requested test without question. *The guys are usually bored shitless, and a change is as good as a rest,* he told them.

"Will that be an end to it then?" asked the Megatron.

"So long as we blow enough of them," assured Rob.

"Good, 'cos I don't want to have to come back here and save your asses again for a while. My head is splitting."

"We'll know soon enough. They'll probably give people a nasty little burning sensation when they go," Rob added.

PART FOUR

"The public will believe anything, so long as it is not founded in truth."
Edith Sitwell

"And it came to pass, when men began to multiply on the face of the
earth, and daughters were born unto them,
that the sons of God saw the daughters of men that they *were* fair;
and they took them wives of all which they chose.
And the LORD said, My Spirit shall not always strive with man, for that
he also *is* flesh: yet his days shall be a hundred and twenty years.
There were giants in the earth in those days; and also after that, when
the sons of God came in unto the daughters of men, and they bare
children to them, the same *became* mighty men which *were* of old,
men of renown."
Genesis 6: 1-4
King James Version

CHAPTER FORTY

Mitch's house, Cambridge, England

Once the others had left, Mitch rang Sarah and arranged to meet her for lunch at a quiet little pub he was fond of. He put on a pair of jeans, brown brogues, and a casual shirt. He gathered up the documents he had been studying at the dining table and slipped them into an old leather rucksack. Timing was critical if he was to put an end to this conspiracy. He took the remaining cash from his safe and squeezed the notes into his wallet. Checking his watch, he strolled out to the Land Rover. Most of the neighbours' cars had either gone with them to work, or were in their garages. He checked the street anyway; looking for anything that shouldn't be there. He didn't drive directly to the pub. Instead, he doubled back a few times to make absolutely sure he wasn't being followed. The last thing he wanted was to put Sarah in any danger.

He recognised Sarah's car, as he pulled into the pub car park. She was already inside, nursing a small gin and tonic. "Hi Sarah. Sorry I'm late," he apologised.

"Hi Mitch. Don't worry, I only got here myself about two minutes ago," she smiled back. "I managed to contact everyone from work on Sunday like you asked, except for Rob," she continued, looking rather concerned. "I do hope he's all right. It must have been a nasty shock for him. I mean, it was for all of us really."

"That's okay, Sarah. Let me get a pint and I'll explain," he replied, briefly squeezing her shoulder.

Mitch told Sarah as little as he possibly could about the events of the last few days; not wanting to worry her. He told her Rob had taken some time off and had gone away with Charlotte for a few days. They had a light lunch and eventually Sarah couldn't contain her curiosity any longer. "Are you going to tell me what's in the rucksack?" she asked, dabbing at imaginary crumbs on her bottom lip.

Mitch smiled and began to explain what it was he needed her to do. He gave her a precise set of instructions. "You're the only person I can trust to do this for me, Sarah," he said, knowing that she would follow everything to the letter. He handed her the rucksack.

Sarah left before Mitch, who had one more important phone call to make before the funeral the next day.

The Steadman's House, Swindon, England
A sharp pain in her right hand woke Enid up with a jolt. *Ouch! What on earth was that?* she thought. Albert's snoring abated for a few seconds then carried on. "Albert? Are you awake? ALBERT!"

"What...?"

"Are you awake?" Enid whispered.

"I am now. What is it?"

"I think something's just happened to my chip."

"Chips? We didn't have chips," said Albert, turning his back on her.

"I mean my identity chip," Enid replied, poking him. "Did you feel anything?"

"What just then, when you poked me?"

"No, you old fool. I mean in your hand. A few minutes ago."

"No."

"That doesn't surprise me. Nothing wakes you up once you're off."

"You just did!"

"I'm putting the light on to take a look," Enid persisted. She switched on her bedside lamp and Albert covered his eyes. "I can't see anything, can you?" she asked.

"No."

"You're not even looking."

"It's probably just a mozzie bite. Go back to sleep."

"I have to go to the loo now," said Enid, climbing out of bed.

"Well turn the light out first," moaned Albert.

"Wait a minute; I'll put the one in the hall on." Flicking the hall switch next to the door, she turned to go back into the bedroom. "What are you doing now?"

Albert climbed out of bed. "I've got to go as well now," he grumbled.

The next day, Mitch's House, Cambridge, England

It was the morning of the funeral and Mitch was up bright and early as usual. He had until 10.00am, so he switched on Breakfast News, while he made a coffee.

"...*Our top story today: There was chaos on the streets this morning as people queued outside Doctor's Surgeries up and down the country. Thousands of people have been trying to get in touch with their GPs complaining of a burning sensation in their hand, where they had identity chip implants. Doctors are overwhelmed, but have stated that there doesn't seem to be any lasting effects. If you are concerned about your implant, please call the hotline number on the screen...*"

Well done Robbie! You did it, thought Mitch.

"...*The Government has denied that there is a problem with the devices, saying that it was an isolated power fluctuation. We can go live now to a Surgery in South London...People here are complaining that at about 4 o'clock this morning they experienced a burning sensation in their hand, where their implant was fitted. Here's what one concerned patient had to say...'I was awoken suddenly, at about 4 o'clock this morning, with a sharp pain in my hand. It felt like a mosquito bite, but when I realised it was coming from where I'd been chipped, I knew it was more serious. We tried to call emergency services, but the lines were all engaged'...*"

Mitch switched off the TV. He wondered if Gideon and Shelby had been as successful.

Selecting a sober dark suit, white shirt and narrow black tie from his wardrobe, Mitch looked out of the window and saw that a storm was threatening to unleash a deluge later. *That's okay*, he thought, *it should always rain at funerals.* He put an umbrella in the car to be on the safe side.

The service was quite short. Simon's father delivered the reading and his sister said a few words about their childhood together. He knew he should resent the girl for selling Simon's shares in the company; it was Simon's 15% that had tipped the balance, but he couldn't bring himself to. Most of the IDSys employees had turned out; Rob obviously couldn't make it.

As they stood by the graveside in the pouring rain, the clouds parted and the sunlight broke through, creating that strange sort of half-light that you often see after heavy thunderstorms. Sarah kept checking that Mitch was okay, as they huddled together under his umbrella. He

191

thought he might lose it a couple of times during the vicar's reading, but he managed to hold it together. Finally, it was over. Mitch paid his respects and gave his commiserations to Simon's parents, as they began making their way back to their cars. Standing by the entrance was a tall man in a light coloured raincoat, covering a blue pin-stripe suit.

"Mitch, I didn't want to interrupt, but I ..."

That was it. Mitch just snapped. "Fuck you, Shackelford," he spat, as he planted a right hook on the man's chin, sending him crumbling to his knees.

A couple of the other mourners helped Shackelford to his feet, but Mitch had already gone. He had an appointment that he intended to keep at all costs.

Later that day

Before setting off for the boat, Mitch decided to drop by his house to check on things. As he pulled into the close, he slowed down and switched off his headlights. He parked a long way short of the entrance to his cul de sac and got out of the car. Keeping close to a neighbour's hedge, he crept along towards the entrance. Before he got to the corner, he spotted a dark coloured car parked up in such a position as to have a clear view of his house. Two men were in the car. *So they do have the place under observation*, he confirmed to himself. *At least they don't know about the boat for the time being.* Retracing his steps, he returned to the Rover and reversed back out of the close.

The Blue Lady, Stubb's Mooring, Lode, England

When Mitch finally got to his boat, he found he had been invaded. Rob, Gideon, and Shelby were in the galley kitchen drinking wine, while a pan full of chilli con carne simmered on the stove. The atmosphere was drenched in the aroma of garlic bread. Mitch's boat was a fifty-two foot, steel wide-beam narrowboat; comprising of a fully fitted kitchen, lounge, bathroom and two bedrooms. He often hid himself away on board to escape the pressures of work. Not many people knew he still had it; Sarah and Simon, naturally, and security was twenty-four hour.

"Well, you three seem to have made yourselves at home," he said wearily.

"I've made enough for all of us," chirped Shelby, looking flushed with wine and success.

"Thanks Shelby. I'll just get showered and changed," he told them.

The narrowboat was a remnant from another era of Mitch's life. He had actually lived on board when he first set up the company – having insufficient funds to buy a house in the area. In those days, it was all he really needed. He remembered the time he and Simon had invited a couple of girls over for Sunday dinner, one summer's day. They'd met them a few months earlier at a thirtieth birthday party for one of Simon's cousins. *What were their names? Sam and Melanie. Or was it Melody?* Anyway, they'd started dating as a foursome, exploring quaint little country pubs and restaurants, visiting local open-air markets, and watching the latest movies at the Grafton Cinema.

One weekend, they'd had the run of Simon's parent's house while they were on holiday. It had been a lovely weekend, and the girls had done most of the cooking. So, when the summer finally arrived, they'd thought it would be a great idea to have Sunday dinner on board Mitch's boat, and they'd do the cooking for the girls. On the Saturday, Simon and Mitch had stocked up with Pimm's and lemonade, and had bought an oversized chicken to roast in Mitch's gas oven. Neither of them were great cooks, but they'd consulted Delia's Complete Cooking Guide and had worked out the time and temperature required. Having put the bird in the oven and with the vegetables prepared, they'd set off to meet the girls in Simon's old Saab convertible. Sam and Melody (?) were sitting in the pub garden drinking Bacardi and cola on ice when they'd arrived at the trendy city centre pub.

"Damn. We didn't get any ice for the Pimm's," Simon had said.

"Don't worry, we'll pick some up from the Off-Licence on the way back," Mitch had replied.

They'd ordered a couple of cold lagers and joined the girls in the garden. "Hope you girls have remembered your bikinis," Simon had joked, as he'd given Melody a quick peck on the cheek.

"Of course we have," Sam had replied. "And I got you a present, Mitch."

Reaching into her bag, she'd produced a captain's hat and had put it on Mitch's head before he could complain. They'd sat and chatted in the garden for the best part of an hour. Then Mitch had decided they'd better get back to the boat and rescue their dinner. They'd stopped on the way to buy a giant bag of ice.

"It'll never fit in my freezer," Mitch had said, but Simon had insisted anyway.

When they'd arrived at the moorings, they could tell something was wrong. A huge red fire-engine was spraying water onto Mitch's boat, while great plumes of black smoke emanated from the kitchen window. "Oh no! The oven..." Mitch had exclaimed.

They'd rushed over to the boat, just as the firemen were tidying up their hoses, and had received a severe lecture from the Fire Chief.

The damage to the boat's interior was pretty extensive. The windows were cracked and broken and covered in soot. The walls and furniture were soaking wet and filthy. Mitch had climbed down the stairs and had made his way to the galley kitchen. He'd opened the oven and pulled out the charred remains of the chicken. Simon had simply shaken his head. "The chicken's off then?" he'd stated matter of factly.

The girls had refused to get on board – not wishing to ruin their clothes, so Simon had run them back into town. He and Mitch had spent the rest of the day trying to clean up and salvage anything that could be saved. The following week, Mitch had had the whole interior redecorated and had bought himself a new gas oven with a thermostat that actually worked. They hadn't seen either of the two girls again. *Those were the days*, he thought to himself.

By the time Mitch had showered and changed, the three friends were already in high spirits. "So what are we celebrating?" he asked.

"Well," slurred Gideon, "Rob pulled off his side of the bargain. How 'bout you?"

Mitch felt himself relaxing and decided the best thing was to join in. "Apart from burying my best friend earlier, I've had an excellent day," he conceded.

"Shit. Sorry Mitch..." started Rob, feeling guilty.

"Pass me some wine," interrupted Mitch. "I hope you two got a result, like Robbie here?" he added, his voice softening.

"Dude, they went for it big time!" exclaimed Gideon.

"They're going to make Vitality withdraw their drinks?"

"And they're going to investigate Colbrite Toothpaste and the cayenne pepper company," added Shelby, triumphantly.

"I think we've finally got them on the back foot," smiled Mitch. "Let's get this lovely meal of Shelby's served up and catch the late news. We must have started to have made an impact by now."

As they settled down in the small lounge to catch the ten o'clock news on Mitch's portable TV, the four of them felt quite pleased with themselves.

"... Our main stories tonight... Bong!... The CEO of IDSys, the company behind the malfunctioning identity chips, speaks out... Bong!... The Government makes a U-turn on its security policy... Bong!... Lewis Hamilton takes pole position in the Japanese Grand Prix..."

They all looked apprehensively at Mitch, who remained poker faced.

"...Earlier today Mitchell Webb, the CEO of IDSys; the manufacturer of the identity chips, confirmed that there was a design problem with the implants. This is what he had to say...'We have recently discovered that there is a design flaw in the RFID chips that may cause discomfort to recipients of the implants. Several of the devices have been found to overheat and cause minor burning to individuals, when a small component within the device fails. We are looking into the problem and don't want anyone to panic, as we believe there is no risk to public safety. We will replace all of the faulty devices at our own cost, and will consider any genuine compensation claims'...This comes on top of the chaos in the highstreet, first thing this morning, as thousands of people..."

"What the hell...?" started Rob. "Design flaw...?"

"Shhh!" countered Mitch.

"...In an announcement from number 10 this evening, the Prime Minister had the following to say...'As a result of today's concerns over the electronic identity chips, the Government has decided to rescind the RFID programme. Whilst we believe there is no risk to people's health, we will stop the further insertion of devices and will set up minor surgery units to remove those already implanted. Again, I stress that there is no risk to people's health. What we have seen is a small malfunction in the device which, although slightly painful for a second or two, has no lasting effects'..."

"The fight-back has started," Mitch announced.

The following morning, Gideon and Shelby were suffering from the excesses of the previous night. As they slowly surfaced, one at a time, they found Mitch and Rob already dressed, catching up on the latest developments in the cramped lounge, where Rob had spent the night.

"Eww, you look awful," he said to no-one in particular; they both looked pretty rough. "It's good to see that our hard work over the last few days is starting to pay off though," he added, flicking the TV over to News 24. "Watch this..."

"...following yesterday's announcement from the Government. There was chaos on the highstreet again this morning as the Food Standards Agency reported a potential health risk from cans of Vitality Health Drink. Supermarkets have been busy clearing shelves and have asked anyone with the following batch numbers..."

"They didn't hang about," marvelled Gideon, glancing at Shelby, who was making toast in the kitchen area.

"...'containing certain elements that may be detrimental to health,' said a spokesman. Over now to the latest business news...Following the announcement by the CEO of IDSys yesterday, the company's shares fell to under £1, wiping almost £120 million off the value of the company. The City is cautious while it waits for the markets to open in China tomorrow morning to see what the knock on effect will be for the Chinese manufacturers of the identity chips. Shares in Vitality Health Drinks are also down as the impact of the product recall, mentioned a few moments earlier, is assessed..."

"Ouch," said Rob sheepishly, looking over at Mitch.

"Looks like I'd better head over to the office and clear my desk," replied Mitch, looking totally unconcerned.

"...and now our main story again, the Opposition has tabled a vote of no confidence in the Government, following the dramatic U-turn on their security policy last night. If successful, there will be a General Election in four weeks time...The Opposition added that they would reconsider plans to rebuild the Channel Tunnel, if elected. Governments in Germany and France have also suspended the introduction of compulsory identity chips, following the revelation of a design flaw..."

"Holy shit," said Gideon.

The Steadman's House, Swindon, England

Albert called to his wife from his armchair in the sitting room. "Enid! Enid! Come in here and watch this." Enid entered the room, wearing a pair of rubber gloves.

"What is it now? I'm halfway through cleaning the oven."

Branston jumped to his feet and began wagging his tail excitedly.

"What was the name of that health drink they gave us?" Albert asked.

"When? What are you talking about?" *I swear he's in a world of his own sometimes,* she thought.

196

"When they tagged us, of course. When else?" He patted the dog, who promptly sat back down next to him.

They'd both seen the news the day before, informing them of the problem with the RFIDs. *'I told you I felt something the other night,'* Enid had said. *'Bloody Chinese technology!'* Albert had replied. *'I'm ringing the Doctor's to see when we can have them removed. I told you no good would come of them.'*

"I'm sorry, dear. I haven't a clue what you're talking about," said Enid, about to go back into the kitchen.

"Look, it's on the telly," Albert insisted. "That lemonade they gave us. I'm sure that's the one."

"If you say so dear. But it's a bit late to be getting a refund now. I put the empties in the recycling bin last week. If there was anything wrong with it, we'd know by now; you know what your stomach's like."

"Nothing wrong with my constitution," muttered Albert. "I've always said, what doesn't kill you only makes you stronger." The newsreader had handed over to their political correspondent, who was discussing the forthcoming vote of no confidence in the current Government. "About time too. At least we'll have the chance to get that useless bunch of Herberts out of office..." Albert started to say, but Enid had a gone already. "Oh, all right then," he said to the dog, who had started pestering again. "Come on, boy, let's go for a walk." Branston jumped to his feet and went to find his lead.

CHAPTER FORTY-ONE

2nd Floor, Palace of Westminster, London, England

Preston Shackelford knocked on the solid wood door.

"Come."

"Have you heard the news, Minister?"

"Yes."

"It's all over. The identity chips, the China treaty ..."

"I am well aware of the consequences, Shackelford."

"The Opposition has tabled a vote..."

"Get out Shackelford. You don't know the half of it."

An indignant and bewildered Shackelford left the Minister's office as instructed.

The Minister walked over to the window overlooking the Thames. Slowly and deliberately, he opened the window.

Moments later, the phone on the antique desk began ringing. After two rings, the phone went quiet, then, seconds later starting ringing again. There was no-one there to answer it.

CHAPTER FORTY-TWO

The Head Office of IDSys, Cambridge Science Park, England

Mitch pulled up in the middle of the car park for one last look at his former company. He had started something that would snowball on until it reached a critical mass. He thought of the lives that would be affected. *At least they would be lives that were free; not manipulated by some hidden, malevolent force, for God only knows what purpose.* He hoped he had damaged the people he held responsible the most: Lindburg, Runnels, Shackelford and their cronies. He looked at the empty car park and felt a pang of guilt. He remembered back to the day that he and Simon had decided to go with Shackelford's offer. *No time for regrets.* The rain that had persisted for the last couple of days appeared to be subsiding, and the sun was making a courageous effort to cheer things up. He looked at the rainbow that had formed over the building, and smiled.

Time to pack up, he told himself. He reversed the Rover up to the front entrance and climbed out. Opening up the back of the Discovery, he found a plant pot to prop open the entrance doors to the building and began the slow task of bringing his personal belongings down from his office to the waiting vehicle. He wasn't sure what his plans were for the next few days, but he knew he needed to keep a low profile. He wondered what to do about Gideon and Shelby. Rob, he knew, would join Charlotte down in Devon for a well earned holiday. They couldn't risk staying on the boat any longer.

His office was nearly empty and Mitch opened the safe behind his desk to clear out the last of his effects. As he stood up again, he saw a large black car enter the car park and pull up on the far side of the building. He went over to the window and recognised the man in the suit, as he got out and headed towards the entrance.

Mitch took a seat behind his desk and waited. "I've been expecting you," he said, as the man entered Mitch's office. "Take a seat." He gestured to the chair opposite with his outstretched arm.

The man noticed the plaster on Mitch's right hand immediately. "Tut tut. Been doing a little do-it-yourself surgery?" he enquired dispassionately.

"Oh, this. It's just a scratch," lied Mitch.

"I am very disappointed in you, Mitch."

"That would be because...?"

"I thought you were an intelligent business man, but you're a fool. You have destroyed your own company. Do you know what it is currently worth?"

"I think they said about £5 million on the news this morning."

"And most of that is fixed assets, Mitch. It is, in fact, worth diddly squat. You have given up what, £45 million?"

"Actually, I sold all but 1% of my stock on Tuesday. Let me see, I think I got something in the region of £47 million, give or take the odd million," replied Mitch, with satisfaction written all over his face. "I think that should be plenty to start a new business with."

"Perhaps you think you've been clever. There will, of course, be an investigation; insider dealing is a crime you know. But it was never just about the money, Mitch. You can't comprehend the trouble you've caused us."

"I can safely say that when I sold my stock, I was unaware of the problem with the RFID chips. I merely sold up because I was no longer a majority shareholder. As for the bigger picture, I assume that's why you're here. Any money you've lost in this venture must be a drop in the ocean, surely. I'd gladly do it all over again if it meant that people like you can't control other people's lives: deciding who can have access to a doctor, social services, even their own bank accounts for fucksake. I really believed that what we were doing was for the benefit of mankind, not their subjugation."

"Don't take the moral high ground with me, Mitch. You did it for the money, which you seem to have managed, quite successfully, to hold on to. Do you really think it will be safe for you to walk the streets after this? Can you imagine how many enemies you have made in the last couple of days? I assume that you and your little band of misfits are behind the Food Standard Agency's investigation into Vitality and Colbrite?"

"Oh dear, you didn't have shares in Vitality and Colbrite as well did you? What about that cayenne pepper supplier?" Mitch watched the casual air of confidence disappear from the man's face. "Ooops, I see that you did," he smiled. "Checked your stocks lately?"

"You foolish, insignificant, pile of useless genetic material. You may have made a nuisance of yourself, but you cannot stop our grand design. You have no right to interfere in the plans of superior beings..."

"Now hold on. You and your Bilderberg buddies may think you have some God given right over us lesser mortals, but no-one gave you permission to..." started Mitch.

"God given right? And which God may you be referring to? The God whose return you are all waiting for? The God who's son died on the cross; to be resurrected after three days? The God who will give you all sanctuary from the devil at the end of days? God your creator?"

Ouch. That hit a nerve, thought Mitch, "I didn't say I believed in God per se..." he started to explain.

"Or perhaps you believe in the Mayan calendar myth; that the world will end in the year 2012 due to some global catastrophe? And you thought you'd cash in before it was too late." The man unbuttoned his jacket. "The Mayans never actually predicted that the world would end in 2012; just that we would enter a new era," he continued.

Mitch had a feeling of déjà vu. "Look, I don't know where this is going..."

"I'll tell you where it's going, Mitch. You and the rest of the human race were created on this Earth to serve your masters..."

"Oh, please. Spare me the Bilderberg rhetoric. I don't give a rat's ass if you and your buddies want to believe that you're superior to the rest of us, through some misguided crap about your bloodlines. I've read the book, seen the film, got the T-shirt," he said forcibly.

"No Mitch. You've read the books we've allowed you to read. You've seen the films we've allowed you to see. We have created and moulded your perception of reality. Do you really want to know the truth? Do you want me to tell you what you have really given up?"

"I'm sure you will anyway," Mitch said, lounging back in his chair.

"Your kind was created from worthless primates, who didn't know how to wipe their own asses. You were created to serve as slaves." The man continued, "But there was a flaw in your make-up. You were spiritual creatures, you see. At first, it didn't matter. The creators liked being treated as gods. Animals don't think of their masters as gods, but humans are different."

"The creators? What do you mean? Like aliens or something?"

"Yes Mitch. Your creators are what you refer to as *aliens*."

"Okay, this is too weird. I know you're pissed off with me, but I really don't need to sit here and listen to..." Mitch paused mid-sentence. The man sitting opposite him had just removed a gun from his jacket pocket and was casually toying with it.

"You see, you *do* have to listen to me Mitch. You have put me to a lot of trouble, and now I want you to know what you have done." He paused while he collected his thoughts again. "As I was saying, your creators failed to deal with the flaw in your make-up. Being spiritual creatures, you needed to believe in a god or gods."

"I take it you're referring to the Annunaki," said Mitch, recalling his late-night discussion with Gideon in the Strand Hotel.

"I'm impressed. Clearly, you have been doing your homework. The ancient Sumerians referred to their gods as Annunaki – those who came down from heaven. Sadly, the stories about the Annunaki are largely fiction; dreamt up to convince creationist sceptics and evolutionist sceptics that a race of benevolent aliens created mankind."

"But isn't that what you just said?"

"I don't recall using the term *'benevolent'*, Mitch. No, the Sumerian clay tablets that have been discovered are mostly forgeries – based on real tablets of course, but with their true intentions made to appear more charitable, naturally. It is only in the last fifty years or so that people were prepared to entertain the existence of extra-terrestrials. Prior to that, people were considered insane for holding such beliefs. The Sumerian clay tablets have served the creators well. But, believe me Mitch, when I say that unlike God, your creators did not create mankind in their own image. They tried, of course, but sadly, the most advanced life-forms on the planet at the time were mammals; more specifically – hominids."

"As opposed to what?"

"Your creators were, in fact, a race of humanoids on a mission to re-populate their old world. We know them as the Tiamatans. They are a tall, powerful race with technologies far in advance of your own."

"What you're trying to have me believe isn't a million miles away from popular alternative genesis theories," Mitch suggested.

"Mitch, when you are trying to hide the real truth from someone, don't you try to minimise the risk of being caught out by telling an *almost* truth? I believe it was Winston Churchill who said: '*In time of war, the truth is so precious it must be attended by a bodyguard of lies'.* This is exactly what we have done through the ages."

"You said they tried to create a race from other animals and their own DNA originally. What happened to those creatures?"

"The fate of those that weren't destroyed immediately is fairly well documented in your Greek Mythology," he replied, with a self-congratulatory smile.

"You mean like Minotaurs and stuff?" queried Mitch.

"Precisely."

"You mean all those myths are *true?*" Mitch looked incredulous.

"Truth is merely a matter of degrees, and reality is seldom what you believe to be the truth. On the one hand you have 100% accuracy, and on the other, 100% inaccuracy. Reality generally falls somewhere between the two, but I digress." He shifted his position in the chair slightly. "Where was I? Oh, yes, the ... er ... spiritual nature of this new species – let's call them '*mankind'* for simplicity although, strictly speaking, they were slightly different from what we tend to think of as mankind today."

Uncertain of his intentions, Mitch was in no hurry to end the conversation, so he asked, encouragingly, "Let me get this straight. These aliens; the Tiamatans - they created man, but they don't look like us?"

"Exactly. Mankind was created to be their slaves. Your life-span was programmed at a DNA level, as was your intelligence; only 12% of the total brain's capacity. You were denied both the knowledge of the gods, and the life of the gods."

"Like the '*tree of knowledge'* and the '*tree of life'* from the Bible?" Mitch suggested.

"Now you're beginning to understand. But don't take the biblical narratives too much to heart. Your history has been re-written more times than the specials board in an Italian Restaurant." He fiddled with his tie, distractingly. "Anyway, to continue; the Tiamatans persisted with their DNA experiments and created domesticated versions of many of the wild animals that co-existed on the planet at that time: cattle, sheep, goats, - even dogs and cats. As time went on, mankind learned how to master these new variations."

The man paused again, seemingly distracted. He didn't appear to be finding this conversation very easy. Mitch took the opportunity to glance out of the window. There was no sign of anyone coming to rescue him.

The man continued, "Regrettably, some of the creators favoured one or two of their human creations more than the others and allowed them to learn more than they should have been permitted. Another of mankind's flaws reared its ugly head: the desire to be, and act, like gods. Instead of dealing with these abnormalities, the Tiamatans banished them from the colony, cutting off the source of their knowledge. Unfortunately, for the creators, these banished slaves began to keep records, and with their strong desire to worship, your many religions were created. These ancient writings formed the basis of what eventually became the Sumerian and Vedic literatures, the Bible, the Talmud and even the Qu'ran, among others."

"Assuming the descendants of these Tiamatans are still around, why don't they just introduce themselves and say; *Hey, we're your gods – now, bow down and worship us?*" asked Mitch. "I mean, if they're so powerful."

"Not descendants; the originals. You see, they can control their own life-span through DNA manipulation and the ingestion of certain high-spin elements. They are also accustomed to a different time frame; four Earth years is equivalent to only one of their years. But you're jumping the gun. No pun intended," he smiled, looking at the gun in his hand. "There was a further complication; some of the Tiamatans took a liking to *womankind*. This had an unexpected... er result. Because they were compatible, they were able to conceive. And they conceived hybrids. These hybrids, sharing most of their DNA with mankind, resembled humans more closely than they did their Tiamatan fathers. Being superior to the human males though, they took positions of seniority in the Tiamatan hierarchy; controlling the slaves. The Bible refers to them as *the Nephilim*. These were the people of great deeds and renown in ancient times: Goliath and his brothers, for example."

"Wasn't he slain by David?" *Careful*, Mitch warned himself. *Don't antagonise him.*

"Unfortunately, many of the Nephilim over-reached themselves. But the real problem was the uncontrollable spread of mankind over the face of the planet. The sheer diversity of culture, language, and religion soon made it impossible for the Tiamatans and the Nephilim to control them."

"Not quite the omnipotent beings they thought they were, I guess."

"But that is about to change. Several attempts have been made to unite mankind under one rule, and one religion. To return, if you like, to the simpler time when gods walked on the planet, controlling their slaves. Alexander the Great, Caesar Augustus, Genghis Khan..."

"All Nephilim, I presume?" prompted Mitch.

"Exactly. But they all failed in their goal. Now, the Nephilim are growing weaker as the original Tiamatan DNA has become diluted by that of mankind."

"So where are these Tiamatans now, if you don't mind me asking?" Mitch enquired, glancing at his watch.

"They are here, in underground caverns. And on Mars..."

Mitch couldn't stop himself from laughing out loud. "Er...sorry. I thought you said Mars. Now if you'd said some planet far away across the Universe, it would be a little more believable."

"See how little progress you have made in over 4,000 years?" His hand tightened on the gun. "If you don't understand something, you either demonise it or worship it. You've even photographed their pyramids and their monuments on Mars, but you're so full of your own importance that you dismiss them as 'natural features' of the terrain."

"Look, I don't want to ruin the punchline, but you don't seem to be including yourself in any of your observations. I assume, therefore, that you're either Tiamatan or Nephilim. So, which is it?"

"I would have thought it was obvious. I am a Nephilim."

"You're not as tall as I would have expected." Mitch tried to force a smile, but he was becoming increasingly nervous. He took a deep breath. "So basically, you guys have taken your eye off the ball and have lost control of the planet. Now you want to take it back before it's too late. But to do that, you need to somehow gain control over our minds?" he summarised.

"Yes, crudely speaking. However, there is another problem that has developed recently. Since the late 1970's – early 80's, there has been a marked increase in the birth of, what I shall refer to as, *advanced human beings*. These children exhibit unusual abilities, usually of a psychic nature. Often referred to as *Indigo Children*, they have become highly attuned to the vibrations of both Tiamatans and Nephilim, and we fear we may be on the brink of being *unmasked* before we have executed our plan, if they are not stopped. They also appear to be immune to our mind control methods." The man paused for several seconds. "I suspect that your colleague, Shelby Taylor, may well have been one of these Indigo Children. She caused us a lot of problems, as I'm sure you know. That's why she had to be taken care off."

They still think Shelby's dead, thought Mitch. "So these ... er ...smooth talking Space Truckers - have they been dipping their rods in the wrong gene pool again?"

"If you mean: *were the Tiamatans responsible for this anomaly?* the answer is *yes*, but not in the way you infer. It appears to be due to a latent gene that was overlooked at your creation. They may well be the next step in your evolution. For this reason, it is imperative that we regain control of the minds of humankind and eradicate these freaks."

"Eradicate? Where are these Indigo Children?" asked Mitch.

"You all lead such busy lives, you don't even notice what's going on around you, do you Mitch?" He let out a long sigh. "Admittedly, it hasn't been widely reported on TV, but many of the newspapers are running with the story. Certain children have been...er...disappearing lately."

Mitch remembered seeing something in a newspaper at the hotel. "But, I thought those kids had learning difficulties or something?"

"Fortunately for us, these Indigo Children are usually quite disruptive at school – you see the lessons are too compartmentalised for their superior intellect – so they usually end up misdiagnosed with ADD, or ADHD, or some other nonsense. Genuine ADD and ADHD cases are treatable with Dexedrine, but your Indigos don't respond to it at all."

"And I suppose Gellar Pharmaceuticals just happens to manufacture Dexedrine."

"Well done. It is quite easy for us to determine those that don't respond to the treatment and take appropriate action. As for the rest of you, the Tiamatans have been looking at ways to exercise some form of mind control over you. Their technology is much more advanced than your own, as you might imagine. But even with their vast knowledge of DNA, they were unable to introduce a virus or create a bacterium that would regain control over mankind. Even adding fluorine to the water supply has had only limited success. So they decided to use ORME technology combined with simple radio frequency signals."

"So *you* know about the ORME particles and their interaction with

DNA?" *How far does this conspiracy go?* thought Mitch. *Was Gideon right all along?*

"We have been using ORME technology throughout the ages. It has an amazing ability to repair damaged DNA, did you know? But, sadly, it can't recreate missing DNA. It has amazing magnetic properties; it will repel both north and south poles, for example. It is an excellent superconductor, and it has levitation properties; which is how our forebears managed to move the massive stone blocks they used to build their pyramids here on Earth."

"I had a feeling they'd be responsible for those too," Mitch humoured him.

"I can tell that you're still sceptical. This material, you see, exists partly in another dimension and can be made to move between the dimensions. When it is molecularly combined with other materials, it can cause them to move between dimensions also. Thus having the effect of increasing or decreasing an object's mass in our own dimension. Do you follow?"

"I'm an engineer not a physicist, but I think I get it," said Mitch. "So it can make things lighter or heavier depending on how you apply it."

"Precisely, but perhaps its most amazing property is that it can be triggered to have an effect on the human brain – specifically, the pineal gland. The RFIDs and the digested ORME were to be the means with which we could subdue and control the masses. It was a simple matter of creating a state of panic, and fear of terrorist attack, to introduce compulsory identity chips. So you see, Mitch, your interference has cost us dearly and time is running out."

"Are you saying the Channel Tunnel Disaster was part of your plan? That's just insane. How long did you think it would take to implant and poison six billion people with your ORME's?"

"We were responsible for the Tunnel Disaster, but we never intended to implant six billion people. Haven't you listened to a word I've been saying? The problem with this planet is the sheer number of you... you... parasites. You have used up nearly all of the planet's natural resources in the short time you have existed. Our forebears were here for 80,000 years – and before that, before this planet was cleaved off their homeworld, they had survived in relative harmony for millions of years. Oh no, Mitch, we don't want control over *all* of you. We don't need control over *all* of you. If this planet's population was reduced by say, two thirds, do you know how much longer the resources would last?"

Mitch thought back to the conversation he'd overheard at the Bilderberg Conference. *Do these people actually think they can get away with wiping out vast numbers of the human population completely unopposed?* he wondered. "About three times as long?" Mitch ventured, answering the original question.

"More, much more. This planet can take care of itself. If its resources are used up at a slightly lower rate, it can self-sustain. Unfortunately, mankind reached a critical mass many years ago; destroying the world faster than it can recover. But it is not too late. A massive reduction in the population is necessary and, as we speak, there is an artificially created asteroid on the far side of Mars; ready to be released on a collision course with this planet, which will achieve just that."

Mitch looked long and hard at the man sitting across from him and realised he was not joking. "So, let's say that I believe you. What is the significance of your timetable?"

"I don't really care if you believe me or not, Mitch. I wanted you to have the big picture, before I killed you."

"Well, I don't quite have it yet." *Try and stall him,* Mitch told himself; the seriousness of his predicament becoming alarmingly clear.

"Resources on Mars are practically exhausted. The migration from there should have taken place in the late 1940's. Everything was in place; including the mass extermination of mankind. Hitler was to have developed the atomic bomb and destroyed the Americas and the Jews. Once the Third Reich was master of the remaining world, the Tiamatans on Mars would have returned and ruled over the human race with their brothers. The Nephilim would retake their rightful places as kings and queens, and everything would have been as it was in the beginning."

"I don't want to put a spanner in the works but, if I'm following this correctly, the Nephilim weren't around in the beginning. How do you know you can trust these Tiamatans?"

"We are their bloodline."

"Okay. So, you're saying Hitler was one of you?" ventured Mitch.

"Yes."

"How many of you are there?"

"That is a problem. Oh, there are probably several thousand of us with varying levels of Tiamatan DNA, most of who are quite unaware. But there are less than three hundred with the purest of DNA, and even fewer who remain in contact with the Tiamatan race. We have been careful to breed within our own families to maintain a high level of purity."

"Look, I er... heard there could be a problem with that," suggested Mitch with an air of bravado he didn't really feel.

"For your information, it only becomes a problem when the DNA has become damaged or corrupted. The ORME material prevents that from happening."

"So how come we don't see evidence of these Nephilim all over the place?" Mitch asked.

"There have been situations where pre-flood Nephilim have been dug up. But fossils or remains of giant skeletons are always sent to the Smithsonian, where they more often than not get lost in some basement or other," grinned the man.

"Pre-flood? Next you'll be telling me Noah was a Nephilim." Mitch shook his head in despair.

"The story of Noah is the Hebrew account of the Great Flood. Other accounts include: Atrahasis; Babylonian, Utnapishtim; Assyrian, Satyavarata; Hindu, and Bergelmir; Scandinavian, to name but a few."

"Well, you certainly seem to know your Noahs," grinned Mitch. He popped a Tic-Tac into his mouth. "But what I don't get is, if as you say, our history is peppered with these Nephilim geezers, why didn't they work together?"

"I'm not sure you're really getting this, Mitch. The Nephilim have always had only one aim – to rule over mankind and to serve our forefathers."

That's two, thought Mitch pedantically.

"Unfortunately in the past, power was devolved to individual Nephilim, who acted on their own interests. In the last hundred or so years, we have been working together, behind the scenes, to formulate a more cohesive plan. We have infiltrated governments, industry, academia, financial and religious institutions. So far, we have taken back control without drawing attention to our presence. But the time is fast approaching when there will be no need for this subterfuge." He paused for a moment. "Sadly for you though, we've reached the end of our little conversation and it's time I put an end to your interference for once and for all." His grip on the gun tightened again.

"Wait! The timeline. I still don't get it."

CHAPTER FORTY-THREE

The Blue Lady, Stubb's Mooring, Lode, England

After Mitch had left, the others began contemplating their future. "I need to go and see Charlotte," said Rob. "She'll be worried to death." He began stuffing his belongings into a carry-all.

"Do you think it's safe? How will you get down there?" asked Gideon.

"I don't know. But I can't stay here. I'll get a train or something."

"I need to go to the police and tell them what happened at DNATech," said Shelby, sipping her third cup of black coffee.

"But they think you're dead," said Gideon, suddenly concerned.

"Exactly. That's why I've got to turn myself in. If Runnels is behind this, like Mitch thinks, then they need to investigate him. Maybe Kim has some evidence at her place that they could use."

"Well, they won't find anything at DNATech; the fire must have destroyed everything on that floor," Gideon conceded.

"Do you really think we might still be in danger?" asked Rob, sniffing a T-shirt before shoving it in the bag with his other things.

"We don't really know what we're dealing with here," replied Gideon. "It could be just a few rich industrialists and bankers, like Mitch thinks, or it could go a lot deeper. I mean, the Government's obviously involved. What if the police are too?"

"Oh come on, Gideon. Surely a conspiracy this huge would need to involve as few people as possible. Otherwise it would leak out," argued Rob. "Not only that, it all seems to be coming down around their ears: we've screwed IDSys, Vitality are in deep shit, Colbright and the cayenne pepper guys are under investigation, the Government will be kicked out of office, who's left?"

Gideon picked up the list of company directors that he and Mitch had downloaded a few days ago. "Mitch has circled this guy..."

"Shackelford? He's the link between IDSys and the Government," said Rob, handing the list back to Gideon.

"He's also a director of Gellar Pharmaceuticals," replied Gideon. "The same as Runnels."

"Mitch might be in danger," Rob realised suddenly. "He's started a domino effect that'll bring down most of the organisations that these guys are involved in. They'll lose a lot of money, not to mention they'll probably be kicked off the boards of any other organisations they're associated with."

"I still say we need to stop Runnels," insisted Shelby, beginning to get quite agitated.

"Okay. I'll take you to the police," conceded Gideon. "But you're not to leave my sight." Noticing her agitation, he added, "I'd cut down on the caffeine if I was you, hon."

"I'll ring Mitch and warn him," said Rob. "Then I'm off to Devon."

While Gideon and Shelby got ready to go to the police, Rob went up on deck and tried the office phone and Mitch's mobile to no avail. "Gideon, I can't get hold of Mitch – I'm heading over to IDSys," he called down the stairs.

Rob thought about taking the Mercedes, but decided it would be quicker by bicycle. Also, Gideon and Shelby would need transport and it had stopped raining at last. Mitch had a top of the range mountain bike hanging on the side of the boat, so he unlocked it and set off across country. *There's another advantage of arriving on a bike,* he thought. *No-one will hear me arriving.*

The cycle-path leading to the Science Park ran through a small copse at the rear of the IDSys building. Rob followed the path round the side of the building. He arrived in time to see a car pull up in front of Mitch's hired Land Rover. He jumped off the bike and climbed into the undergrowth for a better look. He recognised Shackelford the moment he stepped out of the car. What surprised him though, was the fact that in his right hand he carried an automatic pistol.

Shackelford entered the building. *Shit! Now what?* thought Rob. He crept over to the entrance and risked a glance. Shackelford was walking up the stairs to Mitch's office. Rob looked in the back of Mitch's Land Rover, which was parked up close to the main entrance. *There's got to be something in here I can use as a weapon,* he told himself. The best he came up with was a tyre lever. Sticking it down the back of his trousers, he slowly entered the building. Shackelford was out of sight, having gone through into Sarah's office. Rob began to climb the stairs.

CHAPTER FORTY-FOUR

Cambridge Police Station, Cambridge, England

Gideon and Shelby sat in the waiting room; the desk sergeant had told them that a detective would be down to see them shortly. Gideon had driven Shelby to the police station in Mitch's Mercedes, hoping Mitch would understand. Rob had disappeared by the time they were ready to go, *so why not?*

Finally, a man in a shabby suit introduced himself to them as Detective Sergeant Baker and led them through to an interview room. It was a small room with a table and four chairs in the centre. It was painted in what Shelby would have called, *hospital green*. Gideon half expected one of the uniform guys to come in and guard the door.

"Please take a seat. Can I get you anything?" enquired the detective.

"No thanks," said Shelby. Gideon shook his head.

"Now then, Miss Taylor, before we start could you show me some ID?"

Shelby looked through her handbag and produced a driver's licence and some credit cards. "Will these do?"

"Yes, that's fine. Perhaps we can start with the evening of the fire at DNATech..."

"Aren't you gonna start the tape?" asked Gideon.

The detective smiled. "You're not under caution. Let's just go through the facts and I'll get you to sign a statement later. I'll take notes."

"Erm... I think the best place to start is the night my flat door was broken down," replied Shelby.

Shelby told the detective the series of events that culminated with her being locked in her laboratory by Kim Denton. She left details of the

ORME's out, stating that she was concerned about the tests they had performed on the RFIDs; mentioning that one report had not been sent to IDSys, but that Runnels had kept a copy for another client. "Mister Webb was also interested in that report, hence the reason for his visit that day." She added that she'd discovered that Kim Denton had been paid by the other client, possibly to cover up the trial results.

"So let me see if I've got this right," said the detective, laying down his pen. "You're accusing Mister Runnels of murder and attempted murder, based on the fact that he withheld a report that you had produced for Mister Webb?"

"All I'm saying, Detective, is that you should investigate Runnels to see if he is behind the attempted attack on me, and the death of Kim Denton."

CHAPTER FORTY-FIVE

Head Office of IDSys, Cambridge Science Park, England

Mitch stared at the man across the desk from him, trying to anticipate what his next move would be. The man still held the gun in a casual manner; not aiming it directly at him. If he upended his desk on top of the man, could he make it to the door before he could get a shot off? Probably not. Even if he did, what then? There was nowhere to run. If he tried to go down the stairs the man would have a clean shot. If he ducked into one of the other offices or meeting rooms, he would be trapped. Mitch decided his best strategy was to keep him talking and pray for some sort of distraction. "You haven't told me why the timing is so critical," he pleaded.

"You needn't bother sneaking glances at your watch, Mitch. No-one's coming to rescue you. All of your staff have been laid off, remember?" The man paused for effect. "So, you want to understand our timescale. Very well. After the failure in the 1940's," he continued, "My ancestors had a difficult time supplying important resources to their brothers on Mars. Trips in their spacecraft had become easier to detect, now that radar had been invented, but it was a necessary risk all the same."

"Are you guys responsible for what happened at Roswell too?" asked Mitch, still trying to humour him.

"Only in the sense that it was a carefully staged hoax; to draw attention away from the real visitors to Earth. Our great forebears were reduced to scavenging from the very slaves they had created. They were reduced to having to steal vital gold and technology from the discarded lunar landing vehicles on the moon, just to keep their colony's life support systems running. Getting resources and materials to Mars was becoming increasingly difficult to achieve without being detected. In the

1990's, it was necessary to capture several of your unmanned Martian probes. It was then that it was decided to coincide the next attempt to take back control of the planet with the end of the millennium. Conveniently, there are a number of religious texts, across the faiths, which speak of the return of *God* at this time. *A Day of Judgement.* It was decided to choose that time for the great return of our brothers from Mars."

"Hold on a minute. That would have been the year 2000. Why didn't they come back then?"

"That was the original plan. Unfortunately, the President of the United States was impeached in 1998. It took us until 2000 to get another of our kind elected. It is much easier now of course; with electronic voting that we can influence, but back then it was more difficult. Thus, it was decided to change tack and go for the *Doomsday* scenario instead."

"The *Doomsday* scenario?" queried Mitch.

"We decided to prepare mankind for the destruction of the planet by a deep space object, such as an asteroid or even Planet X. The film industry has been an excellent medium for desensitising the masses to this possibility – even to the possibility of extra-terrestrial intervention. The coincidence of the Mayan Calendar and the rumours of a planet beyond the orbit of Pluto have all played their part in creating the right environment for our return to power. Even the Christians, and the other faiths, will give us a bit of leeway on the actual date of the return of their *God*. So the date was set for 2012.

"Hence your artificial asteroid, I assume."

"That really serves two purposes: first off, it wipes out up to one third of the planet's population, and secondly, it prepares people for the possibility that there is a larger body on a collision course with this planet; namely Planet X. Did you know that 40% of Americans already believe that something momentous will occur on 21st December 2012?"

Rob was hiding in the doorway to one of the meeting rooms just outside Sarah's office. He could hear voices, but not what was being said. *Dammit, I need to get Shackelford to come out here,* he told himself. He looked around for something that might do just that. The hallway was open on one side, overlooking the ground floor entrance, reception area and security desk. There was a handrail, with a protective balustrade. *Perhaps if I threw something over the side; down into reception, he would come running out to see what's going on,* Rob considered. *No, he might shoot Mitch first. I've got to try and get closer without being seen.*

"But that's genocide," Mitch stated, ignoring the question. "How can you justify murder on such a large scale?"

"Oh, we've tried before, Mitch. Plagues, wars, HIV, SARS, even Bird Flu. It's the only way to reduce the world's population to a controllable level. At this very moment, our ancestors on Mars are preparing to send fake telemetry to your NASA probe, Dawn. This will confirm the existence of a large planet on the very edge of the Solar System. This planet will be shown to be on a near collision course with Earth," the man continued. "Then, when all appears to be lost, our brothers will step in and save humanity by destroying the rogue planet. They will be revered as humanity's saviours, and we will retake our rightful places as rulers of the world."

"But you can't hope to fool the whole world with a bogus planet. What about our astronomers? You can't have *all* of them in your pocket."

"Mitch, you can't see such a distant object with the naked eye. All of their instruments work on telemetry these days – radio telescopes. It's all very simple; signals from Hubble and Voyager will be blocked. The asteroid will be blamed for most of the interference. Refraction telescopes will be useless due to the dust pollution. They'll only see what we want them to see." The man smiled. Pointing at the TV on Mitch's wall, he added, "That has been our greatest instrument in the propagation of our deception. People blindly accept whatever they are told, if it comes from the *oracle* sitting innocently in the corner of their living room. No matter how big the lie, if it's repeated often enough, people will eventually believe it. Besides, it's no co-incidence that the Digital TV switch over is due for completion in 2012. This was to be the medium with which we could communicate with the RFID implants. They would activate the ORME material in your DNA, suppressing your free will and making you more susceptible to persuasive arguments."

"But you can't have control of *all* of the media. The Bilderberger's influence can't possibly be that wide."

"The Bilderberg Group only represent Europe and the US. We control secret societies that I don't expect you've even heard of: The Club of Rome, Skull and Bones, the Freemasons, the Illuminati, even the Royal Institute for International Affairs and the Council on Foreign

Relations. And yes, we have our own people very well integrated into most of the large broadcasting organisations around the world." He narrowed his eyes, as if troubled by something. "The Internet, on the other hand, is another matter. But we will gain control of its content eventually, and use it to our advantage. We intend to close down the sites we cannot control under the excuse of child pornography or terrorism, and we will very soon be introducing a worldwide law of *false propaganda*, which will silence fools like your friend Gideon Mycroft and his rebel acquaintances."

"One of Gideon's acquaintances, who just happened to be an astronomer, was murdered recently. Do you know anything about that?" asked Mitch, as he began to realise that he had underestimated the scale of this conspiracy.

"There is always collateral damage in any great strategy, Mitch. You didn't seem to worry too much about your staff when you recklessly destroyed your business and *their jobs*. Unfortunately, the student astronomer stumbled across our graviton experiment."

"Graviton experiment?" queried Mitch.

"Yes. Gravitons are the sub-atomic particles that the heated ORME material conducts from one dimension to another. The more gravitons you let through to this dimension, the greater the mass of the target object. It's a bit like how a black hole works: a black hole is a tear in the fabric of our space-time continuum. It allows billions and billions of gravitons to pour into our dimension, giving it its massive gravitational pull. The Tiamatans on Mars are using this technology to increase the gravitational attraction of a portion of the Asteroid Belt to create their artificial asteroid," the man continued to explain.

This is too incredible, thought Mitch. *The guy must be schizophrenic or on drugs, or something.*

CHAPTER FORTY-SIX

Cambridge Police Station, Cambridge, England

Shelby and Gideon had been waiting in the interview room for the return of Detective Sergeant Baker for nearly an hour.

"This is useless, Shelb," said Gideon, getting to his feet. "We should get out of here. I don't like it. If they so much as suspect us of anything to do with a terrorist plot, they can lock us up for months without charge. Then Runnels will get away scot free."

But Shelby was thinking about the white building in her dream. *If it has anything to do with Runnels, then it must be somewhere he's associated with.* "Do you know where Gellar Pharmaceuticals are based?" she asked suddenly.

"Er... I'm sure the address is on Mitch's list. Let's see, here it is: Hoddesdon, Hertfordshire."

"I think we should go over there."

"Yeah right. I'm sure we're just the people Runnels will want to see right now," said Gideon grimly.

"There's something important that I have to do."

"What?"

"I'll know when I get there," Shelby said confidently.

Detective Sergeant Baker entered the room again. "I've talked to my superiors and I've got some bad news," he began.

"You're not going to do anything, are you?" accused Gideon.

"It's not in our jurisdiction. We will pass your statement on to the Hertfordshire Police."

"But what about the murder of Alex Wells and Simon Rockwall?" argued Gideon. "That's your jurisdiction."

"I'm afraid that Mister Wells' case is closed. There were no suspicious circumstances. And Simon Rockwall was involved in a road traffic accident."

"Come on Gideon. We tried our best," said Shelby, getting out of her seat.

"Now they know you're alive, they'll probably want to interview you, Miss Taylor," the detective advised.

"Whatever."

Outside the Police Station, Shelby again asked Gideon to take her to Gellar Pharmaceuticals. This time he relented. "Okay, but we're stopping at Mitch's boat first. I've got some calls to make," he added.

"We should drop by Kim's house on the way to Gellar and see if we can find anything that the police can use," suggested Shelby.

They stopped at Mitch's narrowboat and changed into something Gideon deemed more appropriate for this sort of thing. Shelby changed into stone washed denims under a shapeless donkey jacket she'd borrowed from Gideon, while Gideon preferred his camouflage jacket and black jeans. He checked that he still had Kim's keys in his pocket from the time they'd locked her in her office.

Kim Denton's house, St. Albans, England

An hour and a half later, Gideon and Shelby pulled up as close to Kim's house as they could without stopping right outside. There was yellow police tape across the front door. The house was in a Victorian terrace, with a side alleyway leading to a back garden.

"Looks like the police have sealed the place off," observed Gideon. "I think we'd better try around the back."

They quickly made their way round to the back of the property which, thankfully, wasn't overlooked.

"It doesn't look like she's got a burglar alarm," said Gideon, looking around.

There was a small extension on the back, just under the bathroom window, with a uPVC door and double glazed window. Gideon pulled Kim's keys out from his jacket pocket. Finding the correct key, he opened the door and they went into the kitchen.

Everything was in its rightful place, just as Shelby had expected it to be. She continued down the narrow hallway. "The police haven't even sorted through her mail," she said, pointing to a pile of letters and newspapers on the floor by the front door.

Gideon squeezed past her and began to pick up the mail.

"I'm going to start upstairs," said Shelby. "You see if there's anything useful down here."

220

"Okay, no problem," said Gideon, making his way to the front room. He pulled out his phone to check his call log. He'd three missed calls.

Nearby, a dark blue Audi screeched to a halt. "We've got a signal," said the first man.

"Is it him? Where is it?" asked the second.

"It's the dead girl's boyfriend, and he's here in St. Albans."

"The engineer might be with him. Let's go and find out."

Mostly junk mail, thought Gideon as he sorted through the post. A name on the front page of one of the newspapers caught his eye, but the context didn't seem quite right.

"11 year old Todd Carter still missing!"

He pulled out the list he'd copied down from Runnels' hotel room. "Holy shit! They're not the names of directors or Bilderberg members - they're the missing kids," he exclaimed.

Shelby accessed Kim's PC and began looking through her e-mails. She sorted them by sender and picked out Mark Runnels name. After a few minutes, she found what she was looking for:

From: Mark Runnels, DNATech
To: Kim Denton
Subject: Re: Shelby's return to work
Hi Kim
Thanks for the mail. I'm pleased she's back.

I have invited Mitchell Webb to the office on Monday for a tour of the facility. He has asked for Shelby to show him round. Please arrange this with her first thing in the morning.

After his visit, make sure she doesn't leave the building. Do whatever you have to do to keep her detained. I believe we may have a visit from some animal rights activists later in the day and it would be a shame if she missed them.

Make sure the others leave on time. (I've taken care of the security guard- he knows what to do when they arrive).

There will be another bonus from Orme Metals for you later in the week.

Mark
P.S. Delete this message after you've read it.

She must have meant to delete it when she got home from work on

Monday, thought Shelby.

Gideon could hear a printer operating upstairs, so he followed the sound. "Hi. Have you found anything useful?" he asked Shelby, who was looking through a pile of Kim's letters.

"Runnels was definitely behind the attack on DNATech. I'm printing off an e-mail he sent Kim," she confirmed.

Gideon shoved the list in front of her and tapped the newspaper. "Look at this. Those names I got from Runnels' room are kids."

Shelby looked at the name in the paper and at Gideon's handwritten list. "Todd Carter. He's the second name on the list," she confirmed.

Gideon sat at Kim's desk and pulled up the search engine on her PC. He typed in *'Todd Carter'* and the name came up as a local news item. He tried the third and fourth names on the list. Nothing. Okay, he thought, let's try the first name. He typed in *'Alison Hargreaves'*. There was a recent news item:

"Alison Hargreaves failed to show up at school last Friday morning. The 12 year old attended a special needs school in Middlesex. Her parents are pleading for anyone with information to contact the police..."

"I don't get it," said Gideon. "Why would Runnels have a list of names of missing children?"

"Gideon, don't you see? They're not *all* missing. Yet!" Shelby read the rest of the news item. "Hold on. Both of these kids have ADD," she stated.

"So?"

"So ADD is treated with Dexedrine. Gellar Pharmaceuticals supply Dexedrine."

"So you mean it's just a co-incidence that Runnels had this list because they're on Dexedrine?" asked Gideon.

"No, I'm not saying that. The list obviously isn't *all* of the kids on Dexedrine. Just those that..." She stopped suddenly as an idea came into her head. "When I was a kid, I was diagnosed as having ADD and prescribed Dexedrine, but it had absolutely no effect on me. Maybe it's a list of kids that it doesn't work on," she suggested.

"But why are they missing?"

"That's what we've got to find out. We've got to get this to the police. But first, we've got to go to Gellar. Let's check to see if there's anything else we can use. I'll start with these letters."

"Okay, I'll print off the details of these two kids. Should we warn the parents of the others?" asked Gideon.

"How? We only have names – no addresses, or schools, or anything."

"I don't like it. This has conspiracy written all over it." Gideon picked up a book lying on the table next to the PC. Several of the pages had been marked with post-it stickers. He started reading. "Hey, look at this," he announced a few moments later. "*Lost Secrets of the Sacred Ark by Laurence Gardner*," he read out loud. "Kim's highlighted some pages. Listen to this. It's about the ORME materials... '*I can tell you that for people who have taken it at 2mg injections, within 2 hours their white blood cell count goes from 2,500 to 6,500. I can tell you that stage-4 cancer patients have taken it orally, and after 45 days have no cancer any place in their body.*' Jeez, this is just like Hudson's claims," he continued.

Tears sprang to Shelby's eyes and she blinked them back.

"What is it?" asked Gideon.

"Poor Kim," said Shelby, dropping a letter from St. Albans City Hospital onto the table. "She'd been diagnosed with cancer. She must have been trying to find a cure for herself using ORME material. That must have been the hold Runnels had over her," she sobbed.

"We've got to expose that bastard," growled Gideon.

Outside a blue Audi came to a stop.

"He's in Denton's house," said the first man.

"We'd better contact Runnels for instructions," said the second.

CHAPTER FORTY-SEVEN

Gellar Pharmaceuticals, Hoddesdon, England

Mark Runnels was pacing his office. He was furious. He sat at his PC and looked up the latest share prices. The screen colour matched his reddening face:

"Gellar Pharmaceuticals	no change	FTSE
Orme Metals	no change	FTSE
IDSys	trading suspended	FTSE
DNATech	down 90%	FTSE
Euro Haulage	no change	DAX
Vitality Health Drinks	down 85%	DOW JONES
Colbrite	down 82%	DOW JONES
Pad Ming Spices	down 87%	HANG SENG"

The Food Standards Agency had forced the recall of Vitality's new health drink and Colbrite's toothpaste in the UK. Imports from Pad Ming Spices had been banned. The insurance company had refused to pay for the damage to DNATech. Billions of pounds had been wiped off the share price of the companies that employed him as a director. He was facing financial ruin. What's more, Lindburg wasn't returning his calls and his other friends in the Bilderberg Group were busy insulating themselves from him.

He thumped his fist on the desk. *This is all Webb's fault*, he muttered to himself. He still had a tidy sum invested in Gellar, which had not been affected as of yet. Could he afford to cut and run? He felt completely abandoned. His contacts in the Government were no longer of any use to him and the Minister for Overseas Development had committed suicide this very morning. But he had a clean passport and Brazil was supposed to be very nice this time of year.

The phone on his desk buzzed. "Runnels," he barked.

"We're outside Denton's place and the dead girl's boyfriend is inside. What should we do?"

"Is he alone?"

"Can't tell."

"Torch the place." *It might be all over for me, but I'll take a few people with me,* he thought. He returned to his PC and began the slow process of liquidating his assets. *If Lindburg can't be bothered to return my calls, he's on his own,* he told himself.

Kim Denton's house, St. Albans, England

Gideon was consoling Shelby in Kim's office when he heard the front door letterbox close with a bang. "Shhh, Shelby. There's someone at the front door," he whispered. "We've got to get out the back way."

Shelby pulled herself together. "Do you think you can get through the bathroom window?" she asked Gideon.

Suddenly there was a loud *'whoosh'* from downstairs and they both realised what had just happened. "Holy shit! They've set fire to the place," said Gideon, rushing onto the landing to take a look.

The carpet in front of the door and the wallpaper were already in flames and thick acrid black smoke was beginning to fill the downstairs hallway. "We need water," said Gideon. "Plenty of it."

"Forget it! They've used an accelerant," remarked Shelby, sniffing the air. "Quick – the bathroom."

They both raced into the bathroom. Gideon tried the window, but his shoulders were too wide to fit through. "Shelby, you climb through and onto that roof. You should be able to drop down to the garden from there," he urged. He pushed Shelby through and looked for another way out. The sound of Kim's smoke detector was deafening. The office had a window that looked out over the alleyway and the back garden, but it didn't open.

Meanwhile, Shelby climbed down from the roof of the extension. She could see black smoke filling the kitchen. *Where are you, Gideon?* she asked herself.

Gideon ran into the front bedroom and looked out the window. Flames were shooting out of the downstairs front window. Several of the neighbours were already out the front, watching helplessly. He grabbed the mattress off Kim's bed and struggled back down the hall to the office, choking on the black smoke that was ascending the stairs. Once in the office, he closed the door. Looking out of the window, he could see Shelby standing in the back garden screaming at him to get out.

He picked up Kim's printer and hurled it through the office window. Then he knocked out some loose bits of glass that had stubbornly remained in the window frame. "Gideon, you'll have to jump," screamed Shelby from below.

"STAND BACK, SHELB," Gideon called down to her. The alleyway was quite narrow and he didn't fancy hitting the walls on either side.

He forced the mattress through the opening and it fell onto the ground below the window. *Here goes*, he thought to himself. *I hope that's enough to break my fall.*

Gellar Pharmaceuticals, Hoddesdon, England
Runnels was still at his desk. Getting rid of a large number of shares all at once was having a negative effect on their value. He was getting quite red in the face again, when the phone on his desk rang. "Runnels," he said, trying to sound authoritative.

"I think you'd better come down here. We have a situation brewing outside."

What now? he thought, as he headed for the lift.

A growing band of protesters were gathering outside the perimeter fence. Many carried placards with slogans such as: *'Stop poisoning our water'* and *'Say no! to manufactured drugs'*. There was a man with a megaphone challenging Runnels to come clean about his links to the Bilderberg Group and their involvement in the health drink scandal.

As soon as Shelby saw the large white building with its greenish-grey entrance doors, she knew it was the one from her dreams. A large meshed perimeter fence told unwelcome visitors to 'keep out'. To the front and side of the building were car parks. Tall, electronically operated gates offered the only access point, and behind them was a security hut with two guards.

They'd had a narrow escape at Kim's house. Some of the neighbours had tried to detain them, but they'd managed to give them the slip and were already driving out of the street as a fire engine arrived. "How the heck did you manage to arrange all this, Gideon?" marvelled Shelby, as they stood amongst the angry mob.

"The Internet is a wonderful thing," winked Gideon, still feeling a bit bruised from his fall onto Kim's mattress.

It had taken Gideon just a few phone calls to his activist mates to initiate an Internet invitation to stake out Gellar Pharmaceuticals. "There must be almost a hundred people here," said Shelby, looking around her.

"Stu reckons we could get as many as one hundred and fifty turn up. There are still a lot of people around from the Bilderberg protest."

"It could get a bit dangerous," warned Shelby.

"You wanted to get inside. Now that *would* be dangerous."

"Gideon, I have to get in there," she insisted.

"Why? What for?"

"I can't explain. I just know."

CHAPTER FORTY-EIGHT

Head Office of IDSys, Cambridge Science Park, England

Mitch glanced at his watch again; they'd been sitting in his office talking for over an hour. "So where does Runnels fit in to all this? Is he a... Nephilim too?" he asked. He could feel his shirt sticking to his back, wet with sweat. Try as he might, he couldn't think of a way to escape from the man opposite.

"Runnels? Ha! He is just a small cog in a much bigger machine. Runnels has his uses, of course. He's particularly useful when it comes to arranging accidents."

Mitch felt his anger rising. "So *he* was responsible for Simon's murder?"

"He was indeed, but it is the Nephilim who are the real force behind all this. We are your royalty, your presidents, world leaders; people in positions of power and wealth. Runnels is just one of our faithful servants who will benefit in the long term. You too, could have benefited. But you chose to challenge us. Sadly for you, Mitch, you haven't stopped anything. I have other loyal friends who can step up and take over as soon as I give the word. You have only delayed our plans temporarily. And now, I believe I have wasted enough time on you. I must prevent you from doing further harm. Permanently."

The man stood up and pointed the gun straight at Mitch's head. "I'm afraid I can't let you do that," came a voice from Sarah's office.

There was a loud bang, followed by the hollow clink of a bullet casing bouncing on the hard surface of Mitch's office floor. Blood sprayed across the desk and the man standing in front of Mitch fell to the floor. "Nooooo!" came a shout from outside Sarah's office.

Rob ran into the office with the tyre lever raised above his head, then stopped; mouth wide open, as he took in the scene in front of him.

"I hope you weren't intending to injure anyone with that," said Shackelford disapprovingly.

"Shackelford! What the hell…?" started Mitch.

"I came over as soon as I realised you were in danger," interrupted Shackelford. "I've been waiting just outside, in your secretary's office."

"But I thought…"

"You thought that I was involved with these maniacs? Just the opposite, I'm afraid. I'm employed to uncover people inside our Government that allow themselves to become the pawns of men like him," Shackelford said, gesturing at the man lying face down on the floor.

Mitch looked at the prone body of Lindburg. "What are we going to do about him?"

"We, er… have people who can clean this up," replied Shackelford. "I think you'll find that Mister Lindburg just became another lemming following the collapse of his business empire."

"But you had interests in a lot of the same companies," said Mitch, struggling to understand what had just happened before his very eyes.

"I tried to warn you at the funeral. I saw what was happening and got rid of my stock as quickly as I could."

"You mean you knew about this New World Order stuff all the time?"

"Not at all. I have a certain amount of inherited wealth that I like to invest wisely, and my contacts in the Government help me to make er… informed decisions. I was aware that some of our elected Government were involved with some unsavoury characters and I took appropriate action to protect my investments, whilst building my case to expose them. The Minister for Overseas Development took his own life this morning, and I realised there were far reaching implications. I came straight over."

"But how long were you outside listening? I mean, did you hear some of the crap he was spouting?" asked Mitch, incredulously.

"Long enough to tell that the man was completely delusional," admitted Shackelford. "The Government are in turmoil. Not only here, but in France and China too. There are rumours that some of them were complicit in the Channel Tunnel Disaster and an internal inquiry has been set up. I don't expect that to be made public, but Westminster will clear up its own mess in time."

"What will happen to the people behind all this?" asked Mitch.

"It's rather like pulling on a loose thread; pull hard enough and the whole thing starts to unravel. I think there will be a number of resignations – both inside and outside of Government. People in positions of power will distance themselves from those who have been compromised. Networks will collapse. We'll probably never know who was really behind this, nor indeed, what their real intentions were, but I think it's safe to say that their plans are now in tatters."

"Does that mean it's all over?" They'd both forgotten about Rob.

"I think you'll be quite safe now. I have some rather incriminating evidence, which I can pass onto the police, linking Runnels with the attempts on your life and the murder of Simon Rockwall. Once you cut the head off a serpent, the tail quickly dies. Now, may I use your phone, Mitch? – I need to call in the cleaners. I suggest you two make yourselves scarce."

"Help yourself, Preston. I'm going to find out where Runnels is," Mitch replied. "Rob, where's the nearest PC with the vehicle tracking software loaded on it?"

"The main lab, I guess," said Rob, looking confused.

"Oh, didn't I tell you? Gideon and I left a little present in Runnels' car the other day."

They left Shackelford to his phone call and headed straight to the lab. Rob booted up the PC and opened the vehicle tracking software.

"You got the device ID?" he asked Mitch.

"Here it is," replied Mitch, passing him the small label he'd removed from the device he'd planted in Runnels' car. Rob entered the code.

"There he is," they said in unison.

CHAPTER FORTY-NINE

Gellar Pharmaceuticals, Hoddesdon, England

Runnels stood in the entrance of Gellar watching the angry mob outside. *What on earth is going on?* he wondered. On top of everything else, he needed this like a giraffe needs strep throat.

"Shall I call the police?" asked the security guard.

Runnels pondered the question. There were too few security guards to control the hoards outside. He needed to get out before the police arrived; he didn't want to stick around and answer any questions they might have. "Yes, call them. And have someone bring my car to the side entrance right away."

Gideon was talking with Stu Collins, the organiser of this little demonstration. "Stu, I need you to check out this list of names and see if you can come up with any address or schools for these kids. Chances are, they're all in special needs with either ADD or ADHD. The first two on the list have already been reported as missing. See if you can find out if the other kids that have gone missing lately had been diagnosed with ADD or ADHD."

"Wow! Where did you get this, Gideon? It's written on Strand Hotel paper."

"Let's just say that if you can find out if the other missing kids were taking Dexedrine, we may be able to tie the Bilderberg Group into the kidnappings."

Shelby watched as a silver Mercedes was driven round to the side of the building. "Gideon! It's Runnels. He's going to make a break for it," she called.

"He's mad. He'll have to open the main gates to get out," Gideon shouted back.

The car started to approach the main gates and the crowd began to consolidate in that area. As the gates were opened, two security guards advanced towards the crowd. Behind them, the car revved its engine and started to speed up. As the car passed through the gates it was pelted with eggs and other projectiles. Some of the demonstrators tried to pull the doors open and one was propelled over the bonnet, landing in a heap on the other side of the car. As the car broke free of the mob, it gathered speed and careered down the road.

Several of the demonstrators took the opportunity to charge the gates and enter the inner grounds. Gideon and Shelby were carried along with the others. They could hear the sound of police sirens in the distance.

"Come on Shelby, this is our chance to get inside," shouted Gideon above the din.

The two guards by the gates were knocked over as the mob continued up to the front entrance. Two more security guards came out, warning the demonstrators that the police were on their way. They too were brushed aside as the crowd pushed into the building. Gideon grabbed Shelby by the arm and pulled her to one side.

They were in the reception area, which had a large indoor atrium and a high glass roof. In the middle, an open stairway led to the upper floors and there were corridors branching off in all directions. "You okay?" Gideon enquired.

"Yes. We've got to get to the lifts. This way."

They broke away from the main throng and made their way to the lifts in the far corner of the reception area. When they were safely inside, Shelby pushed the button marked 'B'. Nothing happened. There was a keyhole next to the button. "Damn. How are we going to get down to the basement?" she asked.

"Hold on a sec." Gideon checked the pockets of his camouflage jacket. "Here, I've still got Kim's keys. Do any of them fit?"

Shelby tried a couple of likely candidates on Kim's key-ring. *Bingo*, she thought as one of them turned in the keyhole. She pressed 'B' again and the lift started to descend. She immediately began to feel queasy. The lift seemed to take forever, until it finally came to rest. The doors opened and they found themselves in a long white corridor with a single set of doors at one end. Shelby headed for the doors with Gideon close on her heels. She pushed the doors open, forcing herself to look at the scene that revealed itself to them.

There were rows and rows of people sitting in front of equipment that appeared to be extracting a strange-looking powder from metallic ingots. All of the people were wearing white overalls and strange headgear with what looked like antennae on the sides. It gave them the appearance of giant insects. Despite the intrusion, no-one stopped what they were doing. One man sitting near the front of the closest row looked up, his face expressionless and his eyes dead to everything going on around him. "Oh my God," managed Shelby.

"What the hell are they doing?" asked Gideon.

"I think they're producing ORME's from those bars of metal," replied Shelby.

"But they're like zombies."

Shelby looked at the headgear and realised what Runnels was doing. "Oh my God. He's using the RFID chips to control them. Look there, on the wall, isn't that some kind of transmitter?" she said, pointing to something resembling the head of a mobile phone mast.

"What? But I thought Rob had screwed them all," said Gideon.

"Maybe it didn't work down here. Runnels has been using these people to produce ORME's *and* he's been experimenting on them at the same time."

"I think the police are coming," said Gideon, looking back down the corridor towards the lift. The doors had closed and the 'up' arrow was lit.

Shelby felt like she was going to faint and she leant against Gideon for support. She could feel something welling up inside her. Gideon got a sudden jolt of static electricity and backed away. Shelby stood in the doorway facing the people in the room. The lights began to flicker overhead.

"Shelby, are you okay? What's happening?" he asked.

But Shelby wasn't answering. It seemed as if she too was going into some kind of zombie-like-state. Gideon took a step towards her and his hair started to stand on end. "Damn! Where the fuck is that static energy coming from?" he called out.

He could make out some kind of aura surrounding Shelby. It was like a dark blue light wrapping itself around her. As she stood there with her hands holding her head, the device on the wall began to spark and shake violently. There was a loud explosion and the device fell from the wall, breaking into pieces on the floor. The people in the room slumped forward; some falling off their chairs onto the floor. Gideon looked at

Shelby, just as her legs buckled beneath her, and she fell to the floor. "SHELBY! NO!" he yelled.

As he went over to where she had fallen, the blue light disappeared and the overhead lights calmed down once more. This time he didn't get a shock when he touched her. He felt the side of her neck for any sign of a pulse. *Thank God,* he thought, as his fingers detected her heartbeat. Slowly, she came round and looked a little confused.

"What happened? Did I faint?" she asked.

"I don't really know," Gideon replied, helping her into a sitting position. "Something strange happened to the lights and that thing on the wall..." He stopped talking as the room full of people began to regain consciousness one by one. It was as if a spell had been broken.

Gideon helped Shelby to her feet and they approached the man nearest to them. "Dude, are you okay?" he asked. The man looked confused. Gideon examined the man's right hand. No RFID! "So this is what they did to the guys who refused to have RFIDs implanted," he said to Shelby, suddenly understanding.

The lift doors behind them opened and two police officers came out.

"OVER HERE!" called Gideon. "Can you call for a paramedic?"

CHAPTER FIFTY

Head Office of IDSys, Cambridge Science Park, England

Rob and Mitch studied the monitor. "He's heading towards the M11," said Rob.

"He's making a break for it. Stansted Airport, I'll bet," Mitch replied.

They were joined by Shackelford. "Okay, they're on their way. You two had better get out of here," he said hurriedly.

"But Runnels is getting away," said Mitch. "Come on Robbie, let's head him off. We can probably get there ahead of him."

"Wait!" snapped Shackelford. "You can't get involved anymore. Not if you want to stay out of prison."

"You said you had people who can take care of things. WELL TAKE CARE OF THIS!" demanded Mitch.

Shackelford thought for a moment, then said, "Okay. I'll pull some strings and have the police detain him. Where is he?"

"Heading for Stansted Airport," they replied together.

I need to use your phone again, Mitch. Then will you *please* get out of here!"

Stansted Airport, England

Runnels got out of the car and told his driver to return to Gellar. He had an overnight bag and his passport with him. He planned to take the next flight to Frankfurt, then fly on to Rio de Janeiro. He checked-in his overnight bag and went through to the Departure Lounge.

He had a few hours to wait. *Better freshen up*, he thought to himself. Finding the 'gents', he began to run some water into the sink. There was only one other passenger in there. Two men in dark suits followed him in. One stopped at the door and hung an *'out of order'* sign on it.

"You! Out!" said the man with a plaster stuck over his nose. The other passenger left immediately.

Runnels looked up and recognised the man. "What the hell are you doing here? Did you take care of Denton's house?" he asked.

The man who had hung the sign on the door entered. Runnels looked from one to the other. "What's going on?"

"I'm afraid we are under new management," said the man with the plaster on his nose.

"And we've been given new instructions," added his partner.

The man with the plaster grabbed Runnels and forced him to his knees, twisting his arm up against his back. The other man popped a pill into Runnels' mouth and held it shut. Runnels gagged, then swallowed the pill. "What was that?" he pleaded, as they released him.

"I'm afraid that you will become rather short of breath in a few minutes," nose-plaster replied.

"A few minutes later, you will have a heart attack," added the other. "Very unfortunate. You see, you've been a big disappointment to your superiors, Runnels."

The two men left Runnels sobbing in the 'gents'. As they walked back to the airport car park and climbed into their dark blue Audi A6, a police car pulled up outside the entrance to the airport, its siren blazing and its lights flashing.

CHAPTER FIFTY-ONE

IDComm Headquarters, Cambridge Science Park, England

It was six months since the news broke that Mark Runnels had been found dead in the toilets at Stansted Airport. The cause of death was a massive heart attack, probably brought on by stress. Police were investigating allegations of *mind control* experiments at Gellar Pharmaceuticals, where Runnels had been a director. The Government had lost a vote of no confidence and a general election had been called. The opposition party had been duly elected. There was to be an enquiry into the handling of the Channel Tunnel Disaster. Company collapses in Europe, the US and the Far East had led to a global recession; Mitch himself had narrowly avoided being charged with insider dealing. Several senior business figures had taken their own lives, including the chairman of the Bilderberg Group – who were being investigated by Interpol in connection with a global child abduction ring.

Mitch had set up his new company and had appointed Gideon as his new Programme Manager. Most of his original IDSys staff had joined him, including Sarah and Rob. He'd managed to hold on to his old vehicle tracking system customers and they were entering the bio-chip and PIN market with a new RF proximity chip they had developed for credit cards. The new cards could be read across short distances, allowing customers to swipe their cards in front of special readers to make purchases. The transactions were authorised by a thumb print, which was compared to the data on the proximity chip. Credit card fraud was predicted to fall by over 30% in the next year thanks to its introduction.

"Okay. That just about concludes the meeting," said Mitch, checking his watch. "Any other business?"

"I'd just like to remind everyone that I need your holiday schedules by the end of the week," said Sarah. "May is already looking a bit tight."

The meeting broke up and everyone headed back to their workstations. "You look like you need a holiday more than the rest of us put together," Sarah said to Mitch once the others had gone.

"You know what? This year I'm definitely taking one," Mitch resolved. *In fact, I'll make damn sure I take one every year from now on,* he thought. "How do you think Gideon's working out?" he asked, inviting Sarah to take a seat on one of the sofas.

"I think he's settled in very well. You've got a loyal team there Mitch. Now, where are you planning on going on holiday? Do you want me to get you some brochures?"

Mitch smiled. "Oh, go on then. I'm not going to hear the end of it otherwise. I'm thinking of somewhere quiet, but not too remote."

Down the hall, Rob was in Gideon's office. "So, have you and Shelby got anything on this weekend?" he asked.

"We're going up to Scotland to see Shelby's mum and dad," Gideon replied, rolling his eyes to the heavens.

Rob laughed. "Getting serious then, eh?"

"I think Charlie'll have you down the aisle before me, dude."

CHAPTER FIFTY-TWO

Underground cavern, somewhere on Mars

Enlil finally made contact with his brother on Earth. "Enki? How are your preparations going?

"I'm afraid I have some very bad news," replied Enki.

"What has happened? We are ready to launch our asteroid."

"Our children, the Nephilim, have failed us, dear brother."

"Impossible! We have run out of time. We must come to Earth. We cannot survive on this barren planet any longer."

"Our plan to control the minds of the Humans has failed. We would be met by fierce opposition if we tried to take control by force. We cannot risk the total destruction of the planet. We simply do not have the time to re-plan. You must conserve what resources remain on Mars."

"But they would bow down to us once more if we demonstrated our superior technology. We'll destroy some of their cities."

"I am sorry, my brother. Our creations have developed weapons of their own; sufficient to destroy the world. We have no doubt that they would use them. We have failed."

"Failure is not an option," snapped Enlil. "If they will not succumb to our mind control, they will be subjugated by force, if necessary. Do you still have Nephilim in place?"

"Some, yes. But…"

"Then we proceed with our return as planned."

CHAPTER FIFTY-THREE

IDComm Headquarters, Cambridge Science Park, England

It was January 2011, three years since the collapse of IDSys and the change of Government. Gideon Mycroft was in his new office; Mitch had promoted him to Managing Director of IDComm, having been elected as Chairman himself. Robin Kirk was Chief Engineer, and there were a lot of new faces in the company.

The buzzer on Gideon's desk went off. "Hi Gideon. Rob's here to see you," said Sarah in her usual cheery manner.

"Okay thanks. Send him through."

Rob pulled up a chair across from Gideon. "I've got the production figures from Bulgaria," he said, placing a plastic folder on the desk. "Looks like we're on target again this month."

"Excellent news. Mitch is still in Barbados, but I'll fax the info across this afternoon."

"It's all right for some," joked Rob, as he fingered the gold ring on his left hand. "He wouldn't have even known about the place if he hadn't seen our honeymoon pictures."

"Charlotte always did have good taste. Don't know what happened where you're concerned though," laughed Gideon.

The buzzer went off again. "Sorry to interrupt you two, but I've just heard that the Prime Minister is about to make an announcement on TV. Thought you'd want to catch it."

"I wonder what that's about," said Gideon, feeling a sudden chill in his bones. Okay, you'd better come in." He flicked the plasma TV on and selected the BBC.

"*...can go live to Downing Street for an announcement by the Prime Minister...'People of Britain, I have some very grave news. We have just learnt that a little under half an hour ago an asteroid crashed into the* earth somewhere in central China. The Chinese Government were warned in time to evacuate themselves and several other senior officials, but communications are disrupted and the information we do have is very sketchy'..."

Sarah, Rob and Gideon stared at the screen in complete silence.

"...'have pledged our support and will be initiating an emergency task force with the United Nations to help out in anyway we can. Our thoughts are with those who have perished in this unprecedented natural disaster'..."

Gideon finally managed to speak. "How come no-one saw it coming? I mean..." his voice trailed off.

The picture went back to a rather stunned looking presenter in the News Studio.

"...As you have just seen...the Prime Minister has informed the nation of a terrible disaster that has just occurred in central China. Communications in the area have been knocked out and we are trying to get more information on this tragedy. Never have we witnessed anything on this scale before...we can...wait! We are going over live to the US, where the President of the North American Union is making a statement... 'It is my unenviable duty to have to inform you that about an hour ago China was devastated by an asteroid. We were able to warn their Government only hours before the collision. NASA has stated that the asteroid could not have been detected any sooner due to solar interference. Our major concern at the moment is the resultant fallout making its way towards southern India. We are sending humanitarian aid to the surrounding areas, including environmental suits, drugs and transportation. The whole world is in mourning for those whose lives have been lost in what is one of the worst disasters known to man in the history of this planet'...Now we can cross to the President of the European Union..."

Gideon sat back down in his chair in total shock. *This has got to be a put up job,* he told himself.

"I'd better let the guys downstairs know," said Rob. "Do you think we should send them home, or what?" No response! He headed out of the door towards the labs.

The somewhat disorganised broadcast continued:

"...We have an asteroid expert joining us in the studio. Doctor Marcus, what do you think could have happened, I mean, what sort of *damage would have been inflicted? ... 'It very much depends on the size and composition of the asteroid, but even a fairly small one of, say, thirty miles diameter would have a devastating effect on an area of around 1,500 miles in each direction. We could be looking at a crater of about 300 miles diameter.'... What would happen to anyone close to the impact site? ...'As I said, anyone within 1,500 miles would have been killed instantly by the heat blast. Buildings, bridges, trees – they'd all be destroyed.'...Thank you Doctor Marcus. Er...hold on...We are getting eyewitness reports from India that say the asteroid broke into two pieces as it entered the atmosphere. The larger part hitting China and the other part crashing into the sea, just south of Japan. We are unable to contact anyone in and around Indonesia, Thailand or Japan due to communication failure..."*

The newsreader fiddled with the device in his left ear.

"...We are getting unsubstantiated reports from amateur astronomers that a small astral body was seen moving from the vicinity of Mars to the far side of the Sun late last night..."

Mars? thought Gideon. Something was nagging at the back of his mind, but he couldn't put his finger on it. The phone on his desk rang suddenly. He picked it up and absently responded, "Hello?"

"It's Preston Shackelford; I need to speak to Mitch urgently."

White Sands Hotel, West Coast, Barbados

Mitch woke with a start. He looked at the clock beside the bed – 2.15am. *What on earth is all that commotion outside?* He pulled back the shutters and looked out of the window of his cabin. People were running about and forming little huddles. Someone knocked on his door. "Just a minute," he called out, as he slipped on his bathrobe. He opened the door a crack, "What's going on?"

"Have you seen the news? There's been a disaster in China. It was an asteroid," said the hotel waiter. Without waiting for a reply, he set off towards the next cabin.

Mitch's stomach did a somersault. "A what?" He switched on the TV in time to hear the President of the North American Union concluding his speech. *It can't be. It just can't be. Lindburg can't have been right. Oh my God! What have we done?*

The news programme continued:

"... The President of the North American Union is calling for a New

242

World Order to co-ordinate the humanitarian aid efforts. The President of the European Union has already confirmed his support. It looks like we could be witnessing the beginning of a single World Government. The former British Prime Minister, Cameron Stewart, has already thrown his hat into the ring, calling for the election process to commence as soon as possible. The major central banks have agreed to look into the possibility of replacing the Amero, the Euro and the Afro with a single worldwide currency..."

Mitch switched the TV off.

References

The following webpage references were live at the time of writing. I recommend readers follow these links to find out more information about some of the topics covered in this book:

(1) http://en.wikipedia.org/wiki/Bilderberg_Group
(2) http://www.femalefirst.co.uk/board/about78920.html